AFTER LIFE

T. E. BELL

*For my wife Tina, who is the most
supportive and driving force in my life.*

CHAPTER ONE

THE OTHERS

THE BOY'S BARE-CHESTED body is motionless. A muffled beep fills a white surgical room. Everything is crisp and clean. Large black numeral zeros are stenciled on the room's four walls. A heart rate monitor sits next to a seventeen-year-old boy who is splayed out in a tub-like gurney that's filled to the brim with ice. A thick IV tube runs from a small metal, quarter-inch jack in the side of the boy's right wrist and then up and into the tile ceiling above. He's being fed a morphine and water drip. Two other cables are secured tightly to his neck and back from underneath the chair.

Outside, rain pours over a sprawling field beneath a massive metal and concrete wall. A shrouded figure moves swiftly across the field and toward the wall, hidden under the cover of darkness, dodging search spots from above, a large black duffel bag slung around his back.

The once lively heart monitor finds a steady horizon, filling the air with the piercing sound of a flatline. The door to the room bursts open and a doctor rushes in, a nurse not too far behind. The doctor moves quickly, checking the boy's vitals as his body now heaves and convulses. Fear overcomes the nurse and she freezes. The doctor looks up at the nurse, a small glint of perspiration on his brow, and points to a defibrillator sitting on a small cart opposite the nurse.

"Paddles," the doctor says.

The nurse shakes her head, trying to wish the chaos away with each twitch from shoulder to shoulder. Blood begins to fill the IV drip, and the boy's body thrashes out violently, spilling ice water across the floor.

"Nurse!"

A frigid, mini-tidal wave engulfs her shoes and she snaps back to the moment. She rushes for the machine and slides it next to the body. The cable in the boy's neck bursts free, releasing a steady spray of blood from the open neck port. The doctor throws his hands over the port and applies pressure. He tries as hard as he can to stop the bleeding, but it doesn't seem like it's enough.

The door to the room opens again and two more doctors rush in. The nurse hands over the paddles and the doctor places them on the boy's chest. One of the other two doctors takes his place, holding his hands over the neck port.

The shrouded figure hugs the giant wall, tracing around its perimeter. He pauses for a moment under a guard tower, reaches into his pocket, and pulls out a radio. He holds the radio to his mouth.

"Now," he says.

Gunfire erupts. A wave of bullets crashes into the guard tower above. The guards pick up their weapons and return fire. The once calm night has transformed into an all-out battlefield. The shrouded figure jumps into action, using the cover fire to move to a support pillar just beyond the guard tower. He drops the duffel bag on the ground, pulls out a brick of Semtex wired into a bomb, and then attaches it to the wall.

Bang! A gunshot rings out and a bullet pierces the figure's shoulder. He slams against the wall and slides to the ground. He grasps at the wound and coughs up blood as he crawls on all fours toward the duffel bag and pulls out a simple trigger detonator.

"Charging three hundred," the doctor says as he rubs the paddles together. "Clear!"

The other doctors free their hands from the body as an electrical surge momentarily animates the boy's body—his chest arches toward the ceiling, then slams back into the icy bath below. Everyone looks to the heart monitor, but there are still no signs of life.

The doctor reaches for the power cord and yanks it from the wall. Silence. What blood is left in the boy's neck drizzles out of the port and onto the already soaking red floor. The doctor takes a step back from the table and looks up at a small surveillance camera that's fixed in the upper corner of the room.

The shrouded figure props himself up against the wall. He gasps for air as a beam of light fills his masked face.

"Drop it!" a voice yells from above.

The man flips up the safety switch on the detonator and rolls over onto his back. He looks up into the beam of a hovering GET Gunship. A laser paints his chest.

"Down with GET!" the man yells as he holds up the detonator and pulls the trigger. A ball of flames fills the air.

"Reaper 164. Time of death, 22:37."

"Send in a CC team and prep the room for immediate HD insertion," booms a voice through a speaker system.

The doctor nods to the camera and turns to leave the room. The nurse and two other doctors follow him out, the door shutting firmly behind them. Once the room is cleared, a small four-by-four-foot hatch slides open in the floor. The gurney tips forward and the boy's cold body slides forward into the opening. The hatch closes and the gurney rights itself.

The room is quiet and still except for the gentle gurgle and slosh of the leftover blood dispersing over the water-covered floor as it finds its way down a small drain in the middle of the room.

CHAPTER TWO

EVIE

I HAVE A SMALL corner office. The last time I was promoted there were two corner offices available. One was large with oversized windows and a sweeping view; the other was small and without any of those things. GET promoted two people from the development and diagnostics department at the same time, which was unusual. It meant something had to be wrong. It meant that someone in the next classification wasn't pulling their weight. Worst case, it meant someone had died. Death or incompetence, either way, it throws off the entire GET hierarchal productivity system. The company cannot afford to promote two people from each department to compensate for one department's errors. It simply doesn't work. So when I got promoted, against all rationale, so did Josh Owens.

Josh is what we call a legacy. A legacy is someone who has had a previous or current family member working for GET, more specifically, a family member in the coveted Half-Dead program. Josh's father happens to be a highly decorated member of the HD program and is considered to be one of the very first operatives. Because the company is so young, there are only a handful of legacies at GET. This makes Josh special, or at least *he* thinks so.

His promotion came as no surprise; he had moved up in class about as fast as I had. Not to toot my own horn, but I am the best, pretty much at anything GET has thrown at me, and I have the honorary achievements hanging on my tiny office walls to prove it. Josh, however, never impresses—unless you're talking about his temper, cockiness, or characteristic good looks. Jake's ugly attitude and disgustingly constant advances in the workplace environment far outweigh his chiseled bone structure. With that said, Josh Owens being good-looking? Strike it from the record.

Josh's promotions usually coincided with opportunities and sheer dumb luck—a Hollywood approach to success, you know, simply being in the right place at the right time. This instance was no exception. I'm the only real candidate for promotion, but there *happened* to be a second open spot and Josh Owens was right there to fill it with his shit-eating grin.

I should make something clear. All legacies want to be in the HD program. I've never met one who hasn't repeatedly made that fact known. I've only met two legacies, so I'd say it's safe to generalize in this instance, but being in the HD program doesn't happen overnight—you have to earn it. Only employees and students at or above level 40 can be considered.

Being assigned to the HD program isn't like any other

level of promotion. Once you surpass a level 39 classification you can apply (key word is *apply*) to the HD program. No one, not even a legacy is guaranteed acceptance. Granted, I don't think a legacy has ever been turned away, but I could be wrong.

Josh used his infinite string of "luck" to squeeze his way next to me in a level 40 promotion. With my skill and his heritage we are both one step closer to the HD program, but Josh "happened" to get assigned to the bigger office. What a spoiled, undeserving dick . . . but no hard feelings.

So here I sit, in the small office. It suits me just fine and I really shouldn't complain. I know how lucky I am to not be stuck in a cubicle somewhere like everyone in level 35 and below. I can remember how uncomfortable they are, those cold glass boxes. I hated them, but today I'd be happy anywhere. Today marks the 3,283rd day that I've been a part of GET. When you do the math, that's 2 days shy of 8 years. Might as well be a decade of my life. More importantly, today is the day I received the packet in the mail. I've paid my dues and put in the hard work. I've been training for this for years. And now, today, I finally received the coveted packet. I'm excited, to say the least.

I've always been this way, excitable, especially about the mail. I'm what some might call a geek. I can remember, even when I was really young, rushing home after school so I could be the first one to check the mail as if I were destined to be receiving something extraordinary just for me. I never did, but I always checked. Every day. I love the idea of mail, something tangible and real in a world where so much is transparent and fake. It's almost funny how some things never change. Mail is one of them. I like its stability. I like its history. I like that it survived this long. That the institution made it through The Great Event.

I was seven years old when it happened. My dad had just bought me my first real bicycle. It was a red Schwinn with a white seat and flowing white decals on the frame's side. I loved that bike. It was the single greatest gift I had ever been given. It had white sparkle streamers attached to the ends of the handlebars that glistened when touched by the sun's gaze. My mother had protested the gift, saying it was too dangerous a toy for her baby girl. My mother was overprotective. I can vaguely remember throwing tantrums when she wouldn't let me do something I wanted. My father was always quick to swoop in and give me what she wouldn't. I was a daddy's girl. I wasn't ashamed of it. I owned it.

This sort of ritual drove my mother nuts. Every time my father played the hero it made her the villain—a common juxtaposition that many young parents have to find a balance in. His heroics were, more often than not, met with strong opposition in the form of verbal lashings, but that day, the day of the bicycle, my mother let it slide.

At the time, I thought she was just so mad that she didn't want to see me ride the damn thing, but looking back I now realize her choice to be inside—glued to the television—wasn't out of spite or anger. She was just being a good mother . . . a great mother.

It only took her the whole of about two hours to pack up the house. It was a steady shower of thrown clothing mixed with the thunderous roar of my father's voice. They argued as they packed. My father didn't want to believe what was happening. My mother tried too hard to make him see the reality. We fit as much as we could in the car and, just before dusk, we were on the road. I cried as I watched us drive away from my beautiful red bike.

The only plan they could think of was to head to the Poconos. I had never been there before, but my father had inherited a small cabin years ago when his father had passed. It was set a few miles into the woods off Interstate 390 and abutted Kintz Creek. My parents used to escape there when they were young—before I was born.

It all felt like an adventure, unreal, like a dream. The cabin wasn't much. There was one bedroom, a living room, and a kitchen. The bathroom was a wooden shed with a hole located twenty or thirty yards from the back door. We all slept in the one large bed in the one tiny bedroom.

My father woke me the next morning. He looked more at peace than I had ever seen him. We snuck out the front door as my mother slept off the panic from the day before. This was the first time I really got to know my father. We gathered tinder, kindling, and firewood all morning. He told me how it was still spring and it would remain cold at night until the last of the snow thawed and summer had officially set in. So we gathered wood and piled it neatly in cords just inside the door of the cabin. The insulated walls would keep the wood dry and easy to access.

We lived in the tiny cabin for the next year. I learned to hunt and trap animals in the summer, how to stay warm and conserve energy in the winter, and how to listen, really listen, to the world around me. My father told me that the world we lived in was alive and wanted to talk to us; if we stopped and listened, gave it a chance, it would tell us everything we needed to know to survive. But it was the unknown that drove my mother crazy.

She slowly began to change, becoming more reliant on the fuzzy, garbled stations she tuned in to on a small pocket radio she had found in the back of a kitchen drawer. She would walk the property, adjusting the radio's antenna, hoping to find the perfect height and angle necessary for a clear signal. I don't know what she was hoping to hear. We didn't know it then, but our lives were never going to be the same again. Life would never be the same again.

One day I woke because I felt something was wrong. After searching the cabin I finally found my father sitting on a rock near the edge of the creek. He was strangely quiet; a heavy and dark cloud hung over his head. In his hand, he held my mother's pocket radio. The battery plate on the back was removed and the batteries were missing. I put a hand on my father's shoulder.

"She went to get batteries. I'm sure she'll be home by nightfall," he said.

I knew at that moment that we would never see my mother again. As each day passed and I began to look more and more like my mother, with her long brown hair and green eyes, my father found it increasingly harder to look at me. Those were horrible times, ones I've tried hard to delete from my memory. But through it all, the mail persisted. It was always there and that's why I still love it and still make sure I check it every day. For days exactly like today.

The membership packet has been a distraction all

morning, so I put it in my desk drawer. I don't know why I brought it to work if I wasn't going to look at it, but I did, and now it's eating a hole through the wood paneling in my desk. I haven't gotten a chance to read through it yet. The anticipation is killing me.

I don't actually know what the Half-Dead program is. No one does. Not even legacies—at least they aren't supposed to. Those who are a part of the program are sworn to secrecy and nobody knows for sure what level of the GET building the program exists on. No one even knows what the purpose of the program is—it's *that* important. Occasionally, I'd hear whispers while en route from my office to the watercooler. Until now.

Once you're accepted into the program you're given a packet just like mine. It contains instructional information, and most importantly, a brief understanding of what you have signed up for. Thus, my uncontrollable excitement.

I stare at my desk drawer like a predator about to pounce on prey. My hand drifts slowly toward the handle, but my quest for knowledge is interrupted by a hard knock on the door. I look up and see something that disgusts me.

Josh Owens stares at me from the doorway—all six feet two inches of him. He lifts his hand to his mouth and takes a disturbingly large bite from an apple.

"Fuck off, Josh. I'm trying to work here," I say.

"I just thought I'd zip on over here and see if you know what today is," he says.

"No. What's today?"

Josh invites himself into my office and proceeds to flirtatiously straddle the corner of my desk that's closest to me.

"Today is my last day," Josh says.

"It's not my birthday . . . is it?"

"I never said it was."

"Then why'd you give me such a great gift?"

I give Josh a hard push with my foot and shove him off the edge of my desk.

"For your information, I got into the HD program." Josh puffs out his chest and takes a few steps toward the door. With any luck, he'll just keep on walking and leave, but he doesn't.

"Isn't that supposed to be top secret, need-to-know information?" I say.

I roll my eyes and watch as Josh drops his half-eaten apple in my trash can and heads for the door. He stops for a moment and glares back at me with his annoyingly chiseled face.

"Enjoy your little office, Evie. I'll miss you."

He likes to poke fun at my office whenever he gets a chance. He's infantile with things like that. He reminds me of a schoolboy pulling a girl's hair because of a crush. This is Josh crushing, but it doesn't make him any less of an asshole or any less disgusting, so I flip him the bird as he leaves my office.

I really do dislike him. I could have told him about my acceptance too, but the dumbfounded look on his face when I show up tomorrow is a far better reward than any fleeting satisfaction I could have drawn from rubbing it in his face now. But the thought of working beside him for yet another year, maybe indefinitely, really pisses me off. I think there's a shred of me that thought the HD program would be a fresh start, clean of any of the idiots I'm surrounded by on a daily basis. I thought I'd finally be amongst a class of people worthy of the place in which they sat. This won't be possible with people like Josh Owens there. Perhaps the HD program isn't what I think it is.

I don't just *want* to know; it's about needing to know what a fool like Josh knows. It already isn't right that he knows more than I do about a program we're both in.

I reach for my drawer, yank it open, take the HD packet out, and lay it in front of me. I open the cover and push past the welcome letter. I begin to read. I read about protocol and my new key card. I read that I use the key card to swipe into a special elevator on level one. I read all about how the HD program is held many stories underground. I read that we are to dedicate our lives to this program and in doing so must live, study, and train with our teammates in the HD facility. I read about how we must go through hours and hours of training and classes and how we will all be assigned to teams. Each team will be tested both individually and as a unit. Upon exam completion, each individual will be assigned a job within that team.

I read further about the five different jobs within each team:

1. *The Security Operative is in charge of seeing to the safety of his entire team.*

2. *The Medical Operative is in charge of overseeing the health and well-being of each member of the team.*

3. *The Navigation Operative is in charge of choosing insertion and extraction points for his entire team.*

4. *The Engineering Operative is in charge of maintaining and executing the use of all HD specific equipment for his entire team.*

5. *The Special Operative is the leader of his entire team.*

Besides the fact that they gave names to each of the five positions, they don't really tell you anything about what those positions actually do. I'm frustrated, to say the least. Not only do they choose to use the word "his" when referring to any given job, but they don't explain anything.

I finish reading the last page of the packet and close it. From what I can tell there's nothing important to be known, at least not yet. I don't think the packet could have been more vague if it was deliberately trying to be as vague as possible. I can only hope that tomorrow, when I get to leave level 40 and take my special elevator deep down into the earth, I'll be given an explanation.

I look up at the clock on my wall and decide it's late enough to call it a day. What does it really matter now anyway? It's not like I'm getting fired. I'm moving up, or down, or wherever I'm supposed to go. I guess I'll find out in the morning. I pack up my things and take one last long look at my desk and the little office I was so wrongfully given. I peek out my office door and across the hall at my assistant, Jane, who's still got her head buried in her computer. She's been a good assistant, quiet, but good. I might actually miss her.

"I'm ducking out a little early today, Jane."

"Of course, Ms. Fox," Jane says.

I can't help it. I give Jane a big hug. I can tell by her

limp arms that I've managed to catch her off guard and forcefully place her in a gray area of workplace boundaries.

"Is everything all right, dear?"

"Everything's just great, Jane. Just great."

I give Jane one last smile and head down the hallway toward the elevators and let my imagination run wild with the new possibilities that lie ahead of me. The term *operative* makes me think of some kind of extremely important task. Usually, that task requires a minimal, if not immense, element of danger. That danger in turn comes with the expectation of being fearless in the face of it—something I know I'm capable of. I'm suddenly, more than ever, overcome with excitement.

The last sentence in the packet said: *The Half-Dead program is designed to protect and orchestrate the prosperity and perseverance of the human race.* Whatever I'm in for, one thing's clear: my life is about to change forever.

CHAPTER THREE
AIDEN

LOVE TO DRIVE. It's freeing. I've only had my license for a short time, but there's something relaxing about being in a car. I don't know where my love of the road comes from. I like to think I gained this adoration from my father, who I imagine had an in-depth understanding of how an automobile works. I'd imagine he'd have taught me how to change its oil—a useless tidbit nowadays—swap out a spare tire, or notice a problem just by sound or the way it handles the pavement. It would have been nice to show him I can drive. The gentle whir of my car's electric motor spins up.

"Good morning. Today's date is Monday, October 5th, 2071. Current conditions are sunny and 73 degrees Fahrenheit. Please select your destination," the car says with a British accent.

I don't drive anything special. There are plenty of expensive cars in my GET City high-rise, but I just don't see the point in having a fancy car anymore. With all the new immersive and reflexive self-automation, the damn things practically drive themselves. What a waste. *My* car is practical and economical. It's a Ford—a company that helped build this once great nation. I wonder what Henry Ford would think of our country now, well, what's left of it anyway.

"Set a route for GET," I say to my car.

I pull out of my parking space and make my way up the fifteen underground levels of the parking structure.

"Radio on," I say.

"Good morning, citizens, and welcome to the tenth annual GET Day," a radio host says.

I'd almost forgotten. Every year it's the same thing. Global Energy and Technology, where I work, throws a big parade, shows horrifying footage of people killing and rioting after The Great Event, and then celebrates their rise as saviors for quelling the uprising. As if I'd ever forget how horrible things became when climate change scorched the earth, oil ran dry, and humankind was hurled back to the Stone Age. I'll never forget those times, and I certainly don't need a glaring reminder every year, poking and prodding at the horrible memories of my past.

"Change," I say.

"Please select desired station," the car says.

"One oh one point one."

"You've selected 101.1, classic oldies; is this correct?"

"Yes," I say. There's something about the classics. Call me nostalgic or call me an old soul, but I prefer the songs of before my time to the ones of the now.

I pull out of the parking structure into the bright morning light. I change up my route to GET daily. I find mixing it up keeps things interesting. As I snake through the streets I take it all in. I marvel at the iron giants above me. It really is quite glorious, the shimmering glass and aluminum skyscrapers that fill city blocks—such a display of humankind's ingenuity.

Cars and people move past the buildings every day, not noticing how magnificent they are—heroic and steadfast amongst the otherwise frenetic metropolis. They're a beacon of calm and structure from which everything else can unravel. It's a marvelous accomplishment that we manage to keep these buildings going and in good use.

GET sprang up almost overnight with their mysterious new energy source. They had harnessed the energy and, with a small modification to current power plants, were able to flip a switch and turn the power back on. News stations and people around the streets called it a miracle, others called it magic, and some called it evil. Whatever it was, GET gave me a purpose and I had to be thankful for that.

I often wonder what the world is like in other parts of the globe. Did they have it as bad as we did? Worse maybe? I'd love to go to England one day, after air travel has been restored. Not a single plane has cut through the clouds since it happened. Powering something so massive on self-contained electricity has proven difficult. There have been attempts, but all have ended fatally. For now, global transportation ceases to exist. An inter-global train has been under construction for six years, but there's something about traveling on or under water that irks me.

"Da da da, ooh, da dada da da da," I hum along to "Blinding Lights" by The Weeknd. I don't know who The Weeknd was, but I sure do like his music.

My happiness subsides and I turn down the radio as I pull into the GET parking structure. On the sidewalk, a rough-looking man is slammed to the ground by two GET security guards. I watch as one of the guards digs his knee into the man's back and the other holds the man's arms down. The man kicks and screams. I can hear him through the glass of my car window.

"Down with GET! Down with GET!" he yells.

I turn in to the security checkpoint. Everyone who works at GET has to clear the checkpoint. We've always had to do it, but in the past four months, security has gotten tight. I can see Oscar Watts, a forty-something GET security guard, waiting for me.

I know Oscar, probably better than anyone else in the building. We've built a courteous relationship over the years; he's watched me grow into a young man and I've watched him age. The past four months of scrutinized security measures have given us a witty daily exchange that I have become quite fond of. I come to a stop and roll down my window as usual.

"Morning, Oscar."

"Morning to you too, Mr. Bishop. You know the drill."

"They still at it?" I say, even though I know the answer is undoubtedly yes. I like to give Oscar someone to talk to. It must be lonely sitting in that little hut of his. I'm sure most people look at his job as a burden on their day, ignoring him as he uses a mirror-wand to look under their cars. Or maybe his job isn't lonely at all. Maybe it's a welcomed comfort not having to deal with the idiocy that is the social environment of the workplace.

"Oh, you know how it is with corporate white folk."

He jabs at my status in life. "One little scare from Sector 6 and *everyone's* got to be out to get you." Oscar follows the questionable jab with a sure-fire sucker punch.

I admire his honesty. He isn't intimidated by the fact that I'm a technician and he's only a security guard. In his mind, both of our jobs are equally as important to the company. He's right too, and if you ask me, his job might actually be more important, but what Oscar ever so lightly grazed over as a "little scare" happened to have come a few weeks prior in the form of an IED strapped to one of The Grand Wall's support beams. The bomb, detonated by an unknown Sector 6 terrorist, exploded sometime in the early morning while most of GET slept. The explosion had no problem taking out the support beam and brought two guard towers and a fifty-foot section of the wall down with it. Fifteen GET guards were killed and around twenty-five GET employees were injured. So, I'm curious what a "large scare" might look like to Oscar.

Oscar pushes a button on the handle of a small baton, and it extends into a four-foot pole with an infrared camera on the end. He circles my car and inspects the undercarriage with the camera. I glance over at the man being subdued on the sidewalk.

"They still protesting?" I say to Oscar.

"Seems like every single damn day. They're like cockroaches. They always manage to find a way in," Oscar says.

The guards pull the man's arms behind his back and slap cuffs on his wrists. The man twists his head to the side so his ear cups the pavement, and then just stares at me. A sickly grin spreads across the man's face.

"Save Sector 6," the man says.

I stir in my seat. I can't tell if he's talking to me or through me. Either way, his voice is haunting.

"Save Sector 6!"

Oscar circles back around to my window and retracts the baton. He reaches for a uniquely notched key and slides it into a small box at my eye level. The box opens.

"Take a quick peek for me," Oscar says.

I whip my head around, lean over the doorjamb, and put my eyes up to the box. It pulls a retinal scan.

"Welcome, Aiden Bishop. Please pull forward," a digitized voice says.

Oscar retracts the key and heads back to his post. He waves me on.

"You heard the lady, keep it moving."

"Stay cool, Oscar."

"I wouldn't know it any other way," Oscar says.

I shoot him a smile as I pull forward into the parking structure and the screaming man is thrown into the back of a GET security van. I can't say for sure, but Oscar's and my morning exchanges might just be the most productive and interesting part of my eight daily hours spent at GET. It's not that I hate GET, I'm just bored. I'm better than what I do, but I know I don't have a choice. Everyone has to work for GET. If you don't like it, tough, it's still better than being sent beyond The Grand Wall.

As soon as I pass through the gate, my steering wheel locks up and GET auto drive takes over—another security measure put into place since the attack. It's almost instantaneous once you cross the entrance threshold. It's a hard feeling to describe, but it's like walking up a moving escalator—you feel in control but you aren't.

I'm escorted down five levels and shuttled into my parking spot. Number 555. That's right, I have my very own parking spot. It's not really anything to be proud of. Everyone has their own spot. In fact, it's a little embarrassing. Our names and job titles are written above our space, like a giant reminder to everyone around you that you are just a small spoke in the enormous wheel that is GET.

My placard reads: AIDEN BISHOP ENERGY ENGINEERING REPRESENTATIVE. I'm sure somewhere along the line a human relations or marketing research analyst did a stupid little survey that showed employees work harder if they feel important and invaluable to the company's success. Thus, the humiliating parking space name tag was born. Only a complete moron would work harder because they had a reserved parking spot.

My duties at GET all happen in one place—level 36. There are 51 levels, or floors, in the building, and I'm jammed somewhere in the middle between the upper-level executives and the hungry mailroom newbies.

Level 36 is a maze of 10-by-10 glass cubicles. I heard once, from an older engineer, that the cubicles used to have solid walls, but a lack of productivity led to a decision from higher up. Clear cubicles would allow management to keep an eye on sluggish employees and tell them to kick it in gear. Employees, in turn, would *feel* like they were being watched and be less likely to goof around. After a 20 percent increase in employee efficiency, the transparency proved to be a win-win for GET, so they kept the "walls."

Each cubicle holds a small desk, computer screen, and an Energy Engineering Representative. Everyone looks the same in their GET approved khaki pants, white button-down shirts, and blue blazers. The representatives themselves talk through tiny little earpieces slung around their ears. Some speak German, some French, Russian, and Chinese. We represent GET's interests all over the globe. We're the ears of the company. We report energy influxes or decreases in different parts of the world. We're all assigned regions and expected to give daily reports on energy productivity, if that makes any sense.

I'm assigned to the Arctic. That's right, the least populated region on the entire planet, but I don't speak any other languages other than English, so they stuck me with the freezing, dried-up wasteland that is the Arctic. Communication interference is what I deal with most of the time—magnetic interference to be exact. I'm lucky to get through to my contact once a week. Once a day is out of the question—something my superiors refuse to accept or understand. Needless to say, my job is boring and unrewarding.

So, despite my motivationally transparent cubicle walls, my day usually consists of taking naps, doodling, or counting the clock face.

"You totally pussed out on me this weekend." Or dealing with my cubicle next-door neighbor, Jason Conrad, who has grown up to think his only purpose is to hook up with as many girls as there are days in his life. He's a real jackass.

"I was at Six Degrees of Separation. Drinks were flowing, the women were—"

"I never told you I'd go," I interrupt.

"You said—"

"No. No, I didn't. In fact, I don't remember saying any-thing to you at all, Jason."

"Whatever the case may be, you could have made a killing with those charming blue eyes and boyish good looks of yours. I'm just trying to tell you that you missed out. Big time," Jason says.

"I'm sure I did."

Jason has a way of creeping under your skin and making you feel dirty even though you shouldn't. He likes to make people uncomfortable and invade their space. Maybe he doesn't know he's doing it, but he does it just the same. It's a part of his fabric; the way he leans over my cubicle wall and the way he incessantly pumps a stress ball in one hand. From his greasy, slicked-back hair to his taped-up photos of scantily clad women in his own cubicle, Jason Conrad is a regular creeper, and today is no different.

"What'd you end up doing anyhow? Must've been some weekend. Some indeed. Especially since you rolled up in here twenty minutes late on proficiency day," Jason says.

Holy shit. I forgot it was proficiency day. I'm such an idiot. I'm totally not prepared for this, and they've probably already noticed I'm not in the meeting. I grab what data envelopes I can off my desk and rush to the meeting.

"You're welcome," Jason says as I pass by him. He has a smug look smeared across his face. It takes every fiber of my being not to jump over his cubicle wall and punch the look off of him.

. . .

The boardroom is full. I watch from outside for a moment as the meeting is well underway. I can see my empty chair, like a hollow void eating away at me. I can't believe I'm late for the meeting. Proficiency day is sort of like a test. It's a method in which GET measures whether or not you get to move up a class. You're assigned to one proficiency day a year, and I just screwed mine up royally.

The room is a large, circular, glass office. It hangs out from the side of the building like an enclosed balcony. You can see the entire city from it. Sometimes, during my lunch hour, I sneak in and just stare out at the city. I try to pick out someone I know on the street—an impossible task from this height—or I count my way through the city sectors.

Directly below is Sector 1, The Park, which is part of Upper West. Then Sector 2, Upper East. Sector 3, Mid-City. Sector 4, Mid-City South. Sector 5, Financial. Then, far off in the haze of generations past sits The Grand Wall. On a good day, you can make out the borders of Sector 6 just beyond The Grand Wall, where all the noncompliant citizens are sent.

The wall itself was the very first order of business when GET took control. The Grand Wall was built with alarming speed. It was a measure deemed paramount for the survival of society. A division between Sector 6 and the rest of the city meant progress and a solution to move forward. The Grand Wall was meant to keep the "bad" people out and protect the "good" people on the inside.

It wasn't always called The Grand Wall. In developmental

stages it was referred to as The Great Wall—so named for being part of the solution to The Great Event. The majority saw the name not as progress, but instead as a constant reminder of humanity's greatest tragedy. So, in an attempt to quell unrest, the word "grand" was substituted for "great," and the monstrosity became forever known as The Grand Wall.

It only took seven months for the wall to be constructed. Every able man, woman, and child helped in some form or another. Life was to be put on hold until it was finished. After twelve deaths and countless injuries, the wall had been finished five months ahead of schedule. Now that we were "safe," life could resume.

Martin DeMille, the head of engineering and development relations, is entirely too good-looking for his own good. It annoys me to be in the same room with him and his perfectly coiffed hair, squeaky clean scent, and crisp white shirts. Martin also loves to hear himself talk. Lucky for me, it's that very detail of his personality that lets me slip through the boardroom door and into my seat undetected, or at the very least, unacknowledged.

"If you'll all scroll down to page fifteen, you'll see that at the beginning of last quarter . . ." Martin begins to drone on and on. I can feel my eyes grow heavy and my attention start to waver. Before he can utter another word, my fear of missing the meeting turns into a dreadful lack of interest.

I find myself lost in a daze of curiosity—a curiosity that can only be quelled by staring off at the unknown abyss of Sector 6. I have so many questions about Sector 6. Like how many people live there and do they like it better than here? Or, why are they always protesting?

Martin slams his briefcase shut, an action that snaps me clear out of my daydream. Looking around I realize I'm the only employee left in the boardroom. Martin appears to be ignoring my existence. I grab my things and head for the door.

"Don't think your recent subpar performance has gone unnoticed," Martin says.

"I will try harder," I say.

"Ha. If you think it will help. You're never going anywhere, Bishop."

As I leave, I watch Martin through the glass panes of the boardroom. He stands next to my seat and looks out the windows and over the city. I'm sure he's wondering what I was so fixated on. What could be more interesting than listening to his beautiful voice? Any chance I once had of moving up a class is surely gone. I'm such an idiot.

. . .

There's a beautiful girl. Her long, flowing brown hair dances in the wind with every stride. She's running through a field of wildflowers—brilliant daffodils, dandelions, and baby's breath reach for the warmth of the sun's gaze. Arms extended, like a soaring eagle, she glides—her hands brush against the tops of the waist-high flowers. She twirls, releasing a burst of fluttering orange as monarch butterflies take flight. She falls backward—the velvety give of vegetation breaking and bedding her fall. She smiles up at the world and breathes in a deep breath of crisp, clean air, but her smile doesn't last long. It quickly turns to sadness and fear. The once vibrant sun turns to black, and I can see it eclipse in her vivid green eyes. A single oil slick of a tear creeps down her cheek to her mouth and chin. She whispers two haunting words: "Save me."

I jerk awake. I'm breathing heavily and gasping for air. I wipe the perspiration from my head and sit up. It's just that same damn nightmare, and it's always the same; not a single thing changes about it. I never see myself in the dream, just the girl, the mysterious girl. But it feels like I'm there. It feels so real, like I'm right there with her in the field of flowers, just watching her as if *I'm* the reason that she's so happy.

Seeing her in the dream gives me peace and an extreme sense of excitement I've never felt before in my life. I look forward to seeing her every time I shut my eyes. The whimsical way she feels a part of her natural surroundings combined with her unadulterated joy makes me feel an inner balance that I've always longed for. This girl, a mere figment of my imagination, makes me feel what I can only deduce to be love.

I've never felt this feeling before in the way that I feel it. The dream made it come about. *She* made it come about. And I like it. I can't be sure it's what I think it to be, but the anger I feel when the beautiful dream turns into a horrid nightmare gives me some validation.

I could rip the dream apart, go to a shrink for an analysis, but for what? I know how I feel and I know what it means to me. The only real question I have is: who's the girl?

I look up from my desk. Level 36 is dark. The only light comes from the soft glow of my desk lamp. I stand and peer over the walls of my cubicle. I'm alone. Not a single GET worker left. I can hear the faint sound of a vacuum in the distance, but the janitor isn't in view. It looks like a routine nap of mine turned into a little more than a siesta.

I gather my things. I don't have much—just a light jacket, a small lunch bag, and a few work papers I'll now have to finish at home. As I leave, I walk past Jason's cubicle. What an ass. You know, he could have easily given me a quick little tap on the shoulder and told me it was time to go home. I'll let him have it tomorrow.

The parking garage is creepy at night. Being underground doesn't help, but it's especially creepy when you're the only one in it. I walk briskly toward my car and can hear every footstep bouncing off the concrete walls, like a giant stomping about in a cave. It's dark—only the dingy yellowish-green from overhead mercury vapor lights keep things visible.

Suddenly, I feel the hairs stand up on the back of my neck as if I'm being watched. I quickly stop and whip my head around, but I can't see anyone. If there is someone watching or following me, then they're doing a great job of hiding it. I turn and walk faster now. My car is in sight and I can't get into it fast enough.

I'm in and I shut the door. I let out a deep sigh of relief. For some reason, the human mind and body feel safest when enclosed in a tight space. The idea of having something solid between whatever we fear and us settles the nerves— thus, The Grand Wall. This is strange because it goes against almost every other warm-blooded creatures' instinct. You'll never find a dog, cat, or even a bear for that matter that feels safer when backed into a corner. Instead, they only grow more agitated and will lash out with a violent defense. The only other mammal that closely resembles the survival instincts of man is a rodent. A rat will make a nest in the smallest and safest spot it can find, like between the sheet-rock of a wall in a house. A rat will chew off one of its own limbs to escape a trap. A rat will do anything to survive. I'm not exactly sure what that says about human nature, but it's something to think about.

I reach for the ignition and turn on the car. The steady whine of the electric engine brings comfort.

"Compliant system override engaged," it says aloud.

"Radio on," I say in return.

I'm sure a little music will get my mind off whatever it is that just happened, but the radio doesn't turn on. I reach for the physical radio button and give it a good push. Still nothing. The car remains silent. We're spiraling up the garage levels on our way to the exit, and I can't quite wrap my head around why the radio isn't working.

"Radio. On!" I say with more vigor and enunciation.

My car ignores me once again. I can feel the garage moving faster around me. The tires squeal as they start to lose traction with the ground. Around every corner, my body slams from side to side. The car is definitely gaining speed, and I don't have any way to stop it. I grab for the steering wheel, but its manual controls are locked.

A mere passenger along for the ride, I round the last corner and the car makes a beeline for the garage exit. The security gate is down. In a panic, I jam my feet down on the brake pedal with all my strength. I give the pedal a few demanding pumps before I realize I'm not stopping anytime soon. The car responds by jamming the accelerator to the floor. I watch as the speedometer speeds past forty, forty-five, fifty . . . I unhook my seat belt and try for the door. It's locked. An instant moment of clarity washes over me. I know the only thing I can do is brace for impact. I lean forward, my hands resting against the front dash. I can hear myself begin to scream as the car gains ground on the security gate. I shut my eyes.

A storm of splintered wood rains down on the hood of my car. The little security gate is no match for my hefty sedan, but the trouble isn't over. I open my eyes on impact. Free from the garage, the manual controls kick back in. The steering wheel wobbles frantically. I grab hold, trying to steady it. Oncoming traffic from the street nearly misses me, holding down horns, belting their frustrations, not knowing this seemingly reckless act was of no decision of my own.

Both feet once again find the brake pedal. The tires lock up and let out an ear-piercing shriek. Finally, my car comes to a halt. A cloud of smelly smoke from the burnt rubber catches up and engulfs me. I can feel my heart beating in my throat. That was a close call.

The smoke dissipates and I collect myself. The inside of my car is a mess. The work papers that were once resting neatly on the back seat are now strewn across the front. The remains of my half-eaten lunch are splattered effortlessly across the windshield. *That could have been my head,* I think to myself. The rearview mirror is bent crooked. As scary as that was, I guess it's time to get back on the road and get home.

I gently readjust the rearview mirror. In its reflection, I

spot the figure of a thin man dressed in all black. I whip my head around. I can't trust a reflection. After all, I have just been in a horrifying crash. Who knows what kind of tricks my mind might be playing on me.

Looking over the headrest and out the back window, I don't see a soul. No shadowy figure dressed in black, no cars, and no people at all. Nothing. I can't believe it. I could have sworn somebody or something had been there just a few moments ago. I turn back around and reach for my seat belt.

The loud sound of a truck horn brings my attention to my side window. Before me, traveling at full speed, a giant dump truck crashes into the door. I feel my ribs crack in multiple places. The windshield pulverizes under the pressure, spraying glass fragments across my face. Metal twists and bends. Rubber smokes and squeals. My radio finally turns on.

The car and truck come to rest thirty yards or so from the point of impact. The steady hiss of a cracked radiator masks the lyrics spewing from the radio's speakers. Then pennies. The copper taste of blood fills my mouth. As I fight off my eyes' urge to close and send me into a conscious-less dark unknown, I can't help but think my near-death experience hasn't happened yet, but is about to.

CHAPTER FOUR

THE OTHERS

T HE ROOM IS four piercing white walls and a floor. It's small, only about twenty feet by twenty feet. Each wall has a large black numeral one written on it. There are no windows, just a single metal door in the center of one of the walls. A stainless steel mechanical chair, like a modified barbershop seat, is firmly fastened to the floor in the middle of the room. It's a futuristic cell.

Aiden's body lies flat on the chair. Plastic tubes shoot out from the ceiling, like octopus tentacles, and find a prickly resting place in Aiden's arms, legs, and neck. He wears no shirt or pants, just a small bit of white cloth to cover his genitalia.

Aiden's eyes open wide and frantic. They dart back and forth, looking for signs of humanity. Aiden sees nothing but flashes of white and black lettering.

The single metal door opens quickly. A man and a woman rush into the room and jump to restrain Aiden's arms. A second man, easily in his early twenties with short brown hair, a lab coat, and a name tag that reads NATER, calmly walks into the room. He carries a folded bundle of clothing—white pants, a white shirt, and some slip-on white shoes.

Nater stands and watches as the man and woman remove the tubes from Aiden's body. Aiden screams out in pain. A few spurts of a sticky blue substance gob out of the tips of the tubes. Aiden pulls hard to break free. One arm slams into the woman and knocks her off her feet. Aiden reaches for the man, desperate to free his other arm. The woman, back on her feet, leaps toward Aiden and firmly grabs hold of his flailing limbs.

"WHO ARE YOU? WHERE AM I?" Aiden yells.

Aiden summons what strength he can and lashes out more violently with his arms and legs, but it's no use—they've got him pinned.

"What are you doing to me?" Aiden asks.

The woman pulls out a small metal device from her lab coat pocket. At one end, there's a thick ten-gauge needle, and at the other, a glass vial filled with a green liquid. She reaches forward and lands the needle in Aiden's shoulder. She squeezes and the mysterious liquid enters Aiden's bloodstream. Finally, Aiden's body goes limp.

Everything is slower now, a little hazy. Nater takes a few steps closer to Aiden. He pulls a flashlight from his pocket with one hand and uses the other to hold open Aiden's eyelids. Clicking on the light, he watches as Aiden's pupils chaotically dilate and attempt to dodge the light by rolling into the back of his skull. Nater clicks off the light and places the bundle of clothes on Aiden's lap.

"Make sure these get put on," Nater says. Aiden tries to make out Nater's face, but the green medication makes it hard for him to focus. Suddenly, everything goes dark.

. . .

Aiden opens his eyes. He can see two men carrying him by his arms down a long corridor, his legs dragging behind him on the ground. He can also make out the same man as before, Nater, who leads the way.

The corridor is long. Large black numeral ones adorn every ten feet of the concrete wall. The dragging stops in front of a solid steel door. Nater reaches for the handle and opens it.

Nater enters first. The two men raise Aiden to his feet. He's cognitive enough now to stand and walk on his own. Aiden looks confused and afraid. Nater nods and the two men give Aiden a little incentive push toward the door. Aiden takes the hint and enters the room.

The room itself is large and rectangular, much larger than the last room Aiden remembers. One-half of the room is painted black and the other half is painted white—split right down the middle like a black and white cookie. In the center of the room is a minimalistic table with two chairs placed perfectly at opposite ends from one another.

"Take a seat," Nater says.

Aiden looks back at Nater, then down at one of the chairs. He hesitates just long enough to force the other two men into the room to grab him by the shoulders and jam him in the chair.

"That will be all," Nater says to the men.

The men leave and Nater moves to the doorway. Aiden watches him closely.

"Wait here," Nater says as if Aiden has any other choice.

Nater shuts the door, leaving Aiden all alone. Aiden clasps his arms together. The room is a bit on the cold side—sterile. Aiden waits.

CHAPTER FIVE
EVIE

ARRIVE AT 6:30 a.m. That's what time the packet said to be here, so that's precisely what time I get here. I pull out my nifty new ID card and swipe it at the main entrance. I enter, duffle slung over my shoulder, ready for anything. I find the secret elevator quickly. It's really not so secret. In fact, the elevator sits in plain view of the main entrance on level 1. Right after you cross through the front doors and pass the security turnbuckles, the elevator is in the corner to your right. To the left are six employee elevators, and there, right across from them, the *secret* elevator.

Maybe GET is utilizing the whole hiding in plain sight theory. Anyway, I have passed by this elevator hundreds, no, thousands of times, always wondering what it was used for. I guess I always just assumed it was a service elevator—for the janitors.

The elevator requires my keycard. I touch it to a magnetic fob and the door flies open. Once inside, I notice there are only two buttons and another magnetic fob. One button is clearly marked LOBBY. The second button has no markings at all. I'm in the lobby, so I hit the only other choice. Nothing happens. *Must be the fob,* I think. I reach for my ID card and touch it to the fob. The two buttons light up. I press the unmarked button and the elevator takes off—fast.

When the elevator comes to a stop and the doors open, I can tell the HD facility is in fact deep underground. If I had to guess, I'd say fifty levels. That's deep. I can see a long, concrete-walled corridor and a man. He's tall, dark haired, and looks to be in his mid-twenties.

"Hello, Evie. Welcome. I'm Nater. Please follow me," he says.

I follow him and don't say a word. We snake through the seemingly endless corridors. As I walk, I notice that every ten to twenty feet, painted in black on the walls is the number ZERO. Seems strange, but probably just a way of labeling the floor. Maybe this facility has more than one. But zero? Why zero? I've never heard of such a floor. Ground maybe. Basement maybe. Parking. But zero? Never.

Finally, we come to a door. A placard next to the rectangular steel frame reads: MEDICAL EXAM ROOM. A blanket of panic covers me. I hate doctors. A stranger poking and prodding at me is not my idea of a good time. Nater notices my discomfort.

"No need to worry," he says. "It's just for insurance purposes."

I'm insulted. I'm not some skinny-fat bimbo; I'm in great shape. Ever since The Great Event, I thought it best to be prepared for anything. Being in good shape helps ensure survival, and I might need to survive at any given moment. Something my dad taught me well.

Nater leads me into the room. It's a pretty typical exam room—doctor's table, some health charts, cabinets full of medicine vials, an EKG machine, ultrasound machine, and a few other medical odds and ends. The thing that stands out is the treadmill. I'm not sure why it's here, but I don't really feel like going for a run this early in the morning—with no sleep—no matter how good of shape I'm in.

I step in and take a look around. I'm not sure where to put my bag. Nater looks at me.

"I can take that," he says.

Reluctantly, I hand it over.

I don't like sharing and I don't trust people not to mess with my stuff, but I have to give up my bag. I can tell by the rigid expression on Nater's face that he isn't going to accept an alternative.

"A doctor will be in shortly," Nater says as he leaves the exam room.

I'm only alone for a minute or two until a doctor comes in and tells me to put on a hospital gown. She presses a button on the wall and a holographic dressing curtain creates a barrier around me. After I change, the nurse takes my vitals. She weighs me, takes my blood pressure, and then takes out a table.

"How old are you," the doctor says.

"Sixteen."

"Do you or have you ever smoked?"

"No."

"Drugs?"

"Are you sexually active?"

"Shouldn't you already know? I submitted the full questionnaire with my application," I say.

But the doctor isn't having it. She shoots me a stone-cold look to make it clear she doesn't like asking the questions as much as I don't like answering them.

"No. I'm not," I say.

"Do you or anyone in your family suffer from mental illness?"

"No."

"What about any kind of congenital disease?"

"No. None."

"Asthma?"

"Nope."

"Have you ever had to take another human's life?"

A shiver runs down my spine and I sit up straight. I don't like any of the questions, but I especially don't like this one. It rubs me the wrong way.

"Excuse me?" I say.

"I'm not sure I can put this any more bluntly. Have you ever killed anyone, Ms. Fox?"

"I think we both know the answer to that," I say.

The doctor studies me and then looks down at her tablet and writes something down. I try to see what she's writing, but she pulls the tablet close to her chest. After all the questions have been asked, the exam room door opens and another man walks in. He doesn't say anything; he just carries in my workout clothes and shoves them into my hands.

"Put them on," the man says.

Inside I'm fuming. I can't believe they went through my stuff. And what's with all the damn questions? I'm really mad, but there isn't much I can do. The doctor certainly doesn't look like she cares. She just reaches over and hits the dressing curtain button again. Like a child doing as they're told, I get dressed.

. . .

I've been running on this stupid treadmill for forty minutes. Any anger from before has long gone. All I feel now are my legs beginning to atrophy. It's hard to breathe because the doctor strapped some kind of apparatus to my face before she left. It looks like an oxygen mask on steroids. The tubes are connected to a computer in front of the treadmill. In the reflection of a glass cabinet across from me, I see a whole bunch of digital numbers and graphs on the front of the machine. The data is constantly changing, and I'm sure they're recording detailed information about how my heart and lungs are working together.

Aside from the squid attached to my face, I've got neuron patches stuck all over my body. There must be five on my chest, a handful running up my spine, one on either temple, and fifteen freckling my arms and legs. I must look like a Dalmatian. I wonder how much longer I have to run. Not that I can't; I could run for days if I had to. I've done it before. It's when I learned to run, really run. I remember it like it was yesterday.

It was the morning after the first thaw, about 4 months after my mother had left my dad and me and we had burned the cabin to the ground and decided to move on. Once we left the cabin and reached Route 390, we got the full gist of how quickly and how bad things had gotten. The road was riddled with abandoned cars and trash. Overgrowth from the forest had sprawled onto the pavement. Vines and foliage decorated lamp posts and car windows. In just a little over a year, Mother Nature had reclaimed the planet.

Without another living soul in sight, we quickly searched the ghost highway for resources or anything at all we could use to survive. My father hacked away at the greenery that had swallowed a car whole. He found a book of matches and an empty water bottle, two things that could mean the difference between life and death.

I smashed away at the trunk lid of an old Chevrolet with a rock until it popped open. I screamed. My father came running, fearful that I might be in trouble. I wasn't in danger and I wasn't injured. I had been scared by what was in the trunk. Two bodies, a woman and a child, lay next to one another. They had been there for some time. The woman's arms were wrapped tightly around the child. Their skin had already started melting away from their bones, and the stomach-wrenching scent of rot filled the air.

It was clear the two had been forced into the trunk, and then, without hesitation, someone unloaded a clip of high-caliber ammunition into it. What disturbed my father, so evidently, was they had been murdered. He began to worry and then panic. Once the panic set in he let his instincts take over. He reached for my hand and told me to run.

We ran for days. Then days turned into weeks and weeks turned into months. We stopped to camp, eat, and sleep. We never stopped to take a breath. I was never sure where we were going. I'm not even sure my father knew where we were going. The only clear thing was that we were headed away. Away from the loss of my mother; away from the world that did this to us; away from anything and everything that wanted to get us; away from the gruesome reality of our times.

The treadmill slows. The timer is just about to reach the one-hour mark. It does, and the treadmill comes to a stop. My hands reach for my knees, and I take in deep, heavy gulps of air. A clicking noise from across the room interrupts my recovery. I look up and see the door to the medical room has popped open. Okay, my curiosity is sparked.

I yank the mask from my face and tear the neuro-patches from my skin. I wipe my face with a towel hanging next to the door, and then, I peek out into the hall. I can't see anyone, but a line of blinking green LEDs illuminate a path down the corridor. I step out and follow the lights.

The lights lead me down the hall and around a bend, where they terminate in front of a second door. The placard next to the door reads: GIRLS LOCKER ROOM. Without hesitation, I open the door and step inside. It's exactly what the sign says—a locker room. Rows of benches are sandwiched between large steel lockers. Beyond the lockers and benches are five stall showers.

I walk through the rows of lockers until my name catches my eye. There it is, just before me, a locker with my name on it. Locker number 5. I open the locker hoping to see my duffle filled with my things, but I don't. Instead, there's a red jumpsuit with a hood, some shower supplies, and a fresh towel. Disappointed, I can take a hint. I grab the towel and supplies and hit the showers.

I'm a little confused. Now that I'm in here, I'm not entirely sure I was supposed to leave the medical room. The door had opened, but no one had told me I was *supposed* to leave. Then again, no one had told me not to leave either. The green lights seemed like a clear indication that I was to head in this direction. Maybe this is an exam? Maybe I am being watched? I shudder at the thought of being watched while in the shower.

I turn off the shower and dry myself off. I head back to my locker and put on the chosen red outfit. I'm not happy about the uniform choice. While it seems practical, comfortable, and functional, I don't think I look very good in the color red. I've been told I'm more of an autumn than a spring or summer.

I finish putting on the outfit and take a seat on the bench behind me. Now what?

"Please proceed to the orientation room," a mechanical voice says aloud.

Finally, I think as I get to my feet.

"Please proceed to the orientation room," the voice says again.

"I'm going. I'm going," I reply as if someone is listening to me.

I leave the locker room and close the door behind me.

. . .

Josh Owens is already here. I notice him within the first two seconds I set foot in the orientation room. At first, he's surprised, but then Josh makes it very clear to everyone else in the room that he knows who I am. He raises a hand and I choose to ignore it. He laughs and says something quietly to two other HD recruits sitting next to him. Whatever he says to them forces the other two to laugh right along with him. I'm positive that whatever he said wasn't something flattering.

There are only nine of us in the room. We all look to be around the same age, but I couldn't say for sure. Five of us—including myself—are wearing red. The other four wear blue. These must be our teams. Josh Owens, unfortunately, wears red.

The orientation room isn't what I thought it would be when the mechanical voice from above told me to come here. I had pictured something more in tune with what you might see in a military movie when they are briefing a mission. The orientation room isn't that. It's far from it and more closely resembles a classroom. Rows of stadium seating fill one side of the room. The other half has a platform and lectern—clearly where an instructor would stand.

Before I can take a seat, the door opens behind me and Nater walks in. He stands before an eager room.

"Everyone, this is Evie," Nater says.

Everyone says *hello* in unison like we're in some kind of lame self-help group. I entertain the greeting with a wave.

"I must apologize for the delay. We are still waiting on one more trainee. He should be arriving shortly," Nater says.

The room murmurs with discontent and impatience.

"In the meantime. You have all been divided into two teams: the red team and the blue team. You must sit with your designated teams. You can use this time to get to know one another. We should be getting started shortly." Nater finishes his little speech and leaves.

For some reason, I blame my impending suffering on this last kid we're all waiting on. I find a seat within the reds, but as far from Josh as possible. I park my butt in a seat next to the clear bookworm of the group. The dark skin of her face sits delicately behind the thick frames of Coke-bottle glasses, and she seems extremely nervous being around a group of strangers. She turns in her seat to face me.

"Hi. I'm Tasha," she says.

"Evie."

"I heard."

"Yeah. I guess so."

"I think Nater's a robot," Tasha says with a laugh.

"That would actually make a lot of sense," I say.

"So how do you know Josh Owens?"

"I wish I didn't."

"He's a legacy."

"Oh I know. He's also an asshole. Do yourself a favor and steer clear of him. Who are the other two?"

"The older-looking one, to Josh's left, is Russell. He's 19 and spent the last 3 years working in GET medical on level 41. The smaller one is Gwiz. He wouldn't tell us how old he was, but I don't think he's a day over 14. He got plucked from his final year of mandatory school."

"Some team," I say.

"We are all chosen for a reason."

"This is just training. None of us are guaranteed a spot."

"I guess you're right."

I turn and face the front of the room. A large clock hangs on the far wall. I stare at it.

"Where is this final recruit?" I say.

Josh stands like he's important and starts to introduce himself to the entire class, but I know him too well to listen to anything he's about to say. My mind drifts from the conversation. I wonder what this last guy is like. Is he smart? Is he a total ass? Who does he think he is making everyone else wait?

My thoughts are interrupted by the sound of my name. They already know my name—Nater saw to that—but they expect me to explain who I am. I'm not entirely sure what to tell them. There are so many things I could say. For the first time in forever, I'm nervous. My palms are clammy and the four sets of eyes staring at me demand that I speak. This last guy, the one we're all waiting on, better show up soon. I don't know how much more of this I can take.

CHAPTER SIX

AIDEN

I'VE BEEN WAITING in this room for some time. There's no clock or windows, so it's hard to know for sure, but I'd say it's been about thirty minutes . . . at least. It's a strange place. I'm not sure why the room is painted like a milking cow, but then again there's something familiar feeling about it, about this entire place.

The last thing I remember is the accident. I remember being hit by the truck—stupid idiot, couldn't he see I was in the middle of the intersection? After that everything is blank. I don't remember an ambulance, or hospital, or anything. Next thing I know I'm strapped to a chair in a white room with this a-hole named Nater telling me to do this or do that. I'm confused, to say the least. A good knock on the head can do that. Whatever the case, I'd sure like to know where the hell I am, and the sooner the better.

The door opens and I see a familiar face—it's Nater. Now that I'm fully lucid, I can tell I don't like this guy. Not because of the way he looks or the way he so rudely treated me, but because he reminds me a little bit of myself. A slightly older version of myself, but he's got a way about him that reminds me of me and I don't like it.

Nater holds open the door as if waiting for someone else to enter. Sure enough, another man, in his early fifties with peppered hair and a distinguished look, walks in. He takes one look at me, then turns to Nater and says with a British accent, "I think we'll get on just fine. Thank you, Nater."

I'm blown away. I've never heard a real British person talk before, just my car's silly voice that I'm sure the truck from the crash viciously destroyed. I watch as Nater hesitantly leaves and closes the door behind him. Now I'm alone again, with this new guy. He circles me like a hungry shark. After he's had a sufficient amount of looking, he pulls out the chair opposite me and takes a seat.

"Where am I?" I ask bluntly.

"I'm sure you must have hundreds of questions for me," he says.

You're damn right I do, I think. I don't lash out with frustration, even though there's a decent amount of that building up inside me; instead, I try to control the conversation.

"Who are you?"

"I must apologize for how . . . clinical this must all feel." He sloughs off my question and refuses to give me control. Not today. Not now.

"Maybe you didn't hear me. Who are you?" I push. I will get him to give in. I'm determined.

"My name is Arthur."

"Well, Arthur. I don't know what kind of hospital you are running here, but you can't just—"

"You aren't in a hospital, Aiden. You've been chosen," he interrupts.

"Chosen for what? I was in an accident, I know I was."

In fact, I'm sure I was in an accident. I look down at my arms and legs. I touch a hand to my ribs, but I feel no pain. I see no cuts or gashes. I can feel a certain amount of fear come over me. I hate not knowing what's going on.

"Of course you were. I'm not saying that you weren't," Arthur says.

I sit back in my chair. The hair stiffens on the back of my neck—an all too familiar feeling associated with dread. My body tried to warn me with this same reaction in the garage, but I didn't listen. Now look at me. I have no idea where I am or what's going on. Arthur agrees I've been in an accident, but I'm sure I felt my ribs crack and could taste blood in my mouth. There's only one explanation for my current predicament that comes to mind.

"Am I—"

"Dead? No, not quite."

I'm not exactly sure how one can be *not quite* dead, but Arthur seems to be pretty sure. Before the panic can set in, a small dot in the center of the table begins to glow. Within moments a holographic projection appears. In the hologram, I can see myself on a hospital bed. Nurses and doctors are frantically trying to save my life. I can tell by the amount of blood on the surgical table that I'm losing way too much of it. I'm still confused.

"Is that me? Is this happening or is that happening?" I say as I point to the hologram.

"Both, actually."

As soon as Arthur says "both," my brain begins to work in overdrive. If I had been in the accident and was in fact bleeding out on some surgical table, but at the same time was here, perfectly fine, then *here* must be some kind of middle. I'm not quite dead, but I'm not fully alive either. I'm pretty sure Arthur is reading the stress on my face.

"You're special, Aiden. You've been chosen."

"You said that already," I say.

"As we speak, and we are *actually* speaking, you are sitting on an operating table at Grace Memorial Hospital bleeding to death."

"Then how am I here?"

"You're not here. Well, you are, but not really. Not yet anyway. This is a halfway room."

Why do I always have to be right? Nothing good ever comes from being right all the time. Compromise is the key to survival. If you want a lasting relationship, compromise. If you're trying to settle a deal, compromise. If you want to hang onto your life, you better damn well compromise.

"Is that why it's black and white?"

"Finding balance. That's what this room is all about. It represents being half in and half out. I'm surprised you don't recognize it. After all, you designed it."

"You must be mistaken. I've never been here in my life."

"Precisely. You haven't been here in your *life*. This is the in-between, Aiden. Level one of the in-between. You've just dipped your toe in the vast ocean of what many refer to as the afterlife."

"So what is this, like, the gates to heaven and hell?" I say.

"Like I said, Aiden, you've been chosen."

Now I'm getting angry. He's beating around the bush and it's annoying.

"Chosen for what exactly? Because you're not being very clear about that one teensy-tiny detail." The hologram disappears and I can tell by Arthur's stern face and newly joined hands that he's about to get serious.

"I think the best way to put it is, you have a gift. Usually one gets this gift from a severely traumatizing or near-death experience. The brain processes and stores the terror and fear associated with the event and tucks it away in a deep dark corner. It's in that corner that your brain learns to survive past the life of the body. Scientifically, the brain only ever uses about twenty percent of the body's energy to function normally. But some people, like you, Aiden, have the ability to amplify the amount of energy your brain uses when the body goes into a suffering state. And that's exactly what you're doing right now. Your body is dying, but your mind has taken you here, where, as you can see, you are thriving."

Arthur finishes and waits for me to respond. I'm not exactly sure what to say. That's a lot of crazy-sounding information to take in all at once.

"So this room, this place, I'm imagining it? I'm really just in a hospital dying?" I ask with anticipation.

"Plainly, yes. But this place, this room, is very real. Like I said, there's an entire ocean out there, a whole other world if you will, and *you* have the gift of limbo. The ability to drift between the world above and the world below; two worlds that are very much the same while simultaneously being vastly different. Not everyone can do what you do, Aiden. This is what makes you so special. You are not the first and probably not the last, but like the other gifted individuals before you, you must decide what you would like to do. I imagine on some level you already knew this was coming, hence the black and white room you've created for yourself. The infinite black void of death or the white vibrant purity of life."

I hold my head in my hands. This entire thing is like some kind of sick dream. I pinch myself just to make sure. The sharp pain from the pinch runs up my forearm. I look up to find Arthur smiling at me. I think he thinks it's funny that I still don't believe it. If I had the strength I'd jump across the table and wipe the grin right off his face, but I don't. Something inside me says I need to take this seriously.

"What exactly do I have to decide?" I ask.

"Well, you have two simple choices."

"And those are?"

"One: we can reconnect you with your body in the hospital and you can die."

"That hardly sounds like an option."

"Or, two: you embrace your gifts and realize that life and death aren't always black and white but more a robust shade of gray. You'd be alive, but you would spend the rest of your life dedicated to this gray area. A life half in and half out."

I sit back in my chair. For the first time in this conversation, I find myself at ease. Not because I'm sure of anything that is happening. Not because it seems like I have no other option. And certainly not because I trust the man sitting across from me, but because for the first time, I can plainly see the only viable option for moving forward. For the first time, my life is exciting. For the first time, I actually feel in control of my own destiny. I'm not just some lump on a chair in a glass box. This is my way out and I *have* to take it.

"Well. I certainly don't want to be dead, so let's go with the one where I get to live. You always choose life," I say like I'm some kind of philosophical genius.

"Then I think we are all done here," Arthur says as he stands. "I trust you can show yourself out?"

"But—"

"It truly was a pleasure to meet you. Again, I apologize for how . . . clinical this all must feel," Arthur says.

I take this as my cue to leave. I'm not exactly sure what's supposed to happen next or what lies outside this room. I'm not even sure what my decision means. Arthur never explained that. For now, I'll just have to trust my gut.

Arthur watches me as I head for the door, but I'm not going to turn around. I don't think there's anything else to say. I reach for the door handle—it's frigid to the touch. I open the door, but I can't see what's on the other side. A glaring white light fills it, frame to frame. There's no turning back now. I'm not sure where I'd even go. The only way to move is forward. For some reason, I take in a deep breath and hold it as I step through the door.

. . .

I see the beautiful girl. Her long, flowing brown hair still dances with the wind with every stride. She's running through a field of wildflowers—brilliant daffodils, dandelions, and baby's breath reach for the warmth of the sun. Arms extended, like a soaring eagle, she glides—her hands brush against the tops of the waist-high flowers. But there is something different. She isn't alone. This time, I can see myself running after her. I'm smiling too. We're here together. She twirls, releasing a burst of fluttering orange as monarch butterflies take flight. She falls backward—the velvety give of vegetation breaking and bedding her fall. She extends a hand, inviting me to join her. I reach for it. Our hands meet. She playfully pulls me to the ground next to her. We lie on our backs. She points to the sky, the beautiful soft clouds setting sail across their heavenly ocean. We face one another. We're caught in the moment. We look deep into one another's souls. Her soft, warm lips meet mine. We kiss. I feel a coolness come over me. Her once lively lips fall dead and cold. I open my eyes. Her smile quickly turns to sadness and fear. The once vibrant sun turns to black, and I can see it eclipse in her vivid green eyes. A single black tear creeps down her cheek to her mouth and chin. She whispers two haunting words: "Save me."

I jerk awake. I'm drenched in sweat. I wipe the perspiration from my forehead with the bedsheets. I had my nightmare again. At first, I was excited to be in the dream. Seeing myself be with her was breathtaking, but this dream ended up being far worse than all the ones before it. It has evolved into something far more disturbing. I find myself wishing, for the first time, that the nightmare would stop.

My alarm clock sounds and I forget all about the dream. The events of yesterday come flooding back all at once. The out-of-control car, the accident, the man in black, the pain, the hospital, the halfway room, Nater and Arthur, life and death. Did any of it really happen, or was it just another one of my nightmares? I silence the clock and roll out of bed. My ears ring and my head throbs as I sit up. I grab at the back of my head. At the base of my neck, I feel a small indentation. It feels like a scab, so I pick at it until it falls off onto the floor. I yawn, cupping one hand over my mouth as I release, trapping my own brand of warm, first-light dew. I lift the smell gently to my nose, my eyes wincing with displeasure. It shouldn't be a surprise. My nightmares always result in putrid CO_2.

I swing my feet over the side of the bed and get to my feet, stumbling over piles of dirty clothes and empty leftover frozen dinners. My tinted windows shimmer clear, and I can see the city fifteen stories below—the cars racing up and down the busy streets. The accident. I remember the cracking of my ribs. I slowly lift up my shirt, and a sharp pain shoots down my side. I press my fingers delicately on a large bruise over my ribcage.

I take another painful breath and lean one hand against my window. Despite the horrible nightmares I've been having, I'm just happy to be alive. Then I notice it. I'm almost too afraid to look. Out of the corner of my eye, I can see it dangling from my wrist—the hospital band. I rotate it so I can read what it says. I can see my name, height, weight, hair and eye color, my fingerprint, a barcode with an ID number, and three haunting words: Grace Memorial Hospital.

I rip the bracelet from my wrist and toss it in the trash. I look at the clock. 7:45 a.m. I'm already going to be late for work. I'll just have to deal with this later. Like I said, at least I'm alive. I take a quick rinse in the shower, brush my teeth, throw on my work uniform, and head out the door.

. . .

The hallway is long and green. I don't know why it's green, it's absolutely awful, but it is. Each floor in the building is a different color, or so I'm told. I've never actually set foot on any of the other floors. Not because I haven't wanted to, but because there hasn't ever been a good reason. I've only lived here for a few years. Before my GET City high-rise, I had to live in a GET-sponsored boys' home—a horrible place. I couldn't wait to get out. Let's just leave it at that.

I make my way down the long, straight, seemingly never-ending hallway to the elevator.

I'm not alone. It's rush hour, so the elevator is packed to the hilt. I look around the confined space and inspect each person, wondering what each of their lives must be like, but the more I look the more I realize I couldn't care less about any of these other people; they're just a bunch of coworkers. I say coworkers *very* loosely. GET employs thousands of people and most of them live in buildings just like mine, so I don't actually know any of these people. They live in my building, but I don't *know* them. That's a lie. I do know one of them.

Amidst the khaki-and blazer-filled elevator, in the left-hand corner behind me, a shimmer of vibrant color and the smell of antique perfume, Chanel No. 5, strike a familiar chord. Her name is Barbara Townsend. She's rounding out her sixties, but it's hard to tell—with all the advances in plastic surgery, age has become a blurred line that few seem to even worry about anymore. To say she comes from money would be a huge understatement. She's swimming in it. Her late second husband, Robert Townsend, died from a massive coronary only after he had obtained a board seat at GET corporate—a job that pays eight plus figures and includes executive perks like holiday bonuses, paid vacation, and an extremely hefty retirement portfolio.

The only thing she loves more than her money is her dog, Maybelle, which happens to be a Yorkshire . . . wait for it . . . terrier. She likes to dress nice because she wants people to know she has lots of money. With money comes power, and power only wears bright-colored designer clothing. Barb is somewhat nosey. She likes to know what everyone is doing at every moment. She's the building's resident snoop.

I can tell she wants to say something to me before she even says it. She has a way of making her eyes burn holes in the back of your head.

"I don't recall seeing you at the council meeting last Tuesday," she says.

Everyone in the elevator listens, but only I know she's talking directly to me. I can't believe she's bringing this up, especially now, so close to getting out unnoticed. I decide to answer, but I don't turn to face her. I won't give her the satisfaction. Still, I should be polite.

"So sorry, Mrs. Townsend, I haven't been feeling quite myself," I say . . . another lie.

"Well, I hope it's not something contagious. Heaven knows the last thing we need is some bug like the one ravaging Sector 6 to crawl its way to the Upper West."

"That would be just awful, now wouldn't it?" I say with a heavy dose of sarcasm.

There's something about the filthy rich that gets me. I think it's just the way they generally view the world. They see themselves as the top priority, always. They don't care who they have to step on or step over to get to and stay at the top. That's what gets me, not the fact that they have money, but that their money almost makes them un-human.

"You should be sure to get that checked out," says Mrs. Townsend.

I'm lost in my own thoughts, but the statement registers somewhere in my thick head. "Excuse me?"

"If you aren't feeling well, you should get it checked out. Oh, never mind, but do make sure you attend the next council meeting. It's your duty as a resident. Someone's been stealing the mail."

"The mail?" I say.

"Are you listening to anything I'm saying?"

"Of course. The mail. Someone's stealing it." I really have no idea what she's talking about, but why not play along? Anything to get me, or her, out of this elevator.

The elevator stops at level 1 and the doors open. Level 1 leads to the vast enclosed park between the 4 sides of the building. A digital sky made from millions of tiny LEDs hangs above—it changes with the time of day and creates beautiful artificial skyscapes. Right now it's a plain blue sky with fluffy white clouds.

Mrs. Townsend pushes her way toward the front and forces her way out of the elevator. She composes herself, brushing off any cooties we khaki warriors might have rubbed off on her during her exit. She takes Maybelle from under her arm and plops the little thing on the ground beside her, then looks right at me, like a grandmother teaching a lesson.

"Just make sure you wash your hands *well* and don't let me catch you *not* at the next council meeting."

I have nothing left to say. I quickly reach for the CLOSE DOOR button, and the elevator jets down into the subterranean.

After watching all my other fellow GET employees disappear, one by one, out of the elevator and into the day ahead, it is my turn. I storm across parking level 15. I'm looking for my humble Ford sedan, so I walk right past my parking spot when I don't see it. I notice pretty quickly that I missed it. Two spots directly after mine are empty, so the space number is clear as day.

I turn around and head back a few spots. I realize why I had missed it. A brand-new black Mercedes is parked in my spot. I walk around the car once, just to make sure this is in fact *my* spot. It is. Maybe I'm on the wrong floor? I rush back over to the elevator—the floor number is marked next to the doors, but I'm on fifteen. Even the elevator says so.

I'm back at my spot—in front of the Mercedes. I scratch my head. I'm confused. I've never had this problem in my building before, nor have I ever heard of anyone else having this problem. Maybe someone in Mid-City might have this problem, but not here, not on the Upper West.

"Hello? Okay, very funny. What asshole decided to park in my spot?" I shout out, like the perpetrator must be nearby laughing it up as I stand confused. Then it comes over me—where's *my* car? The accident. I feel a set of keys in my pocket. I rip them out. My Ford sedan key is now replaced on the key ring by a small Mercedes fob. That's strange. I approach the door of the brilliant luxury sedan. Its door pops open.

"Good morning, Aiden. Please select your destination," the car says with a plain, American male accent. I step inside and take a seat. This thing is really nice. It's fully loaded with hand-stitched leather seats, a premium sound system, holographic 3D navigation, and an invisi-ceiling. A hundred-thousand dollars loaded. A car that people like me don't drive, just dream of. Mrs. Townsend might drive one, but not me.

"Global Energy and Technology," I say.

"Certainly. Please buckle your seat belt," it replies.

I buckle my seat belt and start to pull out of the parking spot. The fastest route to GET illuminates in the GPS panel.

. . .

I pull into the security gate at the GET parking structure. I see Oscar coming out from the solidarity of his little hut. I can't wait to see his reaction when he finds out it's me in this fine piece of automotive engineering. He probably thinks I'm just some upper-level executive. Some snob who's going to ignore him completely as he does his job. This should be good. I come to a stop and roll down the window.

"Morning, Oscar," I say with a smug confidence.

"I almost didn't recognize you. Nice ride."

"I hardly recognize myself this morning."

"Well, the good news is you can go right on in."

"What about the inspection?"

"You don't know?" he asks.

"Know what?" I feel stupid. Clearly, I should know something. Does he know something I don't? Is it obvious? Does Oscar know about the accident?

"You've been reassigned. No inspections are required for you anymore. You've got clearance now."

Clearance for what? Everything Arthur had said comes back to me. Maybe Arthur works for GET. Maybe the choices he was talking to me about have to do with accepting a new job. I royally screwed up proficiency day; why would GET want to promote some nobody like me? Then again, Oscar used the word *reassigned*. Maybe that's a bad thing. This nice Mercedes made me assume something greater, but maybe it's a consolation prize for something far worse to come. I swallow my anxiety.

"Oh. Well, have a good day then?"

"You too, Mr. Bishop."

The gate lifts and I pull forward. I cross the threshold and the auto-drive kicks in. The Mercedes circles the garage only once before it pulls into a new parking spot, a better parking spot, on level one. The car shuts off and I look out the windshield. The plaque in front of the spot reads: RESERVED AIDEN BISHOP. What's strange is there doesn't appear to be any job title at all. Now I'm nervous.

. . .

The level 1 lobby is void of the morning mayhem. Casual business goers have replaced the usual rush from the parking structure to the employee elevators. Through the thin human atmosphere, I make out a familiar face—Nater. My stomach sinks. I feel like I might toss my cookies. Nater notices me. My heart tries to break free from my chest as he makes his way straight for me. I'm frozen in place, paralyzed with fear like a deer in headlights. Now I have to believe that everything that happened last night was real; the accident, the hospital, me dying, Arthur, and my choice of life all *must* have happened. I'm worried about what comes next. Nater is upon me.

"I trust the car worked out for you?" he asks.

It takes me a few moments to respond. I can tell by the look on his face that he's tired of waiting. I spit something out.

"Yes. Yes, it did. Have I been promoted?" I get to the point. I like being direct, especially when I'm nervous.

"Follow me, please. There's a full day ahead of you."

Normally I'd snap back with a reworked variation of my previous question in an attempt to force an answer, but Nater's not the kind of guy who'll entertain my bullying. Plus, I'm not sure I even want the answer.

We head through the security turnbuckles and into a single elevator we have to swipe a fob to use. I've noticed the elevator before. I notice everything. Call it one of my many talents. Sometimes, I give myself thirty seconds to walk into a room or open a fridge and try to remember absolutely everything or everyone in there. It's a mind exercise secret agents used to be trained to do. It strengthens the mind's memory cortex and gives the body a faster reflex time in life-threatening situations.

There're only two buttons in the elevator. It seems odd,

but a quick swipe of Nater's fob reveals a LOBBY button and a second unmarked one. The fob reminds me of when I was younger and lived at the GET boys' home. My only friend there was a boy named Spence Gardner. Spence and I used to get in all sorts of trouble together. I think Spence lived for getting in trouble. One time we broke into Headmaster Doyle's office and stole the key fob to the dumbwaiter lift. The little lift was used to send dirty dishes and laundry from each floor to the basement. We'd sneak out of our rooms at night and ride the dumbwaiter up and down, from floor to floor, exploring every secret the GET boys' home had to offer. We'd play pranks on other boys and instructors. We'd rummage through the attic, making up stories for all the trinkets we found. We'd explore the dark, wet basement, pretending to be tomb raiders looking for treasure. But mostly, we'd sneak into the kitchen and eat freshly baked pastries prepared that night for the next day's morning meal.

Nater taps the unmarked button, and the elevator shoots downward. I think of Spence and the bravery we once possessed. I no longer feel as lost or scared of what lies ahead, wherever this elevator should stop. I remember how much I had disliked Nater the other night and the trauma he had put me through, and with such an attitude.

"Where are we headed?"

"Down," Nater says.

"Down where?"

"Just down."

"Talkative this morning. I do remember who you are. From yesterday. You had that damn needle stuck in my arm."

The elevator comes to a stop and the doors open. Nater ignores my testosterone-fueled questioning.

"This way," he says as he steps out of the elevator and into a long cement hallway. The elevator tries to shut and I jam an arm through it, forcing my way out into the hallway and after Nater. I quicken my step to catch up. The walls are covered in gigantic zeros every ten or twenty feet.

"Has this always been here?" I ask as we walk.

"Come on. Hurry. You're already running late."

"Late for what?"

"Orientation," Nater says right before stopping in front of a solid metal door. A placard next to the door reads: ORIENTATION ROOM. Nater turns toward me. "This is as far as I go."

"And I thought we were just starting to get along," I reply with arrogant sarcasm. I instantly feel bad about being so rude. Nater turns, without saying a word back, and disappears down the hallway.

. . .

I enter the orientation room. Beyond the door is a large lecture-like classroom. Nine other teens sit in the seats. A woman, forty-something with rigid posture, jet-black hair, and wearing a military-like uniform, stands behind a podium across from the teens. I notice a small patch on the left breast of her uniform. The letters D and I make up the patch's shape. I've clearly interrupted something. Everyone stares at me like I'm not wearing any clothes.

Then, I notice her. At first, I'm not entirely sure, but a slight adjustment of her hair with her hand confirms it. I'm like a turtle hiding in its shell. I'm overcome with emotion; I'm not sure what to feel. Butterflies fill my stomach. My head and my heart ache. My palms grow damp. I'm sure she can see it. It's the girl from my dream, the nightmare that has been haunting me for weeks and keeping me up nights. I can't believe it. A thick voice interrupts my daydream.

"My name is Instructor Keets. May I help you with something?"

I'm confused and taken off guard. I stumble to put words together. I can't take my eyes off her. The girl from my dreams. I must look like a complete idiot.

"I was brought . . . I'm not . . . I'm not exactly sure what I'm doing here," I say.

"I can see that. I think everyone here can see that," Keets says.

The room laughs in amusement. Except her. She doesn't laugh. I admire that. Maybe she's as perfect as she is in my dreams. Maybe dreams do come true. This all feels so . . . what's the word I'm looking for? Weird.

Instructor Keets is obviously one of those people who thinks embarrassing those who annoy her or disrupt her teaching method is the best way to get across to them. She couldn't be more wrong in my case.

"What's your name?" Keets asks.

"Aiden."

"Aiden what?"

The crowd laughs again.

"Aiden Bishop."

Keets reaches down into the podium and pulls out a tablet. She scrolls down the screen—a roll-sheet no doubt.

She finds what she's looking for. I couldn't care less at this point.

"Ah. There you are. Aiden Bishop. It appears you are exactly where you are supposed to be. However, you are wasting your classmates' time, your time, and most importantly my time. So if you wouldn't mind taking a seat with the blue team, we could get back to business."

Now I realize I'm the only one not wearing one of these red or blue jumpsuits. I'm definitely the odd man out. I head to an empty seat at the end of what looks like the blue row. I stumble once as I sit because my attention is still on the girl—this perfect girl. I can't believe she's wearing red and I'm supposed to be on the blue team. I've got to find a way to talk to her.

I take a seat and glance over at whom I've parked next to. His name's Matthew Hopper—I can tell because his name is written on the front of a small notepad on the desk in front of him. He looks about my age, has chiseled features and a slightly nerdy disposition, and he happens to be watching me intently. I can tell he's dying to say something to me.

"You okay, man?" he says.

"Yeah. I'm good. That girl there—"

"Late on the first day. You sure like to make an entrance," Matt says.

I like him already. He's got my type of sarcasm.

"I didn't know I was late," I say.

"What about your packet?"

"What packet?"

"You never got a packet? In the mail? Nothing?"

When would I have gotten a packet? I have no idea what this kid is talking about. Then I remember Mrs. Townsend mentioning something about how someone had been stealing the mail in our building.

"Nope," I reply.

"Really? That's weird. It had a lot of details about being recruited, what time orientation was, and all of that. Really? Nothing?"

"Nope."

"Well, you didn't miss much anyway, just finished taking roll really. I'm Matt Hopper; people call me Hop." He extends his hand. We shake and I give him my name.

"Aiden Bishop."

"Nice to meet you, Aiden. If you want a piece of advice, take notes. I heard Lieutenant Keets is a real hard-ass when it comes to exams."

"Exams?" I ask.

"Man, you really don't know anything, do you?"

"I don't even know what this reassignment is."

"Reassignment? This is the Half-Dead program."

Matt almost laughs when he says it. He can't believe I didn't know. Everyone knows the Half-Dead program exists, but no one knows what it is or what those involved in the program do. Of course I'd heard of it, but I always thought you had to apply to it to get in. I had never applied to the Half-Dead program because everyone knew you had to be a level 40 or more before you could be considered.

I had applied a while back for a transfer to a creative department instead of a technical department, but I never heard anything back. I just assumed they denied my request.

Maybe they hadn't. Whatever the reason, I think they may have made a mistake. Maybe they think I'm someone I'm not. Then again, Arthur had said I was chosen for something. Maybe he meant this.

"Let me ask you something, Matt."

"Hop, call me Hop," Matt says. I think his little nickname is dumb, but I don't have the heart to tell him. He seems to like it.

"Hop, did you get a Mercedes too?" I ask.

Hop looks dumbfounded. I can tell he hadn't and wished he had. I've sparked his interest and guaranteed myself a question later. He wants to ask now, but Instructor Keets is hell-bent on instructing.

"I formally want to welcome all of you to your first day as HD recruits. Now I know some of you are second-generation legacies and think you know a great deal about our program. Forget it. We start fresh here today. I also know that the majority of you are first-geners and probably have no idea why you're here or what an HD recruit is. Can anyone take a stab at what HD stands for?" Instructor Keets says.

A tall, muscular kid from the red team raises a hand. I can see the girl roll her eyes and cross her arms. I smile at her distaste for this hunk of man meat. If she doesn't like him, then maybe I stand a chance.

"Yes. You there," Instructor Keets says.

"Josh Owens, ma'am, second-generation legacy."

This guy seems like an ass. Anyone who feels the need to make their status known, especially after an instructor acknowledges you, is a total dick who only wants everyone to think he's better than he really is. I can see why the girl doesn't like him.

"Yes. I knew your father, Mr. Owens. We expect great things from you. Could you please be so kind as to enlighten your classmates on the meaning of HD," Keets replies.

"HD stands for Half-Dead. We are unique individuals who possess the ability to sustain ourselves from one world to the next. Our sole purpose is to stop the uprising in Sector 6 and protect what little energy we have left on our planet."

"Very good, Mr. Owens. I couldn't have read it better if I had a GET dictionary right in front of me." Keets takes a little wind out of Josh's sails. Maybe this instructor isn't so bad after all.

"Legacies," Hop mutters under his breath. He is quickly tallying up the reasons to become my best friend here.

"While Mr. Owens has given you the textbook answer to my question, you are much more than that. You are far more important than you might realize. You are in fact a subdivision of Global Energy and Technology, but to the outside world, you cease to exist. Nothing you learn, see, or do here should ever be talked about with anyone other than your fellow recruits. Is that understood?"

Without physically realizing it, I chime in along with the rest of the class with a strong *Yes sir*! It's safe to say none of us are military kids, but Instructor Keets' uniform and the directness of her speech garnered only one simple reply. It's clear she's our drill sergeant and she's got plenty more to say.

"Moving right along. Sector 6. As many of you may know, beyond The Grand Wall the citizens of Sector 6 have been leading a rebellion against our government for some time now. Terrorism, by way of bombings, shootings, arson, and cyber terror, has been crippling our efforts to better society."

Keets hits a switch on the podium. The lights dim and a video projection displays on the wall behind her. We see things that no other citizen of any sector has seen before. We watch footage of militant citizens of Sector 6 destroying buildings, looting stores, beating on GET guards, and setting fires and explosions. The video ends by showing images of clean, calm, and serene water. The lights come back on, and Keets gets right back into it.

"Water. The life force of everything on this planet. It allows us to grow, sustain, breathe, and thrive. Without it, we die. But sustaining water requires power, and here at GET, we are all about power. The citizens of Sector 6 are trying to take away our ability to keep the power on, and it is up to you to keep Sector 6 from succeeding."

The class cheers, except for the girl and me. It seems we're not drinking the entire glass of Kool-Aid. This all seems a little too manufactured, a little too fake, but at least it will give us something to talk about. If and when I manage to work up the courage to say something to her. It always seems like it should be so easy, but it never is.

"Over the next few days, you will be given a series of three exams. These exams will determine exactly where you fit into this program. They will show us whether you are the best fit to be one of five positions: a security officer or bodyguard; a medical officer or drip doctor; a navigation officer or operator; an engineering officer or clinician; and last but certainly not least, a special operative. Better known as a flatliner, death jockey, half-n-half, coffin carrier, or my personal favorite, reaper. Each HD insertion team will be comprised of these five personnel. As the days go by you will learn firsthand what it takes to pull your weight within your team. Your exams will come with and without warning. Remember, we are always watching you. I wish you all the best of luck."

Keets finishes the last of her speech, takes her tablet, and exits the room. Nater enters and plants himself in front of the podium. Now we have to listen to this guy speak. I'm sure this will be good.

"Welcome to HD training and assessment. You will be under intensive screening and examination for the next few weeks. Please take the envelope given to you on your way out. In it, you will be given a number and a time. Each number corresponds to your bunk room. The time is when you are to report for your first exam. Thank you."

Short and sweet. Just like the Nater I've grown to know and love. I'm still confused, but I couldn't care less at this point. The only thing I've got on my mind is trying to talk to *her*.

A bunch of hands shoot up, but Nater ignores them and positions himself by the door. He holds a stack of envelopes. We all take this as our cue to leave. She's the first one to grab her envelope and head out of the room. I can't tell if she's eager or just sick of being in this room. We file out one by one, taking our envelopes along with us. Hop grabs his envelope just before me, and then turns toward me as we exit the room.

"What number did you get?" he asks.

I open my envelope and look. "Two."

"No way. Me too. Bunk mates."

"Yeah. Bunk mates," I say with a lack of enthusiasm. I hope he isn't picking up on it. I like him, but he's a little too excited. We walk down the hall past a GET guard who tells us to keep things moving. Hop's got something on his mind.

"Tell me more about this car," he says.

CHAPTER SEVEN

EVIE

Bunk 1 is small. I'm not sure if the other bunk is this small, but 1 is about as big as my room was in the GET girls' home. My room there was just big enough for myself and my roommate, Susan, who was one of the most private people in the world. She always kept to herself. When she wasn't staring out the window (which was most of the time), she would write in a journal. I often thought about asking what she was writing in that little book of hers, but a journal is private, so I never asked. I quickly realized I spent most of my time watching her. I guess I thought the more I watched, the more she'd realize I was watching and hopefully tell me to stop. At least then I would know she knew I was here and that she knew *how* to speak.

It took her weeks to finally say something to me. I was lying on my bed, staring up at the ceiling when it happened. It startled me. I can remember that I wasn't expecting it.

"You can't believe anything they tell you," Susan said. I knew then that Susan was someone I could trust.

All five of the red team are jammed in here. I don't know why they gave us envelopes with bunk numbers when they clearly just assigned us to rooms based on our team color. Seems like an awful waste of time when they could have just told us we were bunking with our teammates. The entire charade bothers me.

My bunkmates staked claim to the beds of their choice pretty quickly. The room is split down the middle with a stacked bunk bed on either side—between them a small walk space. Against the third wall, opposite the door, is a lone single bed. Next to each bunk and bed are lockers.

Josh took the single bed on the far wall. I think it's unfair, but the rest of the team is too afraid to say anything. Josh is the tallest of the five, and that is good enough reason for them. The two boys, Gwiz and Russell, have banded together over what hangs between their legs and have taken the stack of bunks on the right side of the room. By default, Tasha and I are forced into the bunks on the left.

"You can have top bunk if you want it. I don't mind," Tasha says.

"Thanks," I say.

"I'm a wild sleeper. I'd probably just roll off it in the middle of the night," Tasha says with a smile.

I'm not a fan of brown-nosing, but I do prefer the top, so I don't complain. I decide to look through the locker. There's some small part of me that's convinced they put the contents of my duffle in one of these things. I open the locker closest to my bunk. None of my stuff is there. There's stuff, but not mine. From the looks of the contents, I can only assume the rest are pretty much identical. There are five sets of red jumpsuits with hoods and a mirror mounted to the locker door.

"They really went all out," Tasha says.

I can feel her waiting over my shoulder. I'm not looking to make friends, but I don't want to be rude. She seems nice enough.

"Yeah. You're telling me. Reminds me of the GET Girls' Home," I say.

"You went to the Girls' Home? No way. That's so crazy. What was it like?"

"It wasn't a picnic, that's for sure."

"So you were, like, bred for this."

"I wouldn't say that."

"Don't be crazy. I bet you're going to kick some serious ass here."

"If you say so."

Josh decides to force his way into our conversation and assert his grotesque bravado. He walks over, shirt off, and tries to put an arm around me, but I push it off and toss my things on top of my bunk.

"You couldn't even go one day without me?" Josh says.

"You wish, Josh," I say.

Josh laughs, tosses his shirt over his shoulder, and heads back to his bed.

"You're right. He is an asshole," Tasha says.

I smile, pick up my envelope, and climb up the ladder into my bunk to lie down. I can tell Tasha feels like she's made a friend out of me. I'm going to have to include her now in anything I do. It would be too painful trying to break her little heart. I hear Tasha climb into the lower bunk as if she's mimicking my every action. I stare at the envelope for a moment. I haven't looked at my first exam time yet. I don't know why I put things like that off. Everyone else had already checked theirs before we even got into Bunk 1. They all shared their times with one another as soon as they saw them. Josh's exam is two days away. Both Russell and Gwiz have theirs right after Jake's. Tasha even volunteered her time, although I'm not sure anyone else but me was listening when she delicately said it.

No one questioned me for not offering up my time. I think they think I'm just private. I think they, the boys at least, pick up on my lack of conversational interest.

So I look at the envelope. It has my name on the front and a small HD letter logo in the upper left-hand corner. Other than that, it's a regular old run-of-the-mill envelope. I'm pretty astonished, really, at the lack of technological advancements so far. When I had originally thought of this program, I guess I just assumed everything would be super high-tech. Like retinal scan doors, digital Murphy beds, and dot rations. Dot rations were originally part of the NASA Mars missions before The Great Event. Entire meals were fit onto a tiny dot on a piece of tearaway paper. You simply tear off the piece of paper and throw it in a microwave. In a few minutes, you have yourself a turkey dinner or a vegetable casserole.

None of that technology seems to exist here. The HD facility is an analog fortress fifty levels under a very digital world. Being here feels a lot like how you dream up the future as a child. You draw flying cars, anti-gravity boots, people wearing jet packs, a real glorified view of the future untainted by the harsh realities and limitations of the human condition. Flash forward ten years and you find nothing you drew or thought as a child has come to fruition. The world has but micro-improvements of preexisting things. A jolt to the system that stirs you of wonder and forces you into the reality of adulthood.

I open the envelope. For all I know I could have my first exam five minutes from now. I pull out the slip of paper with my exam time on it. I look. The paper reads: 7:30 p.m. I'm nervous. I never get nervous, but for some reason, I am now. I can't decide whether it's a good thing or a bad thing that I'm one of the first ones on my team to be called in for an exam. Tasha goes before me, but that's it. Maybe one of the blue team has to go in before me. Maybe they don't. Thinking they do calms my nerves a bit, so I'll go with that.

It's probably that kid Aiden too—the one who made us all wait. He's the last to arrive and probably the first to sit in the hot seat. My own imagination is making me upset. What is the deal with that guy? He looked like he had no idea who or where he was. Even Instructor Keets called him out on it. It wasn't nice though, everyone else laughing at him. I don't like it when teachers feel it's okay to make their students look like idiots. They probably do it because *they* got picked on all the time when they were young, so using their power as an adult to make a kid feel stupid makes them feel like the tough kid they never were growing up.

Bullying is disgusting. That's why I didn't laugh with them. It was a little funny, how confused he looked and sounded, but I didn't want to make him feel stupid . . . not like that anyway.

There's something about Aiden. I can't put my finger on it, but the more I think about him, the more I feel it. I feel like I know him. I don't often feel this way, and I'm not just using some cheesy pickup line. I genuinely feel like we have some sort of connection. Maybe I've seen him on the way to GET? Maybe I've seen him at GET? In an elevator or the parking structure. Maybe we've been introduced, and I just didn't notice?

I suddenly feel warmth in the pit of my stomach. I can't believe this. I mean, he is attractive—not in the same blatantly obvious way that Josh is—but attractive in a unique and mysterious way. I'd say he's definitely an acquired taste, but one that gets better the longer you look. His icy blue eyes are magnetic. He looked at me in an odd way in the orientation room, but now I think it was very purposeful—as if he knew who I was too.

I mean, I don't know who he is, but I feel like I do. Deep down, somewhere I do. I hate not being in the know. Even worse, I hate that Aiden's on the blue team. I have to figure out where I know him from. I have to know if he knows me. I have to know why I suddenly feel drawn to him.

This is ridiculous. He probably just has one of those faces. The kind of face that makes complete strangers walk up to him and ask where they know him from. That could be it. I might just be overthinking things. It certainly wouldn't be the first time. If we happen to cross paths and the opportunity presents itself, I'll say something. If not, I'll leave it be. I can't let some boy distract me. I'm here for a reason.

I set the envelope down next to me and stare up at the

ceiling. The bed is soft enough, but the pillow is lumpy. I give it a few fluffs with my hands and get comfortable.

I like looking at the ceiling. That's why I like being on the top bunk. I do this thing where I relax my eyes and let my imagination form different shapes out of the ceiling's tiny imperfections. Sometimes I come up with faces. Other times constellations. The constellations remind me of the time I spent with my father, huddled by a fire, sleeping out under the night sky.

The stars seemed brightest then. In my mind, I know why they looked so bright. I know that The Great Event had rendered them that way. No power meant they had no competition, no glowing cities to steal the show.

My father had told me otherwise. He told me the stars were Mother Nature's million-man army. An army meant for protecting her most magnificent creation—me. They were brightest now because this is when I needed them most. He told me that when night came, the stars ruled the world, shining down on us with the mighty power of the universe. He told me as long as they stood watch, nothing could hurt me.

I find a familiar constellation amongst the cracks and dents above—Orion. I feel the soft mattress beneath me; the pillow softly cradles my head. My four hours of sleep are catching up with me. I've come a long way. Catching a few winks before my exam can't hurt.

As my eyes close, I hear the rest of my team trying to come up with a name for us as if *red team* isn't sufficient. I hear red dragons, red death, and red devils. I wonder if Aiden has to deal with this sort of idiocy on the blue team.

CHAPTER EIGHT

AIDEN

Hop and I enter Bunk 2. We're immediately surprised by what we see: two sets of bunk beds line two of the walls. A single solo bed fills the wall opposite the door. There's little room to move around, it's clear we're only supposed to sleep in here. The space leaves little room for anything else, even if we tried. It's stark. Everything is cold, made of cement and metal, like a prison or what I imagine a military barracks might be like.

A few other blue team members have already found their way into the room and claimed beds for themselves. Two Asian twins have taken the bunks on the left side of the room. The only girl occupies the solo bed.

"What? You guys couldn't wait to choose spots till Aiden and myself got here?" Hop says.

The rest of the room, all three of them, turn their attention to us. Hop points to the twins.

"That there is Sonic and . . ."

"Kyle," Sonic says.

"That's right, Kyle," Hop says. "I don't know why that's so hard to remember."

Sonic and Kyle get up from their bunks and make their way toward us. Sonic extends a handshake.

"Probably because Sonic is so unforgettable," Sonic says.

"Or stupid," Kyle says. "I don't need an introduction. I'm Kyle. Nice to meet you."

"How come you aren't wearing one of the jumpsuits?" Sonic asks.

I shrug my shoulders. Not because I don't have an answer, but genuinely because I have no idea what he's talking about. I never got one of the blue jumpsuits.

"Leave him be. He just got here. He was running late, remember?" Kyle says.

"Sonic and Kyle are twins, in case you haven't noticed. Born together, work together, and will die together," Hop says.

"That about sums it up," Sonic and Kyle say together.

"It's the twin thing. You'll get used to it," Sonic says.

I shake both their hands. My eyes wander to the solo bed against the far wall. I watch as the young woman by the bed ties her long blonde hair up in a ponytail. She's slender, but muscular. Her cut arms define her otherwise seemingly small frame. She looks tough. I've never seen a girl like this before. I'm glad she's on our team. I'm not sure how, but if there are any physical challenges, she seems like a good person to have on our side. She notices my stare.

"Name's Charlie. With an *ie*, got it?" she says.

"I think I got it," I reply.

"No nicknames. Especially not Chuck. That goes for

the lot of you. I hate being called Chuck. If I hear it, I'll knock your teeth out."

"You guys are all Bunk 2?" Hop asks.

"Sure are," Kyle says.

"We wouldn't be here if we weren't," Charlie says. I can tell by her tone that she's a firecracker—quick to explode. She's someone to keep on your good side. She doesn't take any shit from anyone—probably something she picked up over the years on the sheer fact that she's small and a female. She's probably used to getting a lot of crap from a lot of people a lot of the time. She wants all of us to know from the onset that she isn't going to put up with it. I respect that.

"In case you missed it, this is Aiden," Hop says as he lifts his thumb to me.

"Just Aiden? Or you got a nickname like this one here?" Charlie says.

"Aiden is fine," I say.

"Well, Aiden, you might as well bunk up," Charlie says.

Charlie's done with us and lies down on her bed. Sonic and Kyle pull out a deck of cards and use what little space they have to play some hybrid form of hearts. I'm sure they snuck the cards in. I'm not sure how, but they seem like those kind of guys—crafty.

I spot the empty bunks and head over. Hop rushes past me like a kid in a candy shop and jumps up and onto the top bunk.

"I got top," Hop says.

He doesn't leave me much choice, but I don't mind. He's been nice to me, and I'd rather not have to climb up and down the side of the bed every day. Sounds like a real pain in the ass if you ask me. The bottom suits me just fine.

I look around the bunk. I like to know my surroundings. I might as well get the lay of the land. On either side of the bunk are lockers. Each locker has a nightstand with a drawer built into the lower third. I open up one of the lockers to find five sets of blue jumpsuits identical to the ones that everyone else is wearing. They're made of a stretchy nylon-like cloth. I'd never wear this in my former life, but it's safe to say everything is going to be different now. A small circular patch on the breast of the shirt reads: HDR.

"I guess that answers my question about what we do for clothes," I say.

"Man, you really should have gotten the packet," Hop says.

Hop flips up the hood on his jumpsuit and disappears on his bunk. I take the same cue and lie down on mine. It's firm, but it'll do. I can't help but think about the girl. It's strange seeing her in person and not just in my dream. I wonder what her name is.

"Hey, Hop," I say.

"What's on your mind, Aiden?"

"You notice that girl on the red team?"

"Who? The one with the glasses?"

"Nah. The other one."

"Oh. The quiet, brooding one?"

"Brooding?" I ask. I know she didn't say much and seemed to keep to herself, but brooding? I don't know if I'd go that far.

"Yeah. I know who you're talking about. I don't know

her name or nothing though, but I remember seeing her. She seems intense, like she'd kick you in the balls for asking her name. Why? You interested?"

Of course I'm interested. I've only been dreaming about this girl for months now! How and why I've been dreaming about her, I have no clue, but she's important somehow and she's all I can think about. If Hop knew about my dreams, if any of them knew, they'd think I'm crazy. Maybe I am crazy. I'm sure murderers and Sector 6 bombers don't think they're crazy either, but they are. Crazy people can't diagnose themselves as crazy. It's just not possible. So I lie.

"Not in that way. I'm just curious. She looked familiar is all."

"Recruits on opposing teams aren't supposed to know one another. It can be dangerous," Charlie blurts out.

"He never got the packet!" Hop yells.

"Well, it's dangerous. Just remember that," Charlie says again.

I reach for my envelope. My interest in the girl has set a spark in the room; best to keep away from it for a while. I open it and pull out the piece of paper that has my first exam time on it. The time on the paper brings back a horrible memory. One I tried so hard to but could never forget. I was only seven years old at the time. My parents and I had abandoned our house a year before because looters were breaking into homes up and down our street, usually killing anyone they came across, so we got ahead of the curve and hit the road. Like thousands of others, we took to the streets on foot.

We banded together with a few other small families.

We were like a band of gypsies moving from place to place, looking for food and shelter. We'd stay as long as we could in one place before something would go wrong and we'd have to find another. Most of the time it was some kind of sickness that made us move. Fresh water was scarce, and it was all too easy to ingest or pick up a parasite that could kill you overnight. If someone got infected, we left them behind and moved on. We didn't want to. It's just how things were.

Other times, we'd be attacked by roving groups of vigilantes. These groups stole food, women, and children. They terrorized anyone weaker than themselves. If you didn't have anything to steal, they'd kill you, skin you, and roast you over a fire so they'd have something to get by on. They were the very definition of evil.

We had heard rumblings of a safe haven with a decent supply of food, clean water, shelter, and medical care. That would be our plan—to get there. Just a day away from our destination and we were attacked. They came while we all slept. It was a brutal massacre. People ran for their lives; parents tried their best to protect their young. I was hit on the head with a blunt object and went unconscious.

My father and mother had done all they could to protect me. They were both drenched in blood when they woke me. My father hoisted me on his shoulder and carried me a whole day until we arrived at the safe haven hospital. We started with eighty, and by the time they had gone, only thirty of us were left. People lost wives, husbands, and children.

My father put me down, then collapsed. My mother fell on top of him, beating him hysterically with her fists, but his body lay motionless. She beat him and beat him until she lost the last bit of strength she had left. When she collapsed, a rush of doctors and nurses picked them both up and carried them off into an exam room.

The rest was a blur, nothing more than a series of lights and faces. A kind, gentle woman came in and tended to my head. She cleaned it with fresh water and bandaged it with gauze. When she left and closed the curtain, I could hear her arguing with a man, a doctor.

It wasn't long before the curtains to my room opened. I knew what they were going to say before they said it. My parents were dead. A few months later, I was sent to the GET Boys' home.

"What time's your first exam?" Hop asks.

He hangs his head over the side of his bunk. He must have heard me rustling the paper from the envelope.

"Seven," I say.

"Today?" Hop seems surprised.

"Is that bad?"

"I don't know. Seems so soon. Man. They must really want to get you going."

"I don't even know what these exams are going to be like. Am I supposed to study, or what?" I ask.

"I don't think they're going to be the kind of tests you can study for. Just a hunch."

"Yeah. You're probably right," I say. Now I'm nervous. Thanks, Hop. He swings his body back up onto the upper bunk. I relax into my pillow. It sure is lumpy. I give it a few good whacks to soften it up.

Much better.

I seep into the comfort of the bed. I'm afraid to fall asleep. I don't want to have my nightmare again, but I can't seem to help it. I'm tired and the past two days have been quite the ride. I have a few hours before my first exam. Maybe I'll get some sleep. I might need it.

I hear Sonic and Kyle as they argue over their card game. Hop and Charlie talk about what tomorrow might have in store for us all. I focus on individual voices until they combine into a dull, steady hum—a calming technique I taught myself after my parents died.

Before I know it, my eyes drift closed and I'm sound asleep.

. . .

I jerk awake. At first, I think it's because of my nightmare, but it's not. I sit up quickly and listen. I'm sure I must have heard something. A digitized voice comes over an intercom.

"Aiden Bishop. Report to Exam Room 9. Aiden Bishop. Report to Exam Room 9," it says over and over.

I rub my eyes and glance over at a small clock on the nightstand. 7:05 p.m. Damn! I'm going to be late for my first exam. I swing my feet over the side of my bed. They hit the cold floor and I stand. I look around the room. Besides the intercom, the room is quiet. None of my other bunkmates are here. I wonder where they are.

"Aiden Bishop. Please report to Exam Room 9," the intercom says again.

I feel my shirt. It's a little damp from my now seemingly chronic night sweats. I smell too. I can't show up to my first exam late and smelling as bad as I do. The locker. I fling it open and grab one of the blue jumpsuits. I put it on and look at myself in a mirror fixed on the inside of the locker door. I look like an idiot, but I don't have any other choice. I shut the locker and head for the door.

Once I'm in the hall, I'm in new territory. I look to my left and then to my right, but I don't see anyone. Where is everybody? Where do I go? In front of me, I see a sign on the wall. It reads: EXAM ROOMS 1-5 and EXAM ROOMS 6-10. Arrows underneath the text point to the left and right. I have to get to exam room 9, so I guess I have to head to the right.

I move swiftly down the hallway. I'm not nervous, but anxious. I don't know what to expect once I get to the exam room. I hope they still let me take the exam, even though I'm late. I wonder if it will affect my overall score. I wonder if there even are scores. Maybe it's just pass or fail. That'd be nice. Ultimately, all I really hope is that this exam sheds some light on what I'm doing here and makes what Arthur told me sensible. Whatever lies ahead in Exam Room 9, I just have to get there.

As I move through the hallway, I notice that I'm being watched. Small surveillance cameras line the corridors. When I pass by, the cameras rotate to follow. It makes me uneasy, but this is all part of it. That's the point. They have to watch us. They have to study our every move if they are to place us. Don't they? Every other level in the GET building has cameras too, but we've always been told they are for security purposes. Now though, after seeing this place, I'm not too sure. I feel as though GET watches everyone *all* the time. My mind runs freely. I think about where the camera feeds must go and who must be watching them. Then I see it.

The door to Exam Room 9 has no handle. I'm not entirely sure how I open it, but I'm usually good with these sorts of things. After all, this might be part of the exam. I reach out a hand. My plan is to feel all over the surface of the door, but the door slides open on its own.

. . .

Exam Room 9 is dark. The hallway had been bright and cold, but this room is dark and warm. I hear the door shut and lock behind me. Why lock the door? It seems strange, but I can't let it get to me. It's silent. So silent I can hear myself breathe. It takes a moment for my eyes to adjust, and then I take a look around.

In the center of the room, a single overhead light drops a pool of warm light on the top of a table. A single chair is pushed in neatly. I walk over and pull out the chair. I sit. Before me are two items: a piece of paper and a pen. I pick up the pen. Seems like a normal enough pen, not much to it. I examine the paper. Same here. Seems like an ordinary run-of-the-mill piece of paper. There aren't any instructions and no one here to tell me what to do. I'm confused.

"Aiden Bishop," a voice says over another intercom. I perk up. "Your first examination is simple. You have fifteen minutes to use the pen and piece of paper to draw a perfect circle. You may only draw one circle per side of the paper. If one of your circles is not perfect, you fail the exam. If you run out of time, you fail the exam."

"How am I supposed to draw a perfect circle without some sort of tool? I don't think—"

"You now have thirteen minutes remaining," the intercom booms.

This exam is dumb. Not only is it dumb, it's also impossible. What kind of cyborg human do you have to be to draw a perfect circle without some kind of protractor thingy? It's just not possible. And what does this test prove anyway? Nothing. That's what. Unless you think it's important to know how shaky your hand is. Failure is inevitable here and they know that. They do *know* that. That's the point. They want me to fail. I'm sure everyone fails. Failure *is* the point. They want to see how we deal with inevitable failure. Will I still try even though I know I'm certain not to succeed? Well, now I don't feel as bad. If everyone's going to fail, then why waste any more time.

I put my pen to the paper, but something comes to me. I feel a smile creep over my face. I don't like failing. I've been too good at it for far too long. I want to win for a change. I want to pass this exam and show them I'm not like everyone else. I know exactly how to do it.

I remember something I had seen on my uniform. Its letters form a very common and specific shape—a shape that would prove very useful in this circumstance. I put down my pen and put one hand on the breast of my jacket. Running my fingers over the edges of the HDR patch, I find a weak point in the stitching and with one hard yank, I tear it from the blue fabric.

I wipe off any excess threads from my destructive stroke of genius and hold it up to the light. It's a perfect circle.

I toss it down on top of the paper and pick up my pen. Holding the patch down with one hand, I carefully trace around its edges. When I'm done I swipe the patch aside and look at my work. I did a pretty damn good job. I'd say it's perfect.

I'd pay good money to see the expressions on their faces, whoever they are. I can only assume they have cameras hidden in this room, watching my every move. I'd like to imagine Arthur is watching. When I met him the first time, in that mysterious black and white room, he seemed proud. Proud like a father would be of a son. I feel as though he had chosen me personally for this program and there might be a lot at stake for him if I fail. If he wasn't proud before, he most certainly would be now.

I finished the circle. What happens next? Did I not draw a perfect circle? Do they think I cheated? What's taking so long? I'm hungry. I can't remember the last time I ate. This is stupid. I'm done waiting.

"Now what?" I ask aloud.

There's no response from the voice above, but it's only seconds before the door slides open and the intercom comes back on.

"Please proceed to the mess hall," it says.

I stand, push the chair back in, and do as I'm told.

CHAPTER NINE

THE OTHERS

NSIDE THE CONTROL room, it's dark. The only light comes from a wall of monitors. The monitors show footage from cameras all over the HD program. The small monitors show Sonic, Kyle, and Charlie in the mess hall getting some food. They show Hop in the locker room getting dressed after a shower. They show Josh and Russell arm-wrestling one another, Gwiz cheering them on. They show Tasha reading a book, and they show Evie fast asleep in her bunk.

One larger monitor sits centered, surrounded by all the others. On this monitor is Aiden sitting and waiting in Exam Room 9. Besides the monitors, there are two people in the room. One man, shrouded in darkness, sits in a chair and watches the monitors closely. The other, standing behind the chair, is Arthur. Arthur watches Aiden on the monitor and smiles.

"I'm not sure I like that he passed," the mysterious man says.

"What's not to like? He's perfect," Arthur replies.

"It's the way he passed that bothers me. He seems like he might be difficult."

"Still. He passed in under five minutes. That's impressive."

"No one is supposed to pass the first exam!"

The mysterious man slams his fists down on the control board in front of him.

"Then that should tell you something," Arthur says.

"You've said that before."

"No. This is different. Aiden's different. I've been watching him for eleven years. He won't be difficult. It's just not in him. He likes order and structure. He likes to keep his head down, and he's got one of the strongest gifts of limbo I've seen in a long time. With a little bit of training, he could be the strongest. All we have to do is point him in the right direction. He'll follow. You'll see."

"So you're saying he's ready?"

"I wouldn't have pulled him four levels early if I didn't think he was ready. Besides, we're running out of time, and he's exactly what you've been looking for."

"You're playing a dangerous game, Arthur. If he—"

"He won't find out, but even if he did, he's manageable. His gift is too strong a candidate to overlook. He's invaluable. Aiden could be the key to this company's future. He is the solution."

The man doesn't respond to Arthur right away. He just sits and watches Aiden impatiently waiting on the screen, then reaches for a red button just below the monitor, and presses it. On the large monitor, the door to the exam room opens. Light spills into the room and Aiden stands, covering his eyes from the brightness of the hallway.

"I'm trusting you. We'll see how he does, but keep a close eye on him," the man says.

"You're making the right decision. You won't regret this," Arthur replies.

"For your sake, I hope you're right," the man says.

Arthur smiles and turns to leave the room. He got what he wanted, and Aiden performed better than even he could have expected. He leaves the control room, closing the door behind him. The shadowed man places a hand on a joystick and zooms the camera in closer to Aiden as he walks from the table to the door of Exam Room 9.

CHAPTER TEN
EVIE

'M RUNNING THROUGH a field of magnificent wildflowers. All my favorites are there. Brilliant yellow daffodils nestled securely amongst sprigs of delicate baby's breath. Dandelion spores float and flutter in the air like warm weather snowflakes. The sun is full, its warmth like a blanket of light on my skin. I'm filled with joy. I'm laughing. Not to myself, but *with* someone. I can't make out who they are, but I'm not alone.

I'm happy. I can feel the smile on my face. My cheeks are beginning to hurt from how wide and consistent my smile is. I can hear him now—the one who is with me. It's a man. I can hear his laughter harmonize with mine. Our voices echo through the atmosphere. He's chasing me, but playfully. I want him to chase me. I'm sure I instigated it. I like being desired. I like being wanted. I like being loved.

The chase must soon come to an end. I'm growing tired and I don't know how much longer I can glide through these fields, these endless fields of beauty. My arms extend like a goose landing on the shimmering surface of a lake. My fingertips brush the tops of the flowers—their soft petals flirt under my gentle touch. I twirl and fall; the gentle embrace of nature breaking my fall. Orange butterflies take to the air. I've disturbed their momentary home, but they're all too happy to let me stay awhile.

I feel safe. Safe beneath the bed of vegetation. Safe with him. He's upon me. His identity waits in silhouette, the sun beating down over his shoulders. I want to know him. I hold out a hand. I invite him beside me. He takes my hand and everything seems perfect; we just fit. His firm grip and soft skin comfort me. I pull hard, bringing him to the ground next to me.

The sun revealed I close my eyes to give them time to adjust. I feel his lips on mine. They're warm and gentle. We kiss. Nothing in this world could be more perfect at this very moment.

I open my eyes and see him for the first time. It's Aiden. For some reason, I'm not surprised. I'm not taken aback. Somehow, this feels like it should, like it's meant to be. I smile and stare into his beautiful blue eyes. I can see that he loves me. I feel like I love him. I must, for he would never look at me this way if I didn't.

Then I feel it. A slow, fleeting darkness sneaks up on me. I can see the world starting to turn black. The sun has turned into a demon night. Aiden looks scared and confused. I can tell he doesn't see everything that I do. He doesn't see the immense suffering or impending death. I want to reassure him, but my body stiffens. I can barely see him now, as a dark curtain falls over my eyes. They are open and looking, but they cannot see. I cry because I know that these are my last moments in this world, with Aiden. I must give in to the darkness. There's no use fighting it. It's too powerful. This is the only way. I wish I could tell him not to worry, but the thought of losing him overtakes me.

"Save me," I say with my last breath of air.

. . .

I sit up in my bed, nearly smacking my head on the ceiling. I'm sweating bullets and gasping for air. I wipe the sweat from my forehead and pull back my hair. I have a lot of hair, and it's only making things worse. My mind is racing. It felt so real, the dream, but I have no idea why Aiden was in it. I'm not sure I know what to think about the whole thing. The peculiar thing is that it's not the first time I've had the dream. I've had a similar dream a few times over the past few years, but I've never seen the person who was chasing me. I always wake up before that part of it.

It's weird because I only caught a glimpse of Aiden yesterday. How can I already be dreaming about him? Has he always been the person in the dream or am I only now putting him in it? I'm somewhat ashamed and yet it doesn't feel strange or uncomfortable. Kissing Aiden isn't the hardest part for me to accept. What is hard is what happened after I saw it was Aiden I was kissing—the darkness that came over me, the cold, the feeling of death. Somehow I feel like this is some kind of sign or message, but for what? Am I supposed to stay away from him? Or is the exact opposite the right decision?

Regardless, I liked the kiss. I wonder if that's what it

would be like in real life, with him. I feel my cheeks blush red. I never paid much attention to it before, but now I wouldn't mind having the dream again, if for no other reason than to try to figure out what it all means.

Tasha hears me breathing heavily and puts down her tablet and pops her head up to my level. "You okay up there?" she asks.

"Yeah, I'm fine." I don't really want to talk about it, and I hope she leaves it at that.

"You don't *look* fine. You look like hell."

"It was just a bad dream. No biggie."

"Okay. If you want to talk about it, I'm—"

"What time is it?" I interrupt. I'm so caught up in this stupid dream I almost forgot about my exam. Tasha looks at the clock on her tablet.

"Just about 7:20," she says.

"Shoot." I jump out of my bunk and open my locker. I look in the mirror. Tasha was right. I do look like hell. I have a horrible case of bed head and enormous bags under my eyes. Not to mention, I had just sweat like a crazy person in a jumpsuit—literally. I run my fingers through my hair. Any bit of structure would be an improvement.

I was wrong. Now my hair looks worse. Why does it have to be so thick?

"Evie Fox. Please report to Exam Room 9," an intercom voice says. Great. I don't have time for this. I throw my hair up in a ponytail and call it a thing. "Evie Fox. Please report to Exam Room 9."

"You better get a move on, girl," Tasha says.

"I know. I know." I shut my locker and head for the

door. "Oh man, I didn't even ask you how your exam went. Was it hard?"

"It wasn't hard, but . . . ah, forget about it. We're all going to grab some food at the mess hall a little later if you're interested in stopping by after your exam."

"Sure, maybe. I don't know . . . I gotta get going," I say.

As I exit Bunk 1 and follow the signs for Exam Room 9, I hear Tasha calling out to me. She wants me to know that I have to eat sometime and that I can't starve myself. As much as I hate to admit it, she's right, and I am hungry. I'll probably stop by the mess hall and attempt to be a part of this team. That is if I pass this exam.

This place is a maze of hallways, and everything looks identical. A splash of color here or there wouldn't hurt. I feel like I'm stuck in a hospital, a horrible feeling. It smells like a hospital too, that chloroform-sterile smell that after a while makes you want to either pass out or puke. I could do both right about now.

I round a corner and smash right into Aiden. We both hit the ground hard. He climbs to his feet and extends a hand, but I'm already on my feet again and brushing myself off.

"Sorry about that. I didn't mean to take you out," Aiden says.

"Maybe you should just stay out of my way," I say.

"Oh. Yeah. You're probably right. I'm Aiden by the way."

"I know who you are."

"And you are?"

Aiden bobs his head left and right, trying to make eye contact, until finally, boom, we connect. His pale blue eyes pierce into mine, and I feel my stomach drop.

"Evie," I say.

I can't believe I'm acting like such a girl. Not my best moment. My dad would *not* be proud.

"Hi," he says.

"Hey," I reply. "I need to—"

"Sure. Yeah."

Aiden steps aside and I brush past him. *Hey?* What is that? I'm not cool enough to throw out a passing *hey*. Not to mention I would never want him, let alone anyone, to think that's the way I talk. I could have at least said a real *hello*; even a respondent *hi* would have sufficed. I'm such an idiot. I look over my shoulder to see if he's still walking. He's not. He's looking right back at me. I'm not sure what to do, so I snap my head back around. I'm embarrassed he caught me looking back at him. I feel my steps grow smaller.

"Hold up a minute," Aiden shouts.

My small steps come to a halt and my heart quickens as I turn to see him coming toward me. What now?

"Could you make this quick? I've got to get to Exam Room 9," I say, realizing I must sound like a total bitch. Thankfully he ignores my snarl.

"I've been hoping we'd run into each other. I saw you this morning at orientation. I told myself that if I ran into you, I'd say something . . . this is me saying something."

He's shy, I can tell, but he had set his mind to something and stuck to it. He's confident in a nonthreatening way. I like that. It's refreshing.

"Well, it was nice to meet you, Aiden. Thank you for introducing yourself. I'm sure I'll be seeing you around. I really do have to get to—"

"Your first exam. Right. I won't keep you then. Exam Room 9 is down the hall on the left. I just came from there."

"Thanks." I turn and continue on my way. For some reason, I'm smiling. It seemed as good as a first conversation could go. Didn't say too much or too little. I'm pretty satisfied.

Aiden catches up with me and stops me with a gentle hand on my shoulder.

"I'm sorry. I swear, last thing," he says. He's looking for validation, the permission to proceed.

"Okay . . ." I lead him into it.

"I know this is going to sound a little crazy, but I know you. Somehow I know you. Now you don't have to believe me, but I'd really like to get the chance to explain it to you. Could you give me that chance? I don't know what it is about you and me, but I need the chance to find out."

I look at him, surprised. I start to think of all sorts of things. How does he know me? Is he a crazy person? But mostly, did he have a dream about me too?

"Yeah. Sure. After my exam, I was gonna go meet up with some of my teammates in the mess hall. Does that work?" I ask.

"That's perfect. Absolutely perfect."

"I guess I'll see you then. I really do have to get going. I don't want to be late," I say.

Aiden smiles and it makes me smile back. I like his smile. I recognize it from the dream. He slowly backs away and I turn to watch him leave.

"Until then. I'll be waiting, anxiously and on the edge of my seat."

"Okay," I say gently.

"Oh, and Evie?"

"Yeah?"

"Don't let the exam intimidate you. You'll do great," Aiden says as he places his hand over his chest. I notice his jacket is torn slightly where his hand rests. He turns and heads down the hall, finally disappearing around a corner.

CHAPTER ELEVEN

AIDEN

THE MESS HALL is full of recruits. Everyone is here: all of the red team except Evie, Charlie, Hop, Sonic, and Kyle. There are other HD program employees as well: doctors and nurses, instructors, security guards, and personnel. The mess hall itself is cafeteria style. There are long metal picnic tables attached to rows of bench seats. A long line of people stand, trays in hand, waiting for food as they pass by each food station. It feels like I'm back in the boys' home.

Hop slides up next to me. It's clear he's been waiting for me to get back from my exam. I'm sure he wants to know all the details. He'll want to know what I had to do. How long I had to do it in. If it was hard or easy. If it was physical, mental, or both. I don't know if I have the heart to tell him the exam couldn't have been more disappointing, that his excitement is misplaced and he's better off saving it for another time. He just wants to know what to expect so he can relax a little, maybe get some rest tonight, but the truth is, he shouldn't expect much.

"I recommend the hamburgers, and definitely stay away from whatever that is." Hop points through the display glass at a lumpy, oozing, colorless blob. Both of our faces cringe, imagining that the flavor must be even worse than it looks.

"It's a high-protein, high-vitamin, nutrient-rich oatmeal that happens to be free of gluten, preservatives, and chemical processing toxins," a server behind the counter interjects. I look at Hop, and then Hop looks at the server.

"He'll take a burger," Hop says.

"Sure, one hamburger please," I say.

"One thick, greasy slab of red meat coming right up," the server says with disgust. I slide my tray down the counter, and the server plops a burger on it. I reach and grab a bag of potato chips from a basket at the end of the counter. Hop looks at me and holds up a bottle of water. I nod my head yes.

I try not to drink anything other than water. There's nothing better for you and there's nothing your body needs or wants more. I still treat water like it's a precious commodity. It's been a decade since the end of The Great Event, but I can still remember how important, precious, and scarce water was back then. Other than avoiding being killed by other humans, your second and most vital concern was finding fresh water. Bottles of water only lasted a few months after it all started, and without power, purification plants weren't operational.

On the road, we had come up with ways of purifying water on our own, using sunlight, boiling, filtration through cotton or charcoal, but nothing was ever 100 percent pure, and that's if you could even find water. It had grown scarce pretty quick. Our bodies' senses knew the difference too. From its yellowish-brown tint to the way it smelled of earth or dirt. And I can never forget the way it tasted. Let's just say it was pretty disgusting. On a lucky day, it would rain. Rainwater was like the Holy Grail of water. You'd find any way possible to catch and store as much of it as you could. People would kill for it—literally. Now I never take water for granted. Never.

"I'm sitting right over here, come on," Hop says as I follow him to a table where our blue team sits and chows down.

Hop takes a seat. Charlie is sitting across from him. Next to Charlie, Sonic and Kyle steal one another's fries. To round out the table, I sit in an empty seat next to Hop.

"You already met them, but this is Charlie, Sonic, and Kyle," Hop says.

"I can remember their names," I say.

"Does he look like an idiot, Hop?" Charlie says.

"I'm sorry. I've always been bad with names. I'm just trying to be nice," Hop says.

"Don't worry about it," I say.

We all eat our burgers, except Charlie. Charlie fell for the speech and got the blob. She seems to be enjoying it. She strikes me as the kind of person who only likes to put the best things in her body. A real *your body is what you eat* sort of person. My mother was like that, but I take more after my father. I love to indulge in food. I'm blessed with a high metabolism and I like to take advantage of it.

I feel their eyes watching me. No one is saying anything, but they're all thinking the same thing—tell us about the exam. I think it's kind of funny. I've never been the popular kid before, so even if it's a false popularity, I like it. I'll hold on to the feeling until one of them cracks.

"So? Spill!" Sonic says. I thought Hop would be the first one, but maybe he's too polite to pry.

"Spill what?" I play dumb.

"What do you mean *what*? You're the first person on our team to go through the first exam," Sonic says.

"*Any exam*," Kyle chimes in.

"Leave him be. It's none of your damn business," Charlie snaps.

"It can't hurt to ask, you know. I'd sure like to know what to expect," Sonic says.

And there it is—the expectation. Telling them they should expect to fail would undoubtedly crush them. I could explain that's what the first exam is designed to do, but I'm not sure they'd care or really understand. They'd be too hung up on the *fail* part. I could tell them how I had to essentially cheat just to pass. That reminds me, I wonder how Evie is doing?

"Every exam is tailored to the individual. It wouldn't matter anyway," Hop says.

"What do you know? I heard the first exam is the same for everyone," Kyle says.

"He's not supposed to talk about it. That'd be cheating and Aiden's no cheater," Hop says.

"Don't be such a goody-goody," Sonic says.

"You don't have to tell these goons anything if you don't want to," Charlie reassures me. I better put an end to this before things get messy.

"Listen. Guys, it's okay. I don't mind. Really."

"See. He doesn't even mind," Sonic says.

"Just let the man speak already." Kyle jabs Sonic in the ribs with his elbow and Sonic retaliates with a fist smack to his brother's shoulder.

"It wasn't much. I overslept. I got woken up by some horrible intercom alarm and showed up to an exam room." I have them captivated. I could tell them anything at this point and they'd believe it, but I stick with the truth . . . most of it anyway. "No one was in there, just a table and a piece of paper. Another intercom told me I had to draw a perfect circle in fifteen minutes."

They all look dumbfounded, like that can't be it. Surely there must be more to this story. There's a little more—that I cheated and passed—but I figure I won't volunteer that information.

"A circle?" Sonic says.

"That's what he said. A circle," Hop says for me. He looks happy. He smiles. Probably because he's amused at how disappointed everyone else is.

"What does it mean?" Kyle says.

"And that was it? The entire exam? Nothing else?" Charlie fires off in succession.

I feel a little bad they are so upset, but I can't help what happened.

"Sorry to disappoint," I say with a shoulder shrug.

Josh and Gwiz, from the red team, interrupt our mopefest. They've clearly heard all that I've said. I'm sure they're just as interested in the first exam, even if they're trying to act like they aren't. I dislike fake people.

"I wouldn't sell yourself short, Bishop, is it?" Josh says.

He's clearly a bro. If his popping muscles and chiseled face weren't enough, his use of my last name to address me is a dead giveaway.

"Word is you aced your first exam. I'd hardly say that's nothing," Josh's little minion Gwiz says.

It's clear that he's directing it at Charlie. He seems like a real misogynist. The kind of guy who thinks a woman doesn't belong in the workplace. The kind of guy who thinks women should be at home cooking, cleaning, and popping out kids. Charlie is getting angry. She looks ready to jump across the table and crush her tray over his head. I'll play the game to avoid an incident.

"I don't know anything about that. I thought all of the exams are either pass or fail. So I'm not really sure how I *aced* it," I say.

"If you passed, you might as well have aced it. That or you're a liar." Gwiz is trying to defend his stupid remark. He doesn't seem that bright.

"Is there something wrong with passing?" I ask.

"Nobody passes the first exam. That's the point. It's designed to make you fail. To see how you handle it," Josh says. I'm not sure how he knows about the nature of the first exam, but my money's on Josh being a legacy. Who knows what he may already know. He might be someone to watch out for.

"I don't believe you. You're just trying to get in our heads," Charlie says.

"You don't have to believe us, just ask Tasha. She didn't pass and she's supposed to be smart," Gwiz says.

"I guess Tasha is just another loser. Maybe she was assigned to the wrong bunk. Hey, Chuck, you want to take her place? You'd be more than welcome," Josh says as he blows Charlie a kiss.

Charlie jumps up and lunges across the table toward Josh. I step between them. She tries her best to go after him, but I manage to hold her back.

"Fuck you, asshole!" Charlie yells.

Hop jumps right in and reaches a hand over me, trying to diffuse the heated situation.

"I don't think we've formally been introduced. My name is Matt—"

Josh shoves Hop back down into his seat. Evie storms across the mess hall. At some point during the commotion, she'd returned from her exam.

"Hey Josh!" Evie says.

"Not right now, Evie, I'm talking with my new friends," he says.

"If Tasha didn't pass and everyone is supposed to fail, and you fail, doesn't that also make you a loser?" Evie says.

"And how'd you do?" Josh says.

"Fine. Now, why don't you leave them alone."

Josh straightens his posture and clears his throat. It's clear that he can't decide whether or not listening to Evie would make him look weak.

"Catch you guys around . . . if you're all still here," Josh says as he walks away.

"And put a muzzle on that rabid dog of yours," Gwiz says. He grabs a handful of fries off Kyle's tray and shovels them into his mouth as he turns and follows Josh out of the mess hall. Charlie sits back down with a thud. She's a little calmer now, but still fuming.

"What a dick," Sonic says.

We all laugh. It was funny the way Sonic said it. Sonic seems like he might be the clown of the group.

"Sorry about that. I know he's my teammate, but Josh can be a real ass. Always has been," Evie says.

"We didn't need your help. We had it under control," Charlie says.

"You knew him before?" I say.

"We used to work on the same level."

"What is his problem anyway?" Kyle asks.

"They're just legacies. They think they're hot shit, it's in their makeup, but they aren't better than anyone else. They just happen to have been born into it," Charlie says. Her resentment is hard to hide.

Hop shuffles in his seat. He seems agitated by Charlie's answer to Kyle's question, a question he undoubtedly thinks is unfounded.

"Well, I'm going to grab some food real quick. Maybe I'll see you later?" Evie says.

"Yeah, sure," I say.

Evie walks back across the mess hall, picks up a tray, and gets in line. I see Charlie roll her eyes as I sit back down. It's obvious she doesn't approve of Evie and I talking.

"You know, Josh's dad is a legend," Hop says.

"Shut up. Do you think you could get your head out of Josh's ass for like two seconds already? God. You're embarrassing yourself. You don't even know anything about his father," Charlie snaps back.

"I know his picture is up in the Hall of the Deceased."

"The Hall of the Deceased?" I ask.

"It's in the South wing. It's literally just a room filled with pictures and names of reapers," Kyle says.

"It's not *just* pictures of reapers. It's pictures of the *best* reapers," Hop says.

"And what makes a good reaper?" Charlie sarcastically asks. She knows very well that no one at this table knows what a reaper actually does. Some say the reaper is just the boss of the team, responsible for making the tough calls. Some think the reaper is more like what the name implies—death—and is an assassin of some sort. Some think he's more like a farmer, or reaping tool, designed to help manufacture GET's energy source. I haven't really given it much thought, but if I had to choose, the latter seems the most realistic to me.

"This should be good," Sonic mutters.

"Well, I don't know, but I bet I got what it takes," Hop says.

Charlie and the twins burst out laughing.

"I bet," Charlie says between laughs.

"If you ask me, it looks like the only one so far who might have what it takes is our Aiden here," Kyle says.

Hop stands. He's frustrated and wants to leave. He grabs his tray and empties it into the trash. "I'm gonna head back to the bunk."

The rest of the group follow his example and empty their trays. As they do so, I see Evie walking back toward our table.

"We're all going to head back to Bunk 2. You coming?" Kyle asks.

I can't take my eyes off Evie. I want to make sure she knows I want her to come sit with me. There's no way I'm leaving now. Charlie notices my trance and doesn't like it. I can't tell if she's just mad that I'm interested in someone on the red team, or if she's jealous.

"You coming or what?" Charlie snaps.

"No. You guys go ahead. I'll see you soon," I reply.

"Don't take *too* long," Charlie says. She lays on her disgust pretty thick. "Come on, let's get out of here."

Sonic, Kyle, and Hop follow Charlie out of the mess hall. On his way, Hop leans in and tells me to be careful. I know what he means, but I don't think Evie is the type to screw me over. She slides her tray on the table and sits across from me. Then it hits me: maybe Hop is trying to tell me to be careful because she might break my heart. Now that's a possibility.

"Did I scare them away?" Evie asks.

"Nah. They were already on their way out."

"Did you want to go with them? I can—"

"No. I'm where I want to be," I say. She smiles, but it's true. It's not just some line I'm using to try to get her to like me. I'm not sure she'd believe me though if I told her that. She reaches into her pocket, pulls out her jumpsuit's HD patch, and tosses it on the table. I smile.

"Thanks by the way . . . for the help."

"So does this mean you also passed?"

"I did, but don't be too proud of yourself. I'm pretty crafty. I would have thought of something."

"I'm sure you would have."

Evie smacks me in the shoulder with the back of her hand.

"I would have. I don't like to lose, okay?"

"Okay. I got it. I just wonder how pissed the program is going to be now that two people passed their impassable exam."

"Probably pretty pissed. Especially since we cheated."

"We did not."

"Oh really. What would you call it then?"

"Creative interpretation of the rules."

"Oh, I get it."

"What?"

"You're one of those people that don't color in the lines."

"And that's a bad thing?"

"Not sure yet."

Evie takes a bite of her burger. I'm not sure how to follow that. Is she done talking with me? Should I not have told her how I passed the exam? She's so interesting.

"So?" Evie says.

"Sooo . . ." I can't make the connection. I must look like a blundering idiot. "Ah! I'm the one who asked you here."

"I thought that was you," she says. She's trying to be cute and it's working. She's good at it, but it doesn't feel like she does it all the time. There's shyness to her flirting. It's endearing.

I'm suddenly struck by fear—the fear of choice. What do I say? It might seem weird and creepy if I just come right out and tell her I've been having dreams about her. Dreams in which we make out in a field of flowers and then she dies in my arms. Yeah, that might come off a little strong, but there's something that tells me she'll be able to see through anything else I come up with. So, the truth it is. Brutal as it might be, it's the best way to see where she stands.

"I've been having dreams about you, nightmares actually. Well, the first part feels like a dream, but then the second part turns into a nightmare," I say.

She looks at me for a moment in silence. Her face is as white as a ghost. I knew I should have just made something up. Anything else would have been better than the truth.

"Me too," Evie says back.

I don't think I'm hearing this right, so I ask her to repeat herself. She tells me the same thing I thought I had heard—she, too, had a dream about me.

"What's your dream about?" Evie asks.

I tell her everything, and everything I say comes out so easily now. It just flows out of me. I tell her every detail. I tell her about the field of flowers, how at first I couldn't see myself in the dream, but recently I could. I tell her about how I'm chasing her and we both seem so happy. How we laugh together. How we lie on the ground next to one another. How we kiss and how beautiful it is. Then I tell her how I can see a darkness fill her eyes. How her skin turns cold, and I can feel the life leaving her body. I tell her everything.

Her eyes start to well up. Two tears run down her cheeks. Now I feel bad. I don't want to make her cry. I would never want that. I reach across the table and wipe the tears from her face. She nuzzles my hand, accepting the moment of comfort.

She looks at me, different than before. She wants to know more. I can see she wants to understand.

"I'm sorry if I upset you," I say.

Evie puts a reassuring hand on mine. "You said *dreams*. How long have you been having them?"

"Oh, I don't know. At least a few months now."

Evie looks shocked, like she doesn't know how to respond.

"I had a dream about you, this afternoon," Evie says.

I pull back. I don't know what to think. This is odd, very odd.

"Was it—"

"Yes. The same dream," Evie says.

Now I know why she was crying. It wasn't my fault at all. She was crying because she thought she was crazy to have been dreaming about someone she had never even met. But I was having the same dream and that made it okay.

"What do you think it means?" Evie asks.

I want to give her an answer, but I can't. I don't want to lie to her and I really just don't have a clue what any of it, any of this, means.

"I don't know," I say.

Neither of us knows what it means, but we understand that the dream brought us together. Somehow we know we were meant to meet one another and we shouldn't turn our backs on that. Our lack of answers leads to silence, then an in-depth discussion about our lives. We rationalize our predicament and figure talking about our pasts might shed some light on the present.

Evie tells me all about her childhood—what she can remember—and where she was when The Great Event happened. She tells me all about how she and her family struggled in the mountains, how they fought to survive. She saddens when she tells me about her mother leaving and what it did to her father. We laugh together when I find out that she, too, was part of the GET kids program. She tells me about her friend Susan and about the talks they would have about classic cinema. She tells me about how quickly she moved up from class to class within GET and how she applied to the HD program the very second she hit level 40.

I feel like I know her now, but I can tell there's something she's hiding. She's doing a really good job concealing whatever it is, so I don't pry. Not now. It's not the right time. I tell myself she'll let me know when she's ready.

Evie asks about me, and I tell her about my troubles on the streets. I tell her about my mischievous behavior at the GET boys' home. I tell her how I hated my job. I tell her about how my parents died during The Great Event. I decide to even tell her about the accident and Arthur. At first, she doesn't believe any of it, but after studying my face she concedes that there might be some truth to it. After all, they would never let someone into the HD program who hadn't applied and wasn't at least a level 40 employee. I bare my soul to her and she accepts it.

After we're all talked out and the last of the mess hall patrons have gone, we realize it might be time to call it a night.

"I guess I should get going. I told the guys I wouldn't be far behind them," I say.

"Yeah, I understand. Me too. I should get going I mean."

We clear our trays and make our way to the door. The lights to the mess hall turn off and we find ourselves standing in the doorway, the brightness of the hallway spilling into the dark of the mess hall.

"Thanks again," Evie says.

"For what?"

"Oh, I don't know. The exam . . . everything."

"Sure. I mean, you're welcome."

"I'll see you around, Aiden."

Evie leans in like she's about to give me a kiss. I feel the warmth of her breath against my skin. My heart skips a beat, but she doesn't kiss me. Instead, she slips past me, out the door, and down the hall.

CHAPTER TWELVE
EVIE

I FEEL RELIEVED AS I walk back to my bunk. It's still strange how things are, but I'm not alone in how I feel. Aiden seems easy to trust, but maybe that's not a good thing. I kind of wish I had kissed him, but it's too soon. Even though we talked—the best talk I've had in my life with another person, and that includes my own father—I need to remember to be cautious. We're all only two days into the program, and I need to keep my game face on. I can't let my feelings for some boy get out of hand.

But he's not some boy. I know that. I feel that. The way he listens and hangs on my every word or the way he looks at me with the yearning affections of a puppy. He's special. He's not like anyone I've ever met, and that scares me. I don't know what to expect from him. I can usually read people incredibly well. I can usually peg someone's personality within the first few sentences. I'm a profiler, call it one of my instinctual defense mechanisms, but with

Aiden, I can't tell what he's thinking or going to say, and that scares me.

It scares me in an exciting way. I'm not *in* fear of Aiden, but rather, I'm afraid that I'll fall too hard for him. I usually like to be in control, but around Aiden, I don't feel like I need to be. That's what's scary—how I'm so willing to let my guard down around him. Letting your guard down can mean life or death. My father would have told me that. He would have warned me to *never fully trust anyone*. He'd tell me it's safe to give the illusion of trust, but that's as far as I should ever go. The illusion of trust can be used to my advantage. Illusion forces the other person to open up and let me in, while allowing me to manipulate them how I see fit without any moral repercussions.

I can't do that with Aiden. I know that now. I'm not sure if it's because he's too smart for that or because I'm actually starting to fall for him. Nothing scares me more than not being in the know. I guess I could hear my father's reasoning somewhere in the back of my mind when Aiden and I talked. That's why I didn't tell him the absolute truth. I justify it in my mind as simply not offering everything and that if he had asked, I would have gladly told him.

I saw that he could tell I wasn't being completely honest with him. His eyes gave it away. Damn his beautiful blue eyes. They're dangerous. They should be considered a weapon. Find me a weapon that can do more damage to a person than Aiden's eyes and I'll give you a million bucks. To be clear, they aren't damaging in a negative or hurtful way like a gun or brick of C4 explosive might be, but they're dangerous because they demand your soul—something no weapon can take away from you. When he looks at me, he wants all of me, which is good, great in fact, but it sets me up for a broken heart. I'd rather lose a limb than have a broken heart.

Finding out that he never got to level 40 before the selection is concerning. If he really was chosen, I can't help but wonder what GET's motivation is. It seems strange to me that they would allow someone to bend the rules like that. There must be a very specific reason you are required to reach level 40 before you can apply to the program. That's another thing: he didn't even apply. The more I think about it, the more it's obvious GET wanted him for some reason. After all, he did find a way to beat an unbeatable exam. He clearly has the ability to think outside the box. But is that enough to justify bending the rules? GET must want, or need, him really badly, but what is it that they want from him?

I'm struck by what seems to be evident. I'm not sure if Aiden has figured out what I think I might just have. He told me about the accident, then his meeting with this Arthur character and what Arthur told him about choosing between his *gift* and death. Aiden chose life, a decision that comes hand in hand with his gift. A gift that GET seems all too eager to employ. A gift they wouldn't want to gamble to lose. Most likely they created an illusion of their own. They must have caused the accident that night, an act that would put Aiden in a position with seemingly two choices, but any living thing in their right mind will choose life over death, and Aiden did exactly that. They gave him two options, but only one *real* one existed.

He fell for the illusion of choice and chose exactly what they wanted him to. His choice was a calculated and manufactured response set in motion by the choice givers. Not to mention, they earn a few loyalty points for saving his life. GET and the HD program own Aiden now. I'm just not so sure he knows it. Most importantly, I've got to figure out why they wanted him so much in the first place.

I need a shower. All this thinking is making me sweat.

. . .

I open the door to the locker room and I'm met with a dark bag over my head. I fight back without hesitation. I'm not sure what's going on, but I'm afraid. I lash out, kicking and punching. I can feel my fist connect with something firm and warm, probably a man's chest. I scream for help. I raise my right foot and kick in the direction of my landed punch. I feel the tight grip of a hand grab my ankle. They push forward and send me to the ground. I lose my breath with the fall.

I gasp, desperately trying to regain a steady flow of oxygen. With the bag still over my head, I try to get my bearings. I hear a set of heavy footsteps, and then two hands grab my ankles and begin to pull. They drag me across the floor. I kick and scream, but it's no use. I fight in the best ways I can. My arms flail about, searching for something to grab, something to stay the dragging. I don't know where they're dragging me to and I don't want to find out. My hands find the cool metal of a locker room bench post—they're fastened to the floor and make a great anchor point.

I grab tight and hold on for my life. My body yanks to

a halt. I let out a squeal of pain as the tension between pull and anchor stretches my midsection. I feel the pull give for a second, as if a momentary lapse winding up for another larger pull, so I wrap my arm around the bench pole to use the crease of my arm for leverage. Sure enough, the pull this time is much harder, but my arm is proving to be more than efficient. I'm not going anywhere, asshole.

The pulling stops and I feel the grasp of the hands let my ankles go. I quickly tuck my legs up to my body and shuffle backward on my butt. My back slams up against a set of lockers. The room goes quiet. In the silence, I start to wonder if the HD program is watching. Maybe they're sending someone to help me. Who could be doing this to me? Then it hits me. Is the HD program doing this to me? Is this another exam?

I slowly take the bag off my head. I don't have time to see anything. A blunt object smacks me across the forehead. My body goes limp and I topple to the ground. The last thing I see are two sets of boots walking toward me.

A cold splash of water wakes me up. I look around frantically. I'm in a dark and dingy room. A lightbulb swings gently over my head. I'm sitting. My hands are tied behind my back, and my feet are taped to the legs of the chair. The chair itself is bolted to the floor. My head is throbbing, but I can make out a masked figure standing a few feet away, staring at me. I'm suddenly overcome with anger.

"Where am I," I say.

My question is immediately answered with a hard smack across the face. My body jolts to one side. Now I understand why the chair is bolted to the ground. It's easier that way.

It's more convenient for laying on a beating. I must be in an interrogation room.

"Shut up!" the figure says.

"Where am I?" I sputter.

"I ask the questions," the figure says sharply.

Based on the force of the second hit and the taste of blood in my mouth, I'm no longer sure that this is an exam, but I have no intention of talking, especially if it isn't. Try me.

"What's your name?" the figure says.

"Bond. James Bond," I say with a smug grin. Here comes another punch. This time the blow is to my stomach. Once again I find myself gasping for air.

"Who do you work for?"

I'm not going to say anything this time. I just keep my mouth shut.

"I'm going to count to three. One . . ."

I'm good at interrogations, I think to myself. When Susan miraculously vanished from her bed one morning at the GET girls' home and everyone, including Headmistress Baerd, demanded to know where she had gone, I did nothing except smile. Even when Baerd canceled classes and talked with each girl individually, I never even got nervous. And when it was my turn in the hot seat and Headmistress Baerd threatened me with a ruler, I still sat in silence, even though I did know where Susan had gone.

I came back from class one day to find her balancing a chair stacked on top of the bound notebooks she had been using as her diary for the past few years. From that moment on, she told me she trusted me with her very life. Her plan was threefold. Step one: navigate the air ducts and find a way out. Step two: stock up on supplies and food for the journey afterward. Step three: make the escape and never look back.

Susan was already well underway with step one. She had figured out a way to get out unseen, but she had hit a roadblock. The air ducts in each room all led to one place, an exhaust vent on the back of the building. Beyond the exhaust vent was a twenty-five-foot drop to the ground. Once she was down, the vast woods of the Berkshire Mountains would provide enough cover and time for her to slip away undetected. Once she made it across state lines, she would be home free.

She had tried to remove the vent herself, but she wasn't strong enough, and the twenty-five-foot drop was too far to jump without severely injuring herself. Until then, she hadn't figured out a solution. But now that I had agreed to help her, she had a way to solve both—I'd help her remove the vent and secure a rope for her to climb down. I agreed the plan would work, but there was still one little problem . . . we didn't have a rope.

Now that she had formulated and finalized her escape route, and had the help to do it, she started on step two. Every day we went to the cafeteria, we would each sneak out as much as we could, but we weren't idiots. We only took things that wouldn't perish or sour. We took everything from canned peas to bagged cookies. The stockpile was stored in one of her duffle suitcases that we stowed in the overhead vent. The second part of stage two was losing weight.

She figured she'd have to lose about ten pounds to be able to squeeze through the vent. She only ate yogurt for breakfast, salads for lunch, and lean proteins for dinner. She made a workout regimen that consisted of jumping jacks, lunges, and crunches. She lost weight fast, and by the time she had enough food and felt she was ready to go, she looked like she could fit through the vent no problem. She didn't look healthy, but that didn't matter to her.

We still had the problem of acquiring rope. It was the fall and Susan wanted to make her escape when the last of the leaves had turned. She told me this would be the best time to go because the coming winter would be her getaway driver. Once the snows set in, she'd be next to impossible to track down. She'd simply slip into the wilderness undetected. So we had to figure out the rope. Time was running out.

I couldn't believe we had been so stupid. We were allowed to use and play with rope on a day-to-day basis. I brought this to Susan's attention one afternoon while out in the yard during free time. I pointed out a group of girls doing double Dutch with a jump rope.

We managed to sneak the jump ropes back to our room that day. We measured them the best we could. Tied together they might just reach the ground from the vent. Everything was falling into place.

Susan woke me up extra early the morning of November 3, 2065. We would proceed with our day as normal. Our free time was after classes from 4–6 p.m. We would finalize all her supplies and stash them in the ducts, then head to dinner by 7 p.m. After dinner and the room count, we'd make our way into the duct, remove the vent, and she'd climb down to her freedom.

The plan was solid and went off without a hitch. The vent took a little finesse to remove and the rope was a few feet shy of the ground, but everything else went perfectly. She said we'd find a way to tie off the rope to something and we could both go together, but the longer we waited, the better chance we had of getting caught. I told her she needed to move fast and that there was no time to waste.

Susan slid down the rope. I watched as she ran across the yard and slipped into the cover of the forest. I thought about how I'd probably never see her again. How her friendship would mean more to me over time than I could ever imagine. She was gone, for good, and she did what she had said she would do. She escaped and never looked back. Not once.

The next morning, sure enough, they did the room count and Susan was missing. The alarms sounded and Headmistress Baerd brought me to her office. She used the ruler to beat my arm red with blood, but I never even flinched. I found solace in the world outside the office window. Small, puffy white snowflakes floated peacefully to the ground. I remember smiling. The next morning I was assigned to level 1 at GET.

The masked man leans in close to my face. I can smell his scent. It's like a cool eau de toilette.

"Two . . ." he says. I close my eyes. I know what comes next is going to hurt. "Three!" he screams as his fist connects with my jaw. I feel my consciousness dip in and out. My eyes are open, but everything is a blur. I hear the door open and a second set of footsteps comes in. I can't make out a face, just another man's voice. The two argue.

"What's going on here?"

"I'm handling it."

"You told me there's only one in every group. How do you explain this? Nothing good can come of this. You do know this, don't you?"

"I told you, I'm handling it."

"You better because I don't want to have to step in. You got me?"

"I got it."

"Now get this thing under control."

"It *is* under control."

"This is what you call under control?"

"Okay. I get it."

"Just handle it. This is your first and last chance. Otherwise, you'll have to make a call. One or the other."

The argument stops and I hear one set of footsteps leave; then the door closes. I can smell the masked man as he leans in close again.

"Stay away from Aiden Bishop," he says.

I feel my eyes flutter. I can't hold on any longer. My eyes shut and total darkness surrounds me.

CHAPTER THIRTEEN
AIDEN

MY EYES OPEN quickly. I feel the sweat on my face. I had the dream again. I was hoping it would have stopped now that I met her, but it hasn't. It gets worse every time now. Now that I know her, I feel even more protective over her. I'm helpless in the dream, and that angers me. I hate myself for letting her slip away, for letting someone or something take her from me. I can't help but think the dream *must* have some greater significance. I can't help but think the dream is some kind of warning or vision of the future—some event that will happen to us. The thought of the dream coming to fruition makes me sick.

"Hey, you all right?" Hop says. He swings his head over the side of the bunk and looks at me upside down.

"I'm okay," I say softly.

"Well, you look like crap," Hop quickly replies.

"Did I wake you?"

"Nah. We got class in twenty minutes. I was getting up anyway." Hop slips down from the top bunk and grabs a change of clothes from the locker. "I'm gonna hit the shower real quick before class. See you there?"

"Yeah. Sure. Of course."

"Save me a seat?"

"Sure thing."

"You might want to splash some water on your face. Just a suggestion."

Hop leaves the bunk and heads for the showers. I really should have gone for a shower too. I think this is day number two without one. I'm sure I've got a real funk about me. I love showers. They're usually my favorite things about mornings, but not today. Today I can live without showering.

When I was placed in the GET boys' home, I refused to shower for two weeks. Before my parents passed, our only chance to bathe was in leftover water in decorative fountains or under the blessing of nature's tears, but rain was far between, and bathing in the wide open was putting your life at risk. Both options hinged on having soap, something almost as hard to come by as the water itself.

Soap had actually become a kind of currency. It's amazing how much people wanted to cling to the ways of old. They'd give almost anything for the chance to get clean, to feel human and not like some animal. You could trade soap shavings for food and supplies. Hotel mini travel soaps were worth their weight in gold. Light, small, prepackaged, and easy to store and carry. We saw the value in soap as a means of survival. Keeping clean rarely crossed our minds. You get used to the smell pretty quick.

A splash of water on my face will have to do. I slide

out of bed and get dressed. Charlie has already left the bunk and gone to class. She's eager. She's not your typical overachiever. She's more the type who needs to pay close attention in order to do a good job. The kind who needs to study for an extra hour every night so she can retain the information. She's all business and I respect that.

The twins on the other hand are the exact opposite. Not to say that they're geniuses, but they make intelligence look easy. I don't think they've had to study for anything more than fifteen minutes in their entire lives. They have school pegged, and that's why knowing what my exam was like was so important to them. I don't think they take failure very well. They like to be the best, which I can also respect.

I'm in class five minutes before it's supposed to start. Charlie has already marked off our team's area in the class-room with her arms and jacket. I take a seat next to her. She wants me to move her jacket down one seat, but I figure I can ward anyone off if they try to take it. I'm hoping to catch a glimpse of Evie, but she hasn't arrived yet. The rest of the red team is there, but she isn't.

Not too long after me, Hop enters and takes a seat next to me.

"Thanks for holding me a seat," he says.

"You can thank Charlie for that."

Hop reaches over my desk and they pound fists. I roll my eyes. I've never really understood the *pounding fist* thing. The twins arrive and deliver two more fist pounds. There we all sit, together in a row. Only one minute before class and still no Evie. Now I'm worried.

Instructor Keets walks in and puts a binder, clipboard,

and tablet on the lectern. She begins taking roll. She starts with the blue team. She reads off our names and each of us responds, "Here." As Sonic says his part and the roll moves on to the red team, I begin to panic. Why isn't Evie here yet? Has something bad happened to her?

I raise my hand, but no sooner than I do, the door to the classroom opens. Evie walks in quickly, but she's different: she's lost her confidence, her radiance. She looks scared. One side of her face is covered with a huge bruise, and I can tell she's trying not to look at me. She's ashamed. She quickly throws her hood over her head.

"I hope this isn't going to become a thing with you, Evie," Instructor Keets says.

"No sir," Evie replies as she passes through the aisle and heads for an open seat. I reach for her.

"What happened?" I say.

"Nothing . . . exam two," she replies.

I know she's not telling me the truth. Maybe I'm wrong. Maybe it is just part of an exam, but something about her voice tells me she's covering—from what I'm not sure. She brushes me off without another word and heads to her seat. I peek out beyond Charlie to look at her. She won't look back at me.

Charlie elbows me in the side. "Get focused. Some of us are trying to pay attention."

I sit back in my seat. I'll think of something. For now, I'll pay attention. Instructor Keets finishes roll and quickly jumps right into it.

"You are all here for a reason, a very important reason. We briefly discussed in orientation yesterday what the HD program is and stands for, but we have no time to lose. The literary education component of this program pales in comparison to the physical training component. This may be lucky for some of you, as looking around the room I can only imagine the intelligence level of some of you. As you all know, we are at war with the outcasts in Sector 6. They have made it their mission to try to put an end to the way we harvest energy."

"And how does GET make energy?" Russell says.

"I'm getting to that, but thank you for interjecting. We have found a loophole of sorts. We draw our energy from another world entirely. We found that when someone dies, they don't just pass on. Instead, they assume a new life in a second world that runs parallel to ours." Keets gives the room a moment to react.

I'm a little confused, but not surprised. My unexplainable meeting with Arthur seems to make a little more sense now. I now know that I must have met him in this second world. I get a little bit of that creepy-crawly feeling. I can tell by the uneasiness of the rest of the room that none of them have had a similar experience to mine. Maybe this is why Arthur kept saying I was chosen. Maybe I'm special because I have already died . . . or was supposed to. I think I can see where all of this is going.

"All right. That's enough." Keets calms down the room. "Essentially, we harvest our energy as we would any other crop. We extract it and store it. This new energy source is extremely powerful. It's on par with nuclear power of the twentieth century, but far more stable and clean. It's called electromagnetic energy. It's an energy that this other world gives off as a byproduct. Like we do here with CO2. We very simply and easily go into this world and harvest the electromagnetic energy and store it. Some here, some there."

"What do you mean here?" Josh says.

Everyone looks to him in agreement. I try to see if Evie has decided to look at me yet. She hasn't. She's shrunk down in her chair. She looks mortified.

"Every GET facility around the world is a storage facility. You are all at what we like to call ground zero. I'm sure you've noticed the large zeros painted on all of the walls?"

We most certainly have. I can now remember my meeting with Arthur; I had seen the number one on each of the walls. I can only assume, with certainty, that I have been in the other world. Keets pulls up a hologram with her tablet. On it is our GET building and under it, eight levels of a subterranean structure. The structure is split into a series of vertically stacked cells. Each cell is labeled with a number from zero to seven, zero being the closest level to the first level of GET.

"There are seven levels in the world of the dead. Humans have known this for centuries, but instead of believing it as scientific fact, they sloughed it off as religion. All religion in some respect talks extensively about this other world, but there has never been any way to prove it does not exist, nor did anyone necessarily want to. For too long man has been afraid of death. Finding out another world awaits when you die, a very real world that isn't governed by what you do on Earth, would cause chaos. Religion has played an important role in creating a moral balance and order here on Earth, and its done a fantastic job of mystifying the world of the dead—something that we have learned is vital to our survival as a species. Dante Alighieri wrote an epic poem called *Divine Comedy,* in which our entire understanding of the seven layers of the dead was formulated. Each of these seven layers holds more electromagnetic energy than the next, and as such we must have a storage facility on every level. We've laid an energy pipeline, if you will, that passes through these seven layers right up to here at ground zero. Ground zero, other than being a training facility, is used for dispersing the energy to our GET power plants all over the city."

Keets seems to be giving us the condensed version of how this all works. No big business is ever as squeaky clean as they make themselves out to be. As I look around the room, I can see that most of the recruits are eating this up. Something that their individual and collective fears of Sector 6 force them to believe. Evie isn't like the rest. I don't think she thinks GET is as truthful as they are trying to be. They sell a good pitch, but I can tell she's uneasy and untrusting. I don't know why, but something inside me tells me I might want to believe her. I nudge Hop.

"Psst," I whisper.

"What? What is it?"

"Hop, give me your tablet." Hop glares at me with disgust. "Come on, I left mine in the bunk."

"Fine. But hurry up. I'm trying to take notes," Hop says as he reluctantly hands over his tablet.

"Of course." I swipe left to bring up the class seating chart.

I count through the rows and seats until I find what seat Evie is in, then tap on it and select the message icon. I keep it simple and type: WHAT GIVES? WE NEED TO TALK, AIDEN. I finish writing and hit send. My eyes dart between Keets and Evie. I watch and see if she checks her tablet and hope Keets doesn't notice. Keets turns off the hologram and puts the tablet back in the lectern. Her attention is diverted for a moment, and I see Evie open the message and then quickly swipe out of it. No reply. She doesn't even look at me. Nothing. I'm confused. I can't believe she's ignoring me. I'm a little mad. Maybe I only *thought* we had a better talk last night than we actually did. She is on the red team. Maybe she's snubbing me. I sit back in my chair.

"Your role is, like I said, extremely important. You have all been chosen. Thousands of applicants every year, and you ten have been selected. Most of you are here because of certain individual skills that you possess or excel in. Maybe you have extraordinary technical or mechanical skills. Maybe you are strong, fast, and physical. Whatever the reason, you also possess the ability to limbo—at least to the best of our knowledge you do. We've done our homework, and that's ultimately why you have been selected. Not every citizen has this ability. You will all come to know firsthand if you do indeed possess this ability. Some of you were born with it, others developed it over time, but basically, you hold, within each and every one of you, the ability to cross over into this world of the dead. Conversely, you contain the ability to re-enter the world of the living. That is why we call it limbo. You pass under a thin line between both. It is precisely because you have this ability that you are so important. You are by no means alone. You are in good company. Throughout history, there have been long lines of people who have possessed this power. The very first was Siddhartha Gautama, or Buddha, then Jesus Christ after him, then Rasputin and so on."

The entire room murmurs with excitement. For many of them, their entire lives seem to have been revealed—the world explained for the first time. I can barely concentrate. I don't know what to think. All I care about is what Evie must be thinking.

"You all are our first line of defense. Our knowledge of the world of the dead and our technology that allows for the safe passing between worlds have leaked into Sector 6. Now more than ever, we have had a need for the HD program. Sector 6 has made it their mission to sabotage our energy pipeline. From the looks of it, they are making their way from level zero to level seven. If they destroy our level seven pipeline, it's game over. Not just for us, but for the human race. If Sector 6 succeeds, we will quickly slip back into the times of The Great Event, and we all remember what those times were like."

The room grows silent. I can't tell if everyone is simply blown away by the information shock they were just dealt or if they're remembering their lives during The Great Event.

"I think that's probably enough for today. We will convene for your first drip class tomorrow at 9 a.m. sharp in the Screening Room. So get some rest. You'll need it," Keets says as she packs up her things and leaves the classroom.

We all grab our things, but Evie is the first to head for the door. She slides a piece of paper on my desk as she passes. If I hadn't wanted her to respond so badly, I wouldn't have noticed because she placed it so delicately and discreetly.

I snatch up the paper and open it. It reads: IT'S NOT SAFE. I'LL CONTACT YOU. Charlie gives me a shove. I fold up the paper and put it in my pocket.

. . .

I've been sitting in my bunk for three hours. Hop's been pestering me about what I think the world of the dead is like. He's excited, I get that, but it's annoying. I want to tell him I've been there and it doesn't seem all that different than ours, but I'm not sure he'd believe me. I'm not even sure it's a good idea to tell anyone anything anymore. Little does he know I'm only entertaining his incessant talking because I have nothing better to do than wait for a message from Evie.

Charlie has been called to her first exam. Then Sonic, Kyle, and finally Hop. They have all gone and returned, and still no word from Evie. I'm not sure I'll ever hear from her. As each of them came back, they were sadder than the next. Apparently, none of them passed as Evie and I had. I reassured them that's the way it was designed. I told them even I wasn't supposed to pass; I just did. They beg me to explain how I did it, but I find ways to beat around the bush. I still don't want them to know. I don't want to be labeled a cheater. It's bad enough Evie used that word. Besides, maybe she's wrong. I didn't cheat per se. It wasn't like they laid out a rule saying I couldn't rip apart my uniform.

I have waited like this before. When Spence left the GET boys' home, I was devastated. It hadn't been easy for me, assimilating back into a structured society, and now that the only person I connected with was gone, it was far too easy to become what I was—a wild beast, untamed, plucked from the grips of the wild and forced to live in a cage where people looked and laughed at me.

Headmaster Doyle had a school to run, and space was tight as it was. It wasn't long before a new boy was forced to be my roommate. His name was Connor. He hated me from the moment he arrived. He was bigger than me, older too, by two years.

One day Conner *tried* to bully me. I say *tried* because he didn't get very far. He started by calling me names, then proceeded to push me around. Normally I would have done nothing to stop the approach, but I had had it. The bullying had gone on for a little over a year, and enough was enough. Something inside me snapped. I don't know what it was, but *it* snapped. With a fourth push, I lunged back at Conner.

I took him by complete surprise. My weight and his unpreparedness sent him crashing to the floor. We rolled around on the ground a bit—our battle inexperience shining through—until he managed to gain the advantage. He hit me a few times. The pain was excruciating, but it only made me more angry. My rage took over, and I pushed him off me and began my assault.

I pounded on him. I could feel my knuckles blistering open as they made hamburger out of his face. I don't remember much from the incident other than the pure rage that I felt. By the time one of the teachers pulled me off Conner, the entire student body must have gathered around us, their faces stunned with shock. No one thought I was capable of such an act. I was brought to Headmaster Doyle's office, where I waited in the waiting area on a long, flat, and uncomfortable bench that stretched the length of the wall outside the office. I waited for what seemed like an eternity. Finally, he called me into the office. I sat down across from him. He glared at me. I thought that at any minute he'd jump across his desk, grab me by the collar, and smack me across the face, but he never did. He didn't budge. After a good fifteen minutes of mind churning, he finally spoke.

"Good job," he said, and then dismissed me.

A week later I was transferred from the boys' home to GET level 1.

I'm exhausted from waiting. It doesn't look like I'll be hearing from Evie today. The rest of my bunkmates have picked up on my lack of interest in them. It's pretty clear they know I'm waiting to hear from her. I can't tell how they feel about the relationship forming between two opposite teammates, but I'm not sure if I care either. Come to think of it, I'm not even sure I can call what Evie and I have a relationship. We've only talked once. Just because we have some sort of connection that's beyond our control doesn't mean we're anything or will be anything. I should really get that through my head.

A small piece of paper slides under the door, and I jump to my feet. Hop is first to it. He picks up the paper, walks over to me, and hands it over.

"I think you've been waiting for this," Hop says.

I open the note and read it, then fold it back up, tear it into pieces, and throw it in a small trash can by the bunk. I lie back down in my bed. Hop looks at me. He's concerned.

"Be careful," Hop says for the second time today.

I'm not sure what to think right now, and I will be careful. I'm always careful.

CHAPTER FOURTEEN

EVIE

I'M STILL UNSURE if what happened last night was an exam or not. Interrogation has always been a common part of training in the military. It would be no surprise if the HD program were implementing the same techniques. After all, knowing if someone is capable of withstanding interrogation is a valuable piece of information to have. If you can withstand violent interrogation, you're a priceless asset. You're someone who can be trusted out in the field. You aren't a liability, and that's requirement number one when you're an operative in a secret program. Clearly, keeping the HD program under wraps is and always has been a top priority.

What baffles me though is why GET is so concerned with keeping everything a secret. To me, it seems beneficial to have more than one company know how to provide power safely and securely all over the world. The more companies providing power, the more people are able to benefit from it. GET not wanting to share their knowledge makes me suspicious. It makes me think they're up to something they aren't supposed to be. That in some way they are breaking the rules or crossing some unforgivable line in some way, and if last night wasn't an exam, then I know Aiden has something to do with all this. That's why I have to find a way to talk to him again. I have to see if he knows anything else, but I'm not about to risk my neck to find out. For now, I have to assume the worst and be careful.

. . .

I enter the girls' locker room in stealth mode. Finding a hiding spot to talk with Aiden feels dangerous. I like the feeling of danger, but it's definitely what puts me in stealth mode. I tried to think of another place that didn't have cameras, but the locker room was the only one that I could think of. I feel a little bit like a fool, snooping around, holding a towel like I'm here to take a shower, but it's fun, nonetheless. I make sure the door closes behind me, and then I take a look around. I call out. "Hello!"

I want to be sure I'm the only one in here. I don't need another girl like Tasha or Charlie busting in on my secret mission. What's the deal with Charlie anyway? I get that she's a tough girl. She probably grew up in a family full of brothers, but she doesn't have to be so mean about it. She gives off the *don't eff with me* vibe, but I can tell by the way she looks at and defends Aiden that she has a little crush on him. I'm not jealous. Aiden and I don't really have anything going on—technically—but even so, I know Aiden likes me. When Aiden sent me the note in class, I had been expecting it. I could tell by his face when I walked into class he was concerned about me. It's adorable the way he fawns over me.

No one answers my baited hello, so it's game time. I quickly get to looking for cameras. I don't know how long I have to myself, and I know that every minute that passes is another sixty seconds Aiden is growing anxious. Not to mention, we could be called to an exam at any moment. Time is something that I don't have to waste. I check in and around lockers. I look in all the corners and crevices of the room. I even check in the shower stalls and behind the towel bin, but nothing shows up. The locker room appears to be clean.

Just because there aren't any cameras doesn't mean this will be a safe place to talk. The locker room is too public. Anyone could walk in on us unexpectedly during our meeting. Not having cameras is a start because it offers a window of time to be unseen, but it doesn't offer undisturbed secrecy. I don't trust anyone enough to tell them what's going on, and I certainly don't trust anyone here enough to have them guard the door. I get to thinking.

This place has showers, and all showers need drains. The drains to six showers have to lead somewhere, and there has to be an overflow drain. What happens if the showers back up or clog in some way? There has to be a way to keep the locker room from flooding. I grab my towel and toss it over one of the shower drains and turn on the shower. With any luck, the spill will lead me to the overflow drain.

It doesn't take long for the stall to overflow. The lip between the floor and the shower is only about an inch tall. Sure enough, the water finds a way. It spills over the edge of the shower and follows the subtle slope of the floor. The water moves faster than I thought it would. I follow the line right to a far corner of the room and under a bench. I kneel down and see a two-foot-diameter storm drain.

The drain is tricky to get at. The benches are all secured to the floor, and there's only about two and a half feet of room between the bench and the floor. Not the ideal situation when trying to squeeze under something, but I have expertise in getting people to fit through vents; a drain shouldn't be much different, and its diameter wouldn't be a problem for me. It might be a little tight for Aiden, but he'd still fit. I just hope it's not bolted to the floor too.

I position myself as best I can. Gripping the drain with both hands, I use one foot as leverage and the other to keep me from smashing my face on the top of the bench. I pull. I pull real hard. The cover slides right off. I pop my head inside the drain to take a look. I can't see much, but I can hear the sound of running water. The sound echoes and I can tell by the darkness that there's depth to the hole. I take one more look around the locker room. I remove my towel from the shower drain, but leave it running—if anyone comes in they'll assume I'm in the shower. Then, I turn my attention back to the hole under the bench. I slide on my stomach and tuck my feet through first. I slowly push myself farther into the hole. My own weight pulls me downward until I'm hanging from my hands. I loosen my grip and let go.

My feet hit the solid ground only about a foot below. The air is damp and cold. The ground is concrete, but it is split down the middle with a three-foot-wide water-filled channel. It's dark, but when my eyes adjust, I can tell I'm in some sort of tunnel. In either direction, the tunnel goes on for as far as I can see. It probably connects to the main city sewer tunnels. GET takes up four city blocks, so my guess is that's about as long as this tunnel runs.

Where this tunnel goes isn't what I care about. What I care about is how perfect it will be for our secret meetings. It might be a little odd for Aiden to sneak into the *girls'* locker room, but I'm sure he can manage. He seems crafty enough. I have no doubt he can figure it out.

I'll write him a note with instructions on where to meet. I'll tell him what time and how to find the drain. I'll make sure he leaves a shower on for cover. I'll get here ten minutes before him so I can be waiting.

. . .

I check the clock next to my bunk one more time and decide it's time to get going. The note I had left under Aiden's door a few hours ago said to meet me at 9 p.m. It's 8:30 now and I might need a little extra time for something—to account for contingencies. I leave my bunk. I grab a towel from my locker, and no one seems to question me wanting to go take a shower. Once I'm out of Bunk 1, it's only a two-minute walk to the girls' locker room. I hear the door close behind me and I take off.

I'm moving swiftly through the hallways. I can feel my steps growing faster. I slow down a bit. I'm nervous and I don't want the eyes in the sky to pick up on it. This should feel like any other time I might be going to take a shower. I can feel my eyes wanting to look and see what the cameras are doing. I use every ounce of control in my body to stop them. My ears tell me the cameras are rotating with me as I move. They make a faint electronic buzz as they rotate—I pay attention to everything. My heart is pounding out of my chest. I feel like I'm going to faint if I have to walk any farther, but the door to the locker room is in my sights.

I'm in the locker room, but my heart is still pounding. I shut the door and put my back to it. A huge sigh of relief forces its way out of me. This is more frightening than I expected. I wonder what the program will do to me if I get caught? I do as I did in the dress rehearsal and search the room.

"Hello?" I say, hoping that someone will respond if they are in here.

As I move through each row of lockers and check every shower stall, I can tell I'm alone. I remove the drain cover as I did before. It's easier this time. I slide the cover to the side and hoist myself down into the tunnel. The only thing I can do now is wait.

I count off the minutes in my head. We weren't given watches, so I really have no way of telling time other than to count it off in my head. When I left my bunk it was 8:30. Searching the locker room took up about fifteen minutes and climbing down into the tunnel another two or three. That's about 8:48 give or take a minute or so. That leaves twelve minutes for Aiden to show up on time at 9:00. Since I've been down here, I've counted out 960 seconds. That's sixteen minutes. Aiden is officially four minutes late.

I'm worried. I specifically told him in the note *not* to be late. I told him I'd only wait five minutes, and then I would have to leave. It isn't safe to wait longer. Suddenly, I hear the sound of running water overhead. I told Aiden to turn on a shower before coming down the drain.

"Evie?" Aiden whispers. I can barely hear it, but I know it's him.

"Down here," I say quietly.

Aiden's feet push through the hole, then his body. He's taller than I am, so it won't be as far a drop. He hesitates as he hangs, but I tell him to just trust me and let go. He does and his feet plant firmly on the ground.

"Sorry I'm late—"

"Shh, keep your voice down. I'm not sure how well the shower covers us," I say.

He changes to a loud whisper. "Sorry I'm late. I ran into Gwiz in the hallway. I wanted to make sure he went back to Bunk 1 before I snuck in here. By the way, you had to pick the girls' locker room?"

"It was the only place I could think of that doesn't have cameras, and I wasn't about to sneak into the boys' locker room. Besides, this tunnel probably connects to both. You might not *have* to use the girls' locker room." Aiden smiles at me. I can tell he wants to kiss me, but I'm still not sure it's a good idea. He reaches out to touch the bruise on my face. I shy away.

"What happened?" Aiden says. "Why wouldn't you talk or look at me in class?"

"I couldn't," I say softly.

"What do you mean you couldn't?"

"I was told not to."

"Are you really going to make me ask you individual

questions for everything or can you just tell me what's going on?"

Aiden's frustrated. I can see that he's a little hurt I wouldn't let him touch my face. He wants me to know that he's been thinking about me, that he's concerned, but I already know that.

"After we spoke the other night, at dinner, I went to take a shower. The second I stepped into the locker room, someone threw a bag over my head. I fought back the best I could, but they knocked me out."

"You keep saying *they*. Who are *they*? And why did they come after you in the locker room?"

"I'm guessing they chose the locker room for the same reason I did . . . because there are no cameras. And I say *they* because there were two of them. When I came to I was strapped to a chair in a dark room. A man in a mask beat me, trying to get information out of me. At first, I thought it might be part of my second exam. You know, like testing to see how loyal we are, but when a second man came in the room, they argued about what he was doing to me. The second man told him he'd have to make a choice if I got out of control. When the second man left, he told me I had to stay away from you. It sounded like a threat. So I took it seriously. Now I don't know what to think."

"No, you did the right thing. But why do they want you to keep away from me?"

"I don't know. I thought you might be able to shed some light on all this."

"Your guess is as good as mine."

"Are you sure you're telling me everything?"

"Let's not get into who's telling each other everything, shall we?" Aiden says.

I take a step backward. I know I haven't told him everything, but I'm offended.

"Excuse me," I say.

"Listen. Forget I said anything. I didn't mean it."

"It's okay if you meant it. I just thought we could trust one another."

"And we can," Aiden says. He takes a step forward and puts his hands on my shoulders. "We're straying from the point. There's too much of a coincidence here. Think about it. We both have the same dream about one another, we talk to one another in the mess hall, then they take you aside and beat you and tell you to stay away from me. There has to be some connection, some reason why they don't want us to talk."

"That's what I just said."

"No you didn't."

"Well, not in those words, but you know that's what I was getting at." Boys are frustrating. They want us to always spell everything out for them. We can't just talk like normal human beings. Still, we're on the same page at least. "Look, do you believe everything they're telling us?" I say.

"Not entirely. I'm still trying to figure out how I fit into this. Remember, I never even applied. How can I be so important?"

"There has to be something about you. Something you aren't thinking about. Something you might not even know about yourself."

"I swear. There's nothing. I can't think of anything."

"You've got to keep thinking about it. There's always a reason for everything. We just haven't figured it out yet. I'm thinking we have to do some snooping. Something just doesn't feel right. The way Keets explained GET's energy source—"

"Yeah, like it's too good to be true. Like GET's never done anything wrong. Like Sector 6 is some kind of devil and we're the saviors."

"There's something there for sure. We just have to find it," I say.

"Promise me you'll be careful. Look what they did to you already."

"We don't even know who *they* are. Don't you want to find out?"

"Sure I do, but we can't just walk off and start asking questions, now can we? We still have exams. We still have class. They'll expect us to be there for all those things. This isn't that simple. We can't rush into anything. Rushing could get us kicked out, or maybe even killed," Aiden says.

"I can't just sit here, not knowing," I say.

He knows I'm right, but he's afraid. I don't think he's afraid to find out more, but I think he's afraid doing so might mean losing me. I think he's thinking of the dream; how he sees me die in his arms; how he fails to save me. I can tell that would be unbearable for him. So much so that he'd give up anything to keep it from happening.

"It's going to be okay," I tell him.

I grab his hand and squeeze it tightly. I need him to trust me. I'm going to need his help. He looks at me with those piercing blue eyes of his, and I can feel my knees weaken.

"So what do we do?" Aiden says.

"Well, we can't stop talking to one another," I say as I clear my throat.

"I'm not so sure we can keep meeting down here either. Too risky."

"Then what would you suggest?"

CHAPTER FIFTEEN

AIDEN

W E'RE ALL CRAMMED into what the program calls a Screening Room. It doesn't look much different from any of the other rooms in this place—it's cold and monotone—but this room is different in that one wall consists of a two-way mirror. It's evident that today's class will be taught through the act of watching. We're all here, all ten of us. Evie and I try to keep our distance, though every so often we sneak looks at one another. We haven't figured out an easy means of communication yet. Last night we decided to meet in our hiding spot twice a week, varying which days a week and what time each day every week. If we aren't on a schedule, then we aren't predictable.

Instructor Keets walks in and flips a switch on the wall. Lights turn on in the room on the other side of the two-way mirror. This room looks familiar. It's white and has an almost identical barbershop-like chair as the one that I was strapped in when Nater had a nurse stick me with that needle. The only difference in this room is the large numbers on all four walls. They don't read ONE; they read ZERO.

"Good morning and welcome to Drip 101. This is your first lesson on what we call dripping—how you pass from one world to the next. There isn't a door or magical portal that you can walk through. This process is rooted in your biology, and we have a room specifically designed for the entire process. A room that not only ensures your safety, but the safety of those involved as well. This is called a drip room. Drip stands for: Direct Recruit Insertion Process. Coincidentally, it's also what you call it when you have a morphine or water IV inserted into your veins, but that is not where the name comes from," Keets says.

I'm starting to see why they want people to sign up for this program. They're looking for GET employees who are truly committed to the company. They only want ones who are excited and willing to do just about anything. If you ask me, this all looks dangerous. I wonder if this was in the packet. I look over at Hop, who looks nervous too. Not nervous because he thinks it looks dangerous, but because he wants to do well. He puts an awful amount of stress on his shoulders. Some people are just like that. I like to find the easiest solution to every problem.

"Today you'll be watching—the key word is watching—how the drip process works," Keets explains as a veteran recruit enters the drip room. "This is Operative Garcia. He's been with us for about four years now. He's a medical operative, not a reaper, for any of you hoping to get a glimpse of one of our seasoned reapers." Keets pushes a button next to the light switch. It's an intercom. "Garcia, why don't you say hello to our newest class of recruits."

Garcia gives a friendly wave. Tasha, the twins, and Russell wave back, an obvious reaction, but there's no way Garcia can see us. That's not how two-way mirrors work. Garcia takes off his shirt and sits down in the chair. I see two small grayish/black circles on his spine. The door to the room opens and a doctor and nurse walk in. They begin by strapping Garcia's wrists to the arms on the chair. Then the doctor grabs a remote that dangles from a curly electrical cord extending from the ceiling. He presses one of the buttons, and the chair rotates and flattens into a rigid bed about waist high and parallel to the ground. A bright light turns on overhead.

"Now, everyone watch the process carefully. This is ground zero. Two HD medical employees will always control your insertion into level one. However, once you get to level one, it is up to you and your team to perform subsequent drips to get to one of two places: a deeper level or back to level one from a deeper level. Each drip is only good for the assigned insertion point. Remember that. This is why it is so important to pay attention. These procedures will be falling into your hands sooner than you think. Don't worry though. After you are assigned, you will be given hands-on training in the field."

There's a deep sigh of relief in the room because the tension has been lifted. All of this, this entire program has been heavy. It's a lot to process.

The doctor and nurse work together in unison. Their procedures seem so elegant and simple, neither of which are probably true, but it looks as though they've performed hundreds of these insertions. Everything is second nature to them. They place a biometric breathing mask over Garcia's face. Keets tells us that when the human heart is slowed, it is incredibly hard work for your body to pull oxygen from the atmosphere, so the mask makes it easier. It also helps regulate your breathing so your body doesn't overexert itself and make your heart explode.

Next, they run a morphine and water IV drip into Garcia's left arm. Then they strap his ankles to the chair. This ensures his body will relax and prepare itself for the next jarring stage of the process.

"You all don't get the best view from here, but the second part of the process is probably the most disturbing. I'm not going to sugarcoat it; it also happens to be the most painful part. You will all be fitted with three permanent drip ports upon completion of your recruit training. The first two work together and are called neuro drip ports or NDPs. Your NDPs are small circular disks about the size of a quarter. In the center of each is an entry port for optical needles. The NDPs are installed over your C4 and T3 vertebrae, two sections of your spinal column that control your heart rate and your core body temperature. Heart rate and body temperature are two of the most important biological parts of this process. Our ability to control and maintain the desired level of each is key to a successful insertion as well as a vital component in keeping your body alive. Once placed, the optical needles feed us a steady stream of neurological data and response."

Keets pauses for a moment while the nurse makes sure

the two ports are aligned with two small holes in the bottom of the chair frame. She gives an "okay" with a nod of her head, and the doctor hits a second button on the remote. A series of gears and a soft whirring sound initiate the optical needles. Garcia jerks forward, clenching his teeth in pain. Keets reacts to Garcia's gruesome display. "Your body will get used to it over time. The more drips you do, the less painful it is."

Evie is staring at me. I can tell she wants to drip more than anyone else in the room. She thinks the key to figuring everything out lies within the world of the dead, that the sooner she can drip the better. I, on the other hand, think it's just a creative way to kill yourself. Having needles jammed deep in your spine would in any other circumstance most certainly kill you, or cripple you. I'm not entirely sure which would be worse. Either way, it seems like we're putting a lot of trust into the hands of GET and the HD program.

Garcia's body finally softens, relaxing against the cool metal of the chair. The doctor then inserts a half-inch in diameter clear surgical tube into Garcia's third drip port located in his right wrist. Once connected, the doctor hits a third button on the remote. The tube quickly fills with blood. The blood travels up the tube and into the ceiling— no doubt where his blood is stored. A fourth touch of the remote and a large hole opens in the floor just underneath the chair. From it, a large bath-like structure surrounds the chair and Garcia's body. It's clear, so we can all see the bath fill with water up to Garcia's shoulders—just enough to engulf his chest, but not enough to drown him.

"This is the last stage of insertion. The BDP, or blood

drip port, is attached and the ice-bath is installed. These two steps work together just as your NDPs do. The BDP removes half of your body's blood. That's roughly seven percent of your body weight, or just under a gallon of the red stuff. Thus the name of the program, Half-Dead. The clear bath that you see around him is filled with ice-cold water, below-freezing water actually. A small current keeps the water from solidifying, but you can be sure it's cold. You'll all find out soon enough. Once your blood drains, it's contained and stored until you need to be revived. The ice-bath works in conjunction with the loss of blood to lower your heart rate to about ten or fifteen beats per minute. The goal here is to kill you. Not kill you dead, just enough to allow you to pass into the world of the dead, and just alive enough to allow you to be brought back. It's designed to keep you in a constant state of limbo."

"Holy shit," Tasha says.

"Yeah. Gross," Gwiz says.

"I don't feel too good," Hop mutters.

"I think it's awesome," Sonic says.

"You would," Kyle says with a jab to Sonic's ribs.

"I'm with him. Awesome," Josh says with a sick grin.

"Could everyone just shut it? I'm trying to pay attention," Charlie says.

We watch as Garcia's blood leaves his body. The ice-bath turns his skin a pale blue. His eyes are frozen open in a hauntingly lifeless way. The doctor checks a heart rate monitor and life support readout. He presses an intercom button in the room.

"DD 122 successful level one insertion."

Keets pushes the intercom button.

"Thank you. That's enough of a demonstration. Start the reanimation process."

The doctor acknowledges without saying a word, and then hits a series of buttons on the dangling remote. The icy water drains from the bath and follows a tube into the hole from which it came. A small chill shoots up my spine— enough to make my teeth chatter.

"Someone's scared," Gwiz says.

"What's wrong with being scared?" I say.

I hate this kid. Not because he follows Josh around like a lost puppy, but because he reminds me a lot of Conner. He looks for the weakness in people and tries to exploit it. We'll see who's peeing their pants when drip day comes. It most certainly won't be me.

"You've got the right to be scared," Keets interrupts. "Any living and breathing person should be scared. If you're not scared, then you aren't ready to drip. Being scared means you understand the risks. Of which there are many."

I can't tell if I like Keets standing up for me and if that's even what she's doing. If I end up the teacher's pet, I'll have a target on my back.

The reanimation process is more disgusting than the insertion process. Putting blood back in a person and bringing their heart back up to speed is a lot more brutal to the body. Garcia's BDP leaks drops of blood as it pumps back into his body. The bath retreats back into the floor, and the excess water floods the white tile ground. Heaters in the drip room turn on. The last bit of cold water on Garcia's deathly blue flesh sizzles as it evaporates. The doctor watches Garcia's vitals closely, and the nurse takes a manual pulse reading with two fingers on his neck.

The heart monitor shows around sixty-eight beats per minute, and Garcia's once clammy skin restores to a balmy reddish brown. He's still motionless, but the removal of his two NDP optical needles sends a now familiar jolt through his body. His eyes flutter and blink. The last of the blood trickles through his BDP, and the nurse removes the connection. The doctor taps away at the remote again, and the chair returns to its upright position. They unhook his ankle straps, then remove the IV drip, followed by his wrist restraints. Garcia gets to his feet. He's wobbly at first. He needs the support of the doctor to take his first few steps.

"Don't worry, this happens every time you drip. It's extremely taxing on the body. Manipulating your nervous system severs the communication between your brain and the rest of your body's motor functions. It takes a few minutes to regain that connection. An important thing to remember is that the world of the dead, while running parallel to our world, contains a time continuum. For every minute that passes in our world, one hour passes in the world of the dead. And it's compounded by two every level. For instance, one minute on ground zero equates to sixteen hours on level five and so on. When you are reanimated your body remembers the length of time spent in the world of the dead; that's why the deeper you go, the more difficult it is on your body to get back. It also offers the time for a lot more to go wrong. Going deeper is more dangerous, but it does have its bonuses. The deeper levels allow us to store more energy. This is why we are always in need of strong operatives. Only a handful of operatives ever get to go as deep as level seven. It's both a blessing and a curse. An evil necessity if you will."

Garcia makes his way to the glass. He looks at where he thinks all of our eager eyes may be and takes a bow. Charlie starts to clap, and then we all clap. I can think what I want at this point, but the entire process is quite amazing. It's a real miracle manipulation of science and nature. Dripping reminds me a lot of the classic story of *Frankenstein*. A mad doctor straps you to a table, drains your blood, then brings you back to life. I'm sure Garcia doesn't think about it that way. I'm sure he's just happy he made it back alive. Every time you watch your blood fleeing from your body, there's got to be some part of your brain that's thinking you might die.

Keets hits the switch next to the two-way mirror and the drip room goes dark. The lights in the screening room change from their dim hue to a bright and somewhat blinding ambiance. We all grasp at our eyes, rubbing them as they adjust.

"Okay. Any questions?" Keets asks.

"When can I sign up for that?" Josh says.

The class laughs. I don't. He's being a show-off. No one likes a show-off.

"Soon enough," Keets says.

"What happens when things go wrong?" Evie says. I'm surprised she's bringing attention to herself.

"I'm sorry, I don't think I understand the question," Keets says.

"You said things can go wrong. What happens, exactly . . . when they do?"

"Well, there are a number of things that can go wrong. Things that we don't have time to get into at the moment, but if there are no more simple questions, then, class dismissed. We start combat training tomorrow. Bring your A-games," Keets says as she leaves the screening room in a hurry.

The rest of the class follows. They talk amongst themselves as they leave. They're excited and scared, some more than others. Evie looks at me. She didn't like that Keets dodged her question. Maybe we're both reading too much into this. I smile at Evie as we leave. My only hope is that a little warmth from me can calm her nerves enough that she won't try to do anything stupid.

I wonder what it's like in the other world—the world of the dead. For the first time, I can honestly say I'm genuinely interested. I'm intrigued. My initial and naive obsession with knowing what's behind this program isn't as strong anymore. I still want to know, but more than that I want to see what this other world is like. I think we all do, even Evie.

CHAPTER SIXTEEN

EVIE

WE STRETCH FOR twenty, run for an hour, then work on agility exercises for another ten. The plan is to work us to the bone—hell week. After everyone's within inches of feeling like their bodies might give out at any second, we're thrown into combat and weapons training.

Keets is extra hard on us, not because she wants us to be *all that we can be*, but because there hasn't been a real war for her to be a part of. Her father had been part of the Iraqi Freedom War of the early 2000s, and her grandfather had been part of Vietnam. The terrorist attacks from Sector 6 kept GET marshals busy, but our standing army hasn't been needed for decades. Keets is angry because she feels like she hasn't lived up to the Keets family name, so she takes out her frustration on us. If she suffers inside, we will suffer on the outside.

It's hard to tell how much combat training we'll retain. We're shown individual takedown moves at a time and repeat them in unison and in front of a mirror—so we can connect the feeling and visual aspects of our body's motion. Then we're slapped into protective headgear and thrown in a ring with a partner to spar. I'm paired with Charlie.

I resent the gender stereotyping. I wouldn't have any problem knocking one of the guys to the mat. Charlie is more than ecstatic to get in the ring with me. I can tell by her expression that she's been looking forward to this. I don't blame her. I know she doesn't understand what Aiden and I have, and it drives her nuts.

She's more petite than I am, but she comes at me like a raging bull. We're supposed to be practicing Tai Kwon Do force redirection, but she's hell-bent on landing a punch. The first one smacks my gut. She packs quite the power for such a small package. The second punch lands across my lower jaw and triggers my inner beast. I feel the nail-biting agitation build up inside me. My eyes flare and my heartbeat quickens. Charlie goes for a third punch. I block it with my left arm and follow it with a right hook. The punch lands against her temple, and she crumples to the ground. She takes a few moments to get back to her feet, and it's in those moments that I feel like a total badass. I've never hit anyone before, but I think I'm good at it. A new sense of ease comes over me. I'm no longer hopped up on adrenaline. I'm steady, calm, and confident.

Charlie is back on her feet. She rotates her neck in a circle, touching both shoulders with the sides of her head. She still looks angry, but my punch has humbled her—she knows that she'll never get the best of me. My hit, which sent her to the mat, has wounded her pride. She doesn't come right at me as she has before. Now she waits. She's wised up and gone on the defense. If she can't take me down, she'll protect herself. It's at that moment that I learn to respect her. I had thought she was childish with how she had such a blind hatred for me, but I can see she also possesses intelligence and an aptitude for adaptation in crises—two qualities that might be important down the line.

The rest of the time we spar, we're cordial. We aren't out to get one another. We've made a combat pact. We both decide to learn from one another. We study each other's movements—how one attacks, then defends. Perhaps the most important thing that we learn in the ring is we can carry our own, and that's important.

After our session, Charlie and I sit and watch as other pairs square off against one another. Kyle and Russell both fight with courage, but neither of them looks like they're built for it. They mostly roll around on the mat, stuck together like two feuding insects.

Sonic I misjudged. He's paired with Gwiz. Even though Gwiz has height on him, Sonic is fast. He moves like a ninja and has no problem using Gwiz's extra inches and pounds against him. Gwiz spends more time on the mat than anyone else—something that drives him mad with fury.

Tasha and Hop are paired with one another. Hop is kind. He can tell from Tasha's gentle disposition that she's incredibly uncomfortable with the entire affair. Their time in the ring is more reminiscent of a tutorial. Hop leads her through different holds, blocks, punches, and kicks. He lets her use his body as a test dummy. Hop's being a good sport. And a patient one.

I watch now as Aiden and Josh step into the ring. It's the match that everyone's been looking forward to. The blue team has convinced themselves that Aiden is going to be a reaper. Josh, on the other hand, was born for this. While Aiden and Josh are about the same height, Josh possesses at least five to ten more pounds of pure muscle. He's strong, freakishly strong, and I for one don't want to see Aiden get hurt.

Josh is cocky, as usual. He's going into this match with the assumption that he's going to win. I hope Aiden lays him out. I know this is all supposed to be in good fun, and that ultimately we're all supposed to be on the same side, but Josh needs a good ass kicking. He saunters around the ring with his hands in the air, like he's got a crowd full of adoring fans watching him. He does have fans, I guess. Gwiz and Russell are practically drooling over his masculinity.

The two square up in the ring. Josh blows me a kiss out of the corner of his mouth, like the douchebag he is, and I look over at Aiden, ready to see a jealous rage building up inside him, but he's stone cold. He hasn't taken his eyes off of Josh. With a dead stare like that, I'm positive he saw the blown kiss, but I'd be willing to bet he never saw it was directed at me. He's that focused. It's kind of sexy. I can tell right then and there, Aiden is going to win this match-up.

Josh makes the first move. He bounces briskly on his toes, bobbing and weaving as he jabs at Aiden. He's toying with him until he can find an opening, a weakness. Aiden's hands block the jabs as he defends his face. After a few minutes, Josh grows tired of the dance and explodes into Aiden. He pounds on Aiden's stomach and face. The strength of the blows is too much for Aiden's hands to block. Punch after punch he lets them land. It's almost like he wants the hits to keep coming.

I cover my eyes. I can't watch the beating. Through the small cracks between my fingers, I can see Aiden's face starting to bruise up. The helmet helps some, but it can't protect against everything. Then I notice something, something that makes me come out from behind my hands—a strategy. It's brilliant really. Aiden is purposely tiring Josh out—a rope-a-dope. All he has to do is take the hits and conserve his strength. Sure, the punches will hurt, but defending only takes a tenth of the energy as attacking.

Aiden only throws one punch. Josh drops his guard for a split second, and Aiden throws a massive right hook to Josh's jaw. Josh hits the mat. Everyone's stunned, especially when Josh doesn't get back up. Gwiz and Russell look like two kids finding out there's no Santa Claus or Easter Bunny. The blue team is awestruck. Now they think for sure that their predictions of the next great reaper are true. Maybe they're right.

. . .

We're all lined up in a row. It's amazing to think just how large this facility is. Large enough to have its own personal indoor shooting range. There are two targets per lane. One target is about thirty yards out and the other is around a hundred. Weapons handling is something that was briefly explained to us as part of the program, but we haven't had to hold a gun until now. This, I know, is an area where I will excel.

My father had taught me to shoot. He had taught me that guns are not toys. They are made for taking a life, and that should never be taken lightly. The way some of these idiots are looking at these guns makes me sick. They think this is all a game. I doubt any of them have ever used one for its real purpose, but I have. I know what it's like to choose to squeeze the trigger, to watch as a hunk of metal tears through flesh and takes the breath from another living thing. I know what it's like to create death. It's horrifying.

Keets stands firm before us. She holds up a rifle.

"This, ladies and gentlemen, is the main weapon in your arsenal. This is a Remington CAR-20. *The* combat assault rifle of choice here. It has a 16-inch barrel with titanium bedding and a 60-round magazine of extremely lethal .308 uranium rounds. Good enough to kill just about anything in this world or the next."

I'm a little grossed out at how in love Keets is with this rifle. Guns have been outlawed for civilian use since GET took over. After the carnage of The Great Event, no one was sorry to see them go. People willingly volunteered the safe surrender of their personal weapons. Anyone caught with a gun of any kind is either killed or immediately sent to Sector 6. Owning a gun is considered an act of terrorism.

"You will hone your skills. You will be expected to center punch the hundred-yard targets with this weapon. You will not be assigned unless you do," Keets says.

The HD program only wants efficiently trained killers. Check.

Keets whips around and fires two single shots at a target. She clicks a fire select button by the trigger guard, and then pulls the trigger a second time. Now a controlled burst of three shots splatters the distant target. With a second button click and a third final pull of the trigger, a full-auto barrage of bullets shreds the target. She puts the rifle down on a range table and hits a target retrieve button on the side of the lane. The target sails down a cable track and stops just before Keets. She made two eyes, a smile, and a circle around both—a crude smiley face.

"The CAR-20 has three shooting modes: single fire, controlled burst, and fully automatic. You will need to master them all."

Josh and Gwiz nudge each other with excitement. Sonic and Kyle make air trigger pulls with their fingers. Keets pulls a small pistol from a holster resting on her hip. She holds it up so we can all see. It's a semi-auto. She pulls out the magazine, then reloads it and pulls back the slide.

"This is your secondary arm. It is a modified Beretta 98. It holds fifteen magnum rounds in the magazine and one in the chamber. If your primary weapon fails or you are incapable of reaching it, this should always be attached to your hip, literally. It is your lifeline, your last line of defense. This small arm could mean the difference between coming back or not. So please, get familiar with these weapons. You will be allowed to come to the shooting range at all hours of the day or night to practice. In fact, we encourage you to practice. After all, it does make perfect."

Tasha is nervous, sweating. This isn't her thing either. I'm actually starting to question what she's doing here. She doesn't seem to fit in, and she has yet to express a skill that she's better at than the rest of us.

"Put on your eye and hearing protection and pick a lane. If it isn't brutally obvious, the closer target is for the sidearm and the farthest target is for the rifle. These should be comfortable distances for each firearm."

Somehow, Aiden and I end up next to one another. We didn't plan it; it just happens. Now I feel like I *have* to do well. I don't know why I feel the need to impress him, but I do. I want him to be proud of me. I want him to think I'm great. That, and I'm competitive by nature.

I watch Aiden for a few moments to see what I'm up against. I'm fairly confident in my marksman skills, but I know nothing about his skills. Right away I can tell he's handled a gun before. Instead of getting an itchy finger and firing off some shots for fun, he situates himself. He feels the weight distribution of the rifle and adjusts his body for the best shooting position. He studies the sights with his eyes, he steadies his breathing, and he gently squeezes the trigger. He doesn't pull it, just squeezes it. It's supposed to feel like a surprise the first time you engage the trigger. You should be focused on the target and your breathing. Every micron of movement affects the accuracy of the shot. That's all you should be thinking about. The gun will fire when your body is ready for it to.

After the first shot, he looks over the stock and right at me. The lane stalls are made of clear, double-paned, bulletproof glass. He mouths something to me. Our ears are covered with shooting earmuffs, and even if they weren't, the deafening sound of indoor gunfire would be too much noise to render any audible words. He mouths the sentence to me again. This time I can tell exactly what he's saying.

"Are you going to shoot or just watch?" Aiden says.

He's being fresh. He smiles at me once he sees that I understand. I shoot him a sarcastic side smile and pick up the rifle. I get comfortable. The steel of the gun is cold against my cheek. My finger finds a resting place against the subtle curve of the trigger. My eyes focus on the target. I shoot with both eyes open. My father told me never to pinch one closed because it narrows the view of your surroundings. Pinching an eye could mean you don't see the other guy waiting in the bushes, ready to kill you. It's a hard aiming technique to master, but it's incredibly effective if you can.

I feel my eyes de-focus, and the iron sights seem to line up with the center of the distant target. I take in a deep breath and exhale. I always fire right when the last of my breath has left my body. I feel my finger and palm working together between the trigger and handle. The squeeze fires a bullet, and the recoil of the blast shutters the stock into my shoulder. I squeeze a few more times. I reach for the fire selection button and switch it to full-auto. I'm the first to do so in the range. The gun kicks violently as I hold down the trigger, but I contain its fight with the steadiness that is my grip. The last shot is fired and the magazine is empty.

I look up from the sights. I squint a little to see my target in the distance. I'm sure I did well. I always shoot well . . . and straight. Heat escapes from the vented tip of the barrel in the form of smoke. I gently place down the gun and notice that the range has gone quiet. Everyone else is watching me. I guess they didn't expect such a Rambo display, especially not from me.

I'm a little embarrassed, but Keets interrupts. She pushes the target retrieval button on my lane. She seems sure my shots were nothing more than a reckless display of excitement and inexperience. She couldn't be more wrong.

"Let's see what you did here," Keets says.

The target flies down the track and stops in front of my lane. Keets' face drops in shock. I've hollowed out the entire center of my target—all sixty rounds in a nice five-inch center punch. Everyone is awestruck, except Aiden, who shoots me a sharp smile.

"Nice job. Keep up the good work. I think everyone here could learn a thing or two from Evie," Keets says before swapping out my target.

"Thanks," I say as I smile back at Aiden.

CHAPTER SEVENTEEN

AIDEN

I T'S HARD TO tell time down here. We have clocks, but it's hard to remember how many days have gone by. You do your best to keep count in your head, but after a week you inevitably lose count and have to start all over again. The best I can describe the feeling is when you're a kid and not in school, like during the summer. Not having to be anywhere or do anything blurs the lines between days. Before you know it, summer feels like one really long day. What is it about time that humans are so obsessed with? The only time we should really be concerned about is how much of it we have left on this Earth. Then again, I'm beginning to realize that maybe that doesn't matter all that much either. If we die and go to this parallel world, then we have another life of sorts, one that keeps on going. That would mean time doesn't matter at all. It may not even exist if it's infinite. But nothing in nature is infinite. Only mankind can create infinite. Even the sun will burn out one day. Granted, not for like a million bazillion years, but it's not going to be around forever.

That's what it feels like here, one long, timeless, infinity day. Although it's not like the dream of summer. We aren't lost in the beauty of nothingness. We're lost in the never-ending monotony of our daily training. The once varied class assortment has narrowed from GET history, HD program briefing, Sector 6 updates, science of the dead world, understanding energy efficiency, drip biology, and weapons/combat training to just one: weapons/combat training.

At first, the relief of not having to hear Instructor Keets ramble on about spinal columns, the amount of energy needed to run a single apartment, or the latest shooting in Sector 6 was undoubtedly due. But as the days pass, firing guns, beating on one another, and running seem to consume our every waking hour, and it gets old. We never get a day off, just three hours of free time a day. Most of the free time is spent relaxing or sleeping. We never seem to be able to get enough sleep.

In all this time, Evie and I have devised a way to pass conversations without having to risk meeting up in secret or getting caught with chicken scratch on a piece of torn paper. Our need for more steady communication came out of our necessity to make our never-ending day more bearable. I think that's part of what they are doing here. They're grooming us like you would a military platoon. If we're cut off from the rest of the world, then this becomes the only world we know. Our teams have become our family, this facility our home. They want us to look at one another as brothers and sisters. They want us to be able to kill for one another. Killing for one another means we're killing for GET, and that is the ultimate form of loyalty. We're all willing to put ourselves on the line for GET property because that's what we have become. GET has made us into efficient tactical machines, and there's no other place I'd rather be. After all, Evie is here.

Talking is what keeps us sane and grounded. It helps us process our thoughts so we don't let things tip us too far into the deep end. Evie is sure GET has a rotten core, but I'm not so certain anymore. I haven't told Evie. She's so certain. I don't know why or how she is, but she is. I don't want to take that from her. She still thinks everything stems from the world of the dead. With each note, she grows more eager to drip. She wants to explore. She wants to find holes. I love her veracity. It's one of her best qualities.

We still meet when we can. We've gotten pretty good at sneaking around. I feel like a teenager trying to sneak into his girlfriend's house. I'm always pushing to meet, but she's more cautious than I am. They do encourage us to stay with our teams socially. Even though they want us to feel like one big happy family, they like the team division. I'll give it to the program, having two teams does foster competition. The competitive element makes us try harder, work harder, and push ourselves harder. We all want to be the best. So for now, we stick to our notes and meet whenever possible.

The notes we use we derived from one of the oldest tricks in the book. Evie had seen it used in an old movie she saw as a kid. It's pretty simple: we make paper keys. You take a regular piece of paper and place it over a piece of source material. We use the HD Program Packet, which I have to borrow each time from Hop. Evie thinks it's both clever and unsuspicious. I think she likes it because it's like saying *screw you* to the program.

Once the key is over the page, you seek out words or letters you want your message to include. Then you cut out little boxes on the key. When that key is placed over the designated page in the packet, the secret message is revealed in the cut-out boxes. So there is no confusion, we write the page number backward in the upper right corner of the note. Therefore, if we want the other to use page fourteen as the key, we'll write a forty-one in the upper right corner.

We think we're geniuses, but the fact of the matter is, it's not that great of a system. Sure, it's hard enough to crack for unsuspecting eyes, but creating messages is time-consuming, and not every page in the packet has enough words to make good sentences. Most of our messages are limited to broken English with bad grammar. Having a full conversation is painstakingly slow, but it helps the time pass. For now, it will have to do.

Occasionally, Evie will slip something personal into the notes. It doesn't happen too often, but enough. Maybe a tidbit about how she always wanted a pet dog, or how she misses her time spent at the cabin in the Poconos. I always feel lucky on those days. Those are the days I look forward to.

It's been thirty-two days since our first exam.

. . .

I jerk awake. I'm still having my nightmare almost every night, but it's not what woke me. The intercom voice made an early appearance today.

"Blue team, please proceed to Exam Room 2," the intercom blares.

I slide my feet out of bed. Hop jumps down from the upper bunk. He's already wearing his blue uniform. He's starting to sleep in them. For the past week, he's been convinced the second exam could be any second. He wants to be ready. Maybe his predictions have come true.

"Blue team, please proceed to Exam Room 2."

"This is it," Hop says.

I rub my face and look for a fresh jumpsuit in my locker.

"Oh yeah?" I say.

"Sure is. This is our second exam. It's a team exam."

"You don't know it's a team exam. Just because we're all being called to the exam room doesn't mean it's a joint exam. Maybe we're all taking an exam in the same room together. Ever think of that?" Sonic says as he laces up his shoes.

Charlie's dressed and ready to go. She has turned getting ready in the morning into a science. She has to be the fastest girl in history at getting ready. "Come on. Hustle it up. Let's just stop wondering what's gonna happen and go find out," she says.

I'll tell you what I wonder. I wonder what's going through Evie's mind. For days now she's been talking about the next exam. It's finally here and, for some reason, I think Hop is right.

. . .

Exam Room 2 is small. There are only enough seats for the ten of us. Both teams fight over who gets the front row. I end it by taking a seat in the second row. Once we're all sitting, we wait for Keets to come in. That's how things go. We always arrive before Keets does. The room is small, but it's different in that one wall has two doors. One door is marked with a blue plaque and the other with a red one. It's pretty obvious our teams will be separated at some point. What's not clear is what awaits us on the other side.

Sure enough, Keets enters the room. She takes her usual position in front of us and calls roll. I'm not entirely sure why; anyone can see that there are ten butts sitting in the only ten seats in the room. Calling roll must be a part of protocol—something Keets' military background would never permit her to break. Once we're all checked in, she pulls up a holographic map. It looks like a city. The city is laid out on a standard grid. On the far corners of the grid, between all the other buildings, subways, and storefronts are two large individual buildings that stand out from the rest of the map. One building is red and the other is blue.

"Ladies and gentlemen," Keets says in her all too famil-iar way of addressing us, "welcome to your second exam. Today's exam is a team examination."

Hop gives me a nudge. He likes to be right. It's not often that he gets to be, so he makes everyone know it when he is.

"This exam is designed to show us how well you will work together as a team, something your lives will depend on when you are assigned and in the field. This map shows you the overall layout of the simulation. Yes, that's right, this city is a simulation. You are not *actually* in a city. The barriers of buildings will feel and look real, but I assure you they are not. Many doors will lead to nowhere, streets are cyclical, and they do not go on forever. If you run down one long enough, you'll come out on the same street on the opposite side of the map."

"It's like one giant video game," Kyle whispers to Sonic. A whisper that if I could hear, it most certainly means Keets could too.

"It is like a video game. Thank you for your input. However, unlike a video game, your feelings are real. If you get hit, shot, fall, or do anything stupid, you will most certainly feel it."

Everyone in the room looks nervous. The mention of being shot doesn't sit well with the lot of us. Keets has a fine-tuned skill of picking up on our anxieties, as any good profiler would.

"Not to worry. The weapons you will be using do not kill, but I will get to that shortly," Keets says. She points to the red and blue buildings on opposite sides of the map. "These two buildings are designated with your team colors. One red and one blue. They are on opposite sides of the map from one another because you will not all be working together. There can be only one victorious team. Both teams will start at their base. Within that base, there is a flag. The objective of the exam is to get your flag into the opposite team's base. The first team to do so wins."

"What do we win?" Charlie says.

"That's a dumb question," Gwiz blurts out.

"Come on now, that's enough. You don't win anything but the bragging rights," Keets says.

"How do we pass or fail?" Evie always asks the hard

questions. You have to admire her commitment to pushing Instructor Keets' buttons.

"This exam is different. You don't pass or fail. By participating you pass. This exam is really made for us. By watching all of you, we will get a better grasp of your individual strengths and weaknesses. We want to assign you to the position that suits you best. This is another step in the many that allow us to do so."

"Got it," Evie says.

I can tell she didn't really care what the answer was. She just likes to rattle the cage.

Keets turns off the map.

"The weapons you will be using are exact replicas of the CAR-20 rifle and HD sidearm. However, they are loaded with non-lethal electro, or E-rounds. E-rounds do what their name implies . . . they electrify, but just because they are non-lethal doesn't mean they don't sting like a bitch. When shot with an E-round, your body is electrocuted for 60 seconds. That's 60 seconds of sticking a fork in the toaster. It'll shake you, maybe even bake you, but it will not kill you. During those painful sixty seconds, you will not be able to move or fire either of your weapons, giving your opponent a timed tactical advantage."

Russell turns in his seat and points his fingers at Hop and pretends to pull the trigger. He looks at Gwiz and they both laugh. Hop takes a huge gulp of air. His nervousness is radiating from his body. It's no wonder the bottom feeders picked up on it. Just one drop of blood and they're ready to pounce. I lean in toward Hop.

"Don't let them get to you, okay? You're going to be

just fine," I whisper. I'm not sure I believe it, but as long as Hop does, that's all that's important. We're going to need everyone working to their full potential.

"Other than that, there's only one other rule. Once you cross a street, you aren't allowed to move backward, only forward. If you or any member of your team crosses a street and then moves back across it, that person will be ejected from the exam. And I can tell you, losing a teammate never ends well for the rest of your team. Just focus on your objective, and the stronger, better team will prevail."

It's clear that Keets thinks the red team is going to win. They are the physically stronger team, but now I have a vendetta. I want to win, bad. I don't like being seen as weak. Underdogs we may be, but I'll think of something. By the looks of them, I can tell my team is counting on me. No pressure. I am a little conflicted seeing as Evie is on the red team. Shooting her and making her suffer like that isn't something I ever thought I'd have to do. Deep in my mind, I know that she'd shoot me just for thinking about not shooting her. She doesn't like pity, nor does she dish it. I'll just have to step up to the plate. Maybe I won't even have to. Maybe someone else will handle that one little detail.

"If you look to your left, you'll see two doors. Those are your locker rooms for the exam. You must suit up and load up. Once you are all ready, you will be permitted to enter the exam. Once you are all in your bases, you will hear an alarm sound. The alarm designates the start of the exam. You will know when the exam has ended because that same alarm will sound again. That's about it. Good luck."

Keets leaves the room. The red and blue doors slide open.

. . .

"Does this look right?" Kyle says as he pulls at the straps of a blue vest fastened around his torso.

Sonic takes one quick look, winds up, and slugs Kyle square in the chest.

Kyle stumbles back. "Hey!"

"Looks right to me," Sonic says with a laugh.

The vests were in each of our lockers in the locker room. Thin blue stripes across the chest and over the shoulders mark us as the blue team, but they also provide a degree of cushioning in the event we get a foot or stock of a CAR-20 jammed into our chests. Still, they're pretty useless and awfully goofy-looking. If anything they just inhibit our movement.

We're in the blue base. There's not much to it. It's really just a large empty room. In the middle, there's a platform with a blue two-by-two-foot flag gently placed in a flag holder. The alarm hasn't sounded yet, so I can only assume that the red team is taking a little longer than we had. My guess is that Tasha is holding them up. She's probably hyperventilating in the corner and refusing to leave the safety of the locker room. Josh or Gwiz probably want to drag her in and use her as a shield, but Evie would force them to give her the time she needed to muster enough courage to make the entrance on her own.

Hop is pacing.

"So, what are we going to do?" he says.

I can tell this question is directed at me.

"What do you mean?"

"Our plan. What's our plan? Please tell me you've been thinking of a plan."

"I've been thinking," I lied. I haven't really been thinking. A few random ideas, but nothing that sounds like it would work. Nothing worthy of sharing. Nothing I think will lead us to victory.

"Well, we've got to think of something. And fast," Hop says.

"Would you calm down already? You're making me nervous. I sweat when I'm nervous," Kyle says.

"Then you must sweat a lot," Sonic says.

"I say we just grab the flag and storm right at them. By the time they know what hit 'em, they'll be jolting about in little heaps on the ground and we'll be long gone, nothing they can do about it," Charlie says. She aggressively uses her rifle to accentuate her plan.

"That's the dumbest idea I've ever heard," Hop says.

"Oh yeah, why?" Charlie forces herself up in Hop's face. Hop backs down.

"Because they're stronger than us. We wouldn't stand a chance head-to-head with them in an all-out firefight. I mean, tell 'em, Aiden. Evie alone could take out all of us," he says.

"Bullsh—"

The sound of the alarm fills our base.

"Great. Now, what are we going to do? Josh's probably riled them all up, and they're for sure halfway here by now. And what do we got? Not a plan! That's for sure," Hop says.

"Can you shut up. You're scaring the kids," Charlie snaps.

"Hey, who exactly are the kids in this scenario?" Sonic says.

I have it. Like a blast of lightning, I know how we can win this thing. I have to contain my excitement. They can't think it's foolproof because it's not. I need their A-game, and arrogance isn't going to get us very far. Keeping them afraid might work in our favor. Fear is a survival instinct and can be extremely powerful if you can keep a hold on it.

"Guys," I say. No one seems to hear me over their bickering. "Guys!" This time they hear me. "Hop is right."

"Sure he is," Charlie says.

"Come on now. Hear me out. Charlie, you're right too."

"We're listening," Kyle says.

"Let's look at what we know. We know they are stronger. We know Josh has probably asserted himself as their team leader. We know Josh is completely full of himself."

"Is there a point to all of this?" Charlie says.

"Josh won't leave anyone behind in their base to guard it. He thinks he can beat us. He thinks he knows it for a fact. He'll think attacking with all guns blazing will defeat us."

"So what do we do?" Hop says.

"We defend," I reply.

My plan is really quite simple. It's inspired by the very mission of the HD program. They told us our main job as HD operatives is to defend the GET power source. So maybe that's the key to this exam. Flex our defensive skills and create an opportunity. I beat Josh in the ring with this strategy and I can beat him again with it.

We set up shop and wait for them to attack. I'm sure that's what they'll do, and we'll be waiting for them. We form a line one street in front of our base. We each hide, sheltered behind different objects. The city they created for us is extensive, right down to the steam coming out of vents in the streets. There are parked cars, mailboxes, working doors, and traffic barricades. Each of us waits, concealed from our impending attackers. We space ourselves about twenty feet apart. That way we cover enough ground that they can't just slip by us undetected. It's also a small enough gap that one of us can't be isolated and picked off. This plan is going to work. It has to.

The red team is here and right on schedule. It doesn't take Josh long to navigate through the city. We've worked out hand signals so we don't have to give up our positions with words. I can see them, all five of them, about forty feet in front of us. They're closing the gap fast. I look over at Charlie. I've positioned myself in the middle so I can command either side of the street independently. I motion to Charlie. I hold up five fingers and point in the direction of their approach. She relays the info to Kyle, who's to her left. I turn around to my right and relay the same info to Hop.

The four of us are lined up out here in the street. Our fifth man, Sonic, is safely tucked behind the walls of our base. He's waiting for our cue to emerge, bearing our flag that's neatly secured to his hideously impractical blue vest. The thing about Sonic is that he's fast and agile. He's probably the fastest out of anyone here, including the red team, but that's all he has to be.

The plan is simple. We draw the red team in close enough to ensure they're easy targets. Once we take down all five of the red team, we'll give the cue and Sonic has sixty seconds to get his butt across the street. Once he's across the street and past the red team, he's home free. He could walk his way to their base if he wanted to and put up our flag. Why? Because they can't backtrack; it's against the rules. The hardest part of the plan is the coordination of taking out the red team.

A perfect execution would give Sonic a full sixty seconds to make the trip across the street. In a much more grounded world, it'll probably take a good thirty seconds just trying to nail them all. That means Sonic will only have thirty seconds until the first shot red team member can potentially shoot him and ruin the entire plan. Our victory relies on a matter of seconds. We have a very narrow margin for error.

They're within sidearm range now. An easy enough shot with the handgun, but an almost nonexistent shot with the CAR-20. I make the first move. It's now or never. I pop up from behind a mailbox drilled to the pavement. I open fire. I use short, controlled bursts. The first few pulls of the trigger don't land any hits, but my fourth connects with Russell. His body writhes and jiggles with an electric charge.

"Fire!" I cry out.

The rest of my team jumps into action. A steady barrage of E-rounds fills the street. The red team fires back. I count off the seconds in my head from sixty.

SIXTY.

Josh makes quick work of shooting Hop, but not after Hop manages to take down Gwiz.

FIFTY-FIVE.

Kyle goes for the weakest and takes out Tasha with three rounds to the chest. Evie retaliates, sending Kyle to the ground with a full-auto E-round barrage. It's okay if we lose teammates, just as long as we take the red team down with us. I fire a warning shot at Evie. She ducks behind a car.

FORTY-EIGHT.

We have to end this. We're running out of time. I'll have to sacrifice myself. It's the only way. I gesture to Charlie, telling her to watch for Evie. Shooting me might be too good for her to pass up.

I make a run for it. I relinquish the safety of my trusty mailbox and run straight for Josh. I think I take him by surprise because the look on his face is priceless. He never would have thought in a million years that I had it in me to take him on like this. After the surprise comes his determination. He doesn't want to be made the best of again. He raises his rifle, but I'm too close now for a clean shot. He fires and misses. I slide, ripping the rifle from his hands. He immediately goes for his sidearm.

FORTY.

I skid to a stop and turn on a dime, gun aimed.

"Sonic, now!" I yell as loud as my lungs will allow. I can see how this all plays out.

I'm first to fire, but hear the distant whir of Evie's E-round leaving the muzzle of her rifle. Charlie had to move from her hiding spot to get a clear shot at Evie, which put her only a short distance from Josh. Josh doesn't have time to turn on me, so he fires at Charlie just as she pulls the trigger on Evie.

THIRTY-SEVEN.

Within milliseconds all four of us hit the ground, convulsing and twitching. Damn, these E-rounds really do sting, but it doesn't matter because through the pain I can see Sonic running his little heart out. He ducks, weaves, and bounces off the pavement. He holds no weapons, just our flag. Sure victory is in our grasps. It feels good to be on top. I gave it my best and my best bought Sonic thirty-four seconds to make it across the street.

Sonic does it in twenty-nine.

CHAPTER EIGHTEEN

THE OTHERS

Winston Parker gazes out his top floor office window—floor 51. His reflection reveals a manicured black and white head of hair. Time has wrinkled his forehead, and crows have made nests in the corner of his eyes. His face is streamlined and hairless, but the brutal weathering from the sun has made his skin tough and leathery. He bears the look of a Marlboro Man, untamed and wild, stuffed in a three-piece suit as to keep up appearances. His left hand rests in the pocket of his blazer. He's in no hurry and probably never has been, but it's clear that he's waiting for something.

He looks out and down at the world he has created. The world he forged out of the ashes of The Great Event. He looks at the city from his perch; a lingering question tickles his tongue and hovers over his lips. His steely blue eyes look to the distant horizon for answers, but it has none. Reaching into the breast pocket of his blazer, he pulls out an antique pocket watch, older than his oldest wrinkle—a timepiece from before his time—and holds it in his right hand. A hand scarred and tattooed from years of seething gunpowder. He was, or is, a gunslinger. He'd taken lives with that hand; his fingers and palm bear the proof. How many lives is hard to say, but even the crisp white cuffs of his shirt can't hide his hand's fury. Winston Parker is what you'd call a dangerous man.

It's 5:31 p.m. He closes the lid of the watch, gives it a quick wind, and, frustrated, jams it back in his breast pocket. A knock at the office door sends his trigger hand swiftly down to his right hip—a reflex developed from years of living on edge—but no smoke-wagon rests there.

Putting down his guns was a necessary step in taking control of his company. A step that, more than ten years later, he is still getting used to. Trust has never been easy for him. Trusting someone means you have to give up a part of yourself. Winston Parker doesn't like to give up anything. He's a taker. He takes what he wants and gives very little in return. Grabbing the bull by its horns isn't just a saying in his life. It's how he lives his life. Trust, in his mind, means death, and that's why he always carries a gun on his hip, or at least used to. That was the hardest part. Trusting others to get the job done. Even the dirty ones—especially the dirty ones.

"Come in," Winston says in his firm, gristly voice.

The door opens and Arthur walks in. He's quick about it. He knows he's one or two minutes late. He shuts the door behind him—this is a private meeting—and stands at attention. It's hard to tell if Arthur fears Winston Parker. Most men would and they'd be right in doing so—after all,

Winston Parker is a dangerous man—but Arthur isn't most men. He's been to hell and back, many times in fact, and it takes more than a powerful gunslinger to send Arthur running for the hills.

Arthur has spent more time in the world of the dead than any two HD operatives combined, and that includes two of the oldest. Those who know him best, which is few, jokingly call him Skim Milk because he only spends about two percent of his waking hours above ground zero. In his forty-something years on this planet, he's lived three, maybe even four lifetimes below. Long enough to have seen everything and anything. Arthur has grown a thick skin, impenetrable to almost all things in this world or the next. To think he fears a dangerous man like Winston Parker would be a mistake, but every man has to fear something. Otherwise, you're not a man at all. Whoever said fear makes you weak must not know what it's like to be strong. Arthur has never had that problem. With a shred of luck and timing, it could just have easily been Arthur standing in Winston Parker's shoes, reveling over *his* empire.

"Sorry I'm late," Arthur says.

"I only flew a few thousand miles. All the way from our GET Europe headquarters, to find out how your golden goose performed."

"He did well. Quite well in fact. As expected."

Winston turns and redirects his gaze on Arthur.

"Really?"

"Yes. The blue team won. He set a record."

"Is that what you want to call it? A record?" Winston laughs under his breath.

"It was a brilliant display of team leadership. He figured out how the red team was going to attack and he used their plan against them. He sacrificed himself and his teammates all so one could slip through. He's the only recruit who seems to be realizing that all it takes is one person. That one individual can change the course of everything. That's not to say they aren't all strong. This is a very strong class of recruits. Maybe one of our best. But Aiden is extraordinary. He also seems to understand that life is not as important as success. I think he's the clear choice for Reaper."

"He hasn't been faced with life and death in the field. I'd think it unwise to draw that conclusion this early," Winston snarls.

"I'm almost certain—"

"Almost? We *have* to be sure. You know that."

"I do," Arthur replies.

Winston takes a deep breath. He glares at Arthur. His rigid face leaves nothing to be desired. He's angry and unsure. Damn trust. "What about Evie?"

"What about her?"

"Please don't make me repeat myself."

"She's doing fine. She excels above many of the others. Her shooting skills and intellectual capabilities are off the charts. We've noticed she has a small problem with authority, but it's not out of control. If it weren't for that I'd say she'd be nominated for Reaper as well, but the legacy Josh seems to have a better handle on his team."

"Josh is an idiot, but we only need one. You said so yourself," Winston says.

Arthur shifts his weight. He's uncomfortable with

how Winston views the recruits' lives, something he and Winston disagree on all the time, but now is no time to gripe, not when he's trying to push his prize pony. He keeps his mouth shut.

"I think she's dangerous," Winston says.

Arthur holds back a chuckle. A smile creeps over his face. Winston notices and it makes him sick. If he had his gun he might have taken this opportunity to use it.

"With all due respect, sir, I disagree," Arthur says.

"Of course you do. You treat them all like they're your children. It's disgusting. If you give them the chance, they'll bite your head off. Just so you don't forget, we're creating killers. Every last one of them. If anything sets them off—"

"They are all on course for completion," Arthur reassuringly interrupts.

"What about the notes?"

"What notes?" Arthur asks.

"Somehow I knew you wouldn't know. Evie and Aiden have been communicating in secret."

"I can assure you—"

"It's happening. I'm pretty sure they've been meeting in person as well. There are gaps in our surveillance, but there are enough dots to make a straight line." Winston walks toward Arthur like a lion hunting prey. "We need Aiden. GET needs Aiden. We do not need her. I just want you to remember what you told me a month ago."

"If Evie poses a problem, I will deal with it," Arthur says calmly.

"That's what you told me the last time. It's clear she didn't listen."

Winston returns to the window and looks out at the sprawling city. Cars race by, people crowd sidewalks and storefronts; from up above, everything seems so quiet and delicate, like a newborn baby asleep in its crib. From here Winston Parker feels like a god.

"Look at them, all of them, down there on the streets. They're leaving work, picking up food from the grocery store, going home to their two kids and dog. They go to bed and wake up the next day and do it all over again, not realizing everything I do for them. They're so oblivious to everything that happens outside of the wall, from outside of their walls. They look like ants from up here. So tiny and helpless just doing as they do. The city is a living, breathing organism. It's mighty, but fragile. It's only as strong as its weakest citizen. Everyone serves a purpose. Even the citizens of Sector 6 serve a purpose. Little do they know, all of their lives, no matter how in control they feel, are balancing on the edge of a sharp knife. One little slip. One little chink in the chain. One little ripple. That's all that is needed, and if that ripple is strong enough and happens at the right time and in the right way, it will grow into a tidal wave. And this, everything they have come to know and love, will come crashing down around them."

Winston turns back to Arthur.

"I want to move up the third exam," he says abruptly.

"Their drip exams aren't scheduled for another few weeks," Arthur says.

"Evie is dangerous and I want to know why."

"They aren't ready."

"You yourself said all of them are some of the best recruits we've ever had. Were you lying?" Winston says.

"No," Arthur says firmly.

"Then move up the exam."

Winston Parker turns his back to Arthur for good. This conversation is over. He gazes out the window again. His reflection reveals a sultry grin. He likes having control. For, in Winston Parker's mind, Arthur is the dangerous man.

CHAPTER NINETEEN

EVIE

WE JUST GOT word that our free time is going to be cut from three hours a day down to two hours. There are only two possible reasons for this happening that come to mind. One: The program is entering its last phase of training and they need more hours during the day to get us ready for our third exam and our assignment. Two: Something is wrong.

I think it's because of option two. Given the sketchy nature of GET as a whole, I'd say something must have happened that pissed off the higher-ups. In return, they retaliate by slashing the one part of the day that we have some control over. If my instincts serve me well and option two is in fact the reasoning behind the freedom slashing, then what was it that encouraged this wrath? The only thing I can think of is Aiden. Aiden and his clever plan that allowed him to lead his blue team to victory in exam two. I say *his team* because that's exactly what it is. He's the clear leader of the blue team. He never asked nor pushed for it. The rest of the team forced him into the role, but it suits him. I'm not sure he realizes he's the leader, but he is. I'm still not sure why the blue team winning would piss *them* off?

Maybe Aiden broke a rule. It wouldn't be the first time he's done that on an exam. *Cheating*, in Aiden's mind, is a very loose term. What most might consider cheating, he'd consider a minor bending of the rules to achieve an easier means to success. What some might see as an unfair advantage, Aiden would see as an intelligent workaround. He views problems with a very different outlook than most. His barometer for right and wrong is a little skewed, which does worry me a little. I'm conflicted because everything else about him—his kindness, intelligence, and gentle disposition—leads me to believe he's a great guy. Not to mention the physical attraction I feel getting stronger and stronger with the passing of each day. I'm not proud of it, but sometimes, when I read one of his latest notes, I find myself imagining kissing him and thinking of our dream and that place and how wonderful it was when our lips met. I know he feels the attraction too, he more so than I, and earlier too. I could tell from the very first moment we met. His eyes went soft with want and his voice tender and clear, but we can't lose ourselves. Not now.

Our little bit of free time has me in a frenzy. It's not that I think it's not fair, but it gives Aiden and me far less time to communicate. Now I have a little less than two hours to think of what to say, devise the key, put the entire note together, and then deliver it. It shouldn't really be a problem. On average, I can make a half-page note in about an hour, but that's not the tricky part. The tricky part is finding a clear window to deliver it. Note delivery usually takes a solid hour if not more. You have to scour the halls, find the gaps in the surveillance because the camera variance changes daily, and make the delivery. It takes patience and patience takes time.

It doesn't look like I'll get a note out today. I'll finish it, but I won't have a large enough window to deliver it. I'll include an explanation in the note. The new restraints mean notes every other day now. Aiden will take it the hardest. I know how much he looks forward to the notes. I do too, but when we meet I try not to show it. Sometimes, I literally feel myself holding back in the notes. I'll write something sentimental or what I would consider cute and I'll go back and change the word or sentence, sometimes deleting it altogether. Some days, when I'm feeling a little more lonely than normal, something dear to me will spill out and I'll leave it be. It helps me feel better. It can be therapeutic.

Today would not be one of those days. I'll tell him all about how I think something he did made the program heads mad. I'll jokingly blame him for the free-time cut. I'll also tell him how it puts a staggered stranglehold on our secret communications. He'll reply as he always does, in a timely manner. He never writes as much as I do. It's either because he's not as fast as I am at making a key or because he's just a guy, and guys aren't great at communicating with girls. I like to think I'm just better at it than he is. He'll say I'm crazy for thinking he's the reason for the time cut. I'm not sure he realizes how important the program is making him out to be. It's easy to see that they favor him. The reason for which I'm still trying to figure out. He'd also tell me that a note every other day doesn't work for him and that he'll figure something out. I doubt he will. I know he'll try, but I've worked it over in my head and I don't think it's possible.

I'll make sure I send the note as soon as I can. I wouldn't want him to worry too much. Something else I don't think is possible.

. . .

We all walk down the long corridor in a single file line. Nater is escorting us. I'm guessing by the blue team's presence that they, too, received the notice. The notice said we would be moving ahead with the 3rd exam at 0800 hours. I was surprised when it was delivered. We had just finished the 2nd exam. There had been weeks in between the first two. Having the 3rd and final exam just a day after the 2nd seems odd. I suddenly feel like my prediction is validated. My team has been nervous. Even Josh, who never acts nervous, looks like he's going to puke. I laugh a little bit inside, but I have to admit, I'm feeling the same. None of us are ready for another exam. We are all still exhausted from yesterday.

We walk together in silence, the fatigue written all over our faces. I see Aiden up ahead. He looks tired too, but he seems excited. I'm not sure what the exam will entail. It could be anything, but I think it's going to be our first drip session. It's the only thing we haven't done yet. Keets told us it would happen, but not when. We were supposed to have a physical examination beforehand, but it looks like that isn't going to be happening.

I've been waiting for the opportunity to drip. I'm more than interested to see what this world of the dead is like. I also think GET and the HD program aren't telling us everything. It's clear they are keeping us on a strict need-to-know basis. If I'm going to risk my neck for something, I want to know exactly what that something is.

We pass by the girls' locker room and I notice something troubling. A GET employee is on a ladder installing additional cameras in the hall. One of which points continuously at the girls' locker room door. Now I know something is wrong. Aiden notices too and looks over his shoulder at me. I immediately motion for him to turn back around. I'm sure that's clear enough for him to know that I know what he just figured out.

We round the corner and enter a door marked: DRIP LAB. When we enter, Keets is there waiting for us. She doesn't say anything yet; she just motions for us to keep coming in. Once we are all there, Nater leaves, shutting the door behind him.

The room is much larger than the drip room we had observed a few weeks back from the screening room. While the other room contained one drip chair, this room contains ten chairs set up in a large circle. The feet of the chairs face outward and the heads toward the center. A doctor and nurse stand in the middle of the circle. It's clear they will be administering our drip. Each chair has a name badge on the front of the headrest. There is a badge for each of us. Without instruction, we all gravitate to the chair with our name on it. We now stand in a circle. I'm sandwiched between Russell and Tasha. Aiden is next to Josh and Charlie, which is only a few chairs from me. Everyone looks petrified.

"Welcome, ladies and gentlemen, to your last and final exam. This is your drip test. The purpose of this test is to see how your mind and body handle the transition. Don't be confused by this room. You are all in the same room for the convenience of our technicians; if something goes wrong it's easier for us if you are all in the same place. I can tell by looking around the room that you are afraid of what might come on the other side. You have every reason to be afraid. New experiences can be scary. However, you needn't worry too much because you are being inserted into safe zones. This means that each of you will be inserted into an isolated drip safe zone, quarantined by HD operatives on the other side. You will be by yourself. Keep that in mind also. Each of you will be inserted in a different safe zone location. This is not how it will be on a real HD mission, but for the purposes of the exam, it allows us to individually monitor your interactions with the world of the dead. How you act and react to situations presented to you in your safe zone will be taken into consideration when choosing your HD assignment. Lastly, your only real requirement for passing this test is to survive it. If you are successfully reanimated, then you pass. Are there any questions before we get started?" Keets says.

Not a single person speaks up or raises a hand.

"Good. Then take your seats and try to relax." Keets points to one wall of the room. It shimmers slightly—a two-way mirror. "We will be watching and monitoring you from the control room on the other side of that wall. Good luck, everyone."

Keets leaves the room. The doctor instructs us to remove our shirts and take our seats. Thankfully, they told us girls to wear our sports bras. Kyle seems uneasy or embarrassed to remove his shirt. His brother Sonic helps him off with it. Originally, I thought Tasha would be the fish out of water here, but Kyle seems to be the most uncomfortable. We all take our seats. I hear Russell mutter the words *here we go* under his breath. The nurse makes her way around to each chair and fastens each of our wrists to the cold metal of the chair's armrests. My hands are trembling. I don't feel afraid, but my body thinks it knows something I do not.

The doctor places three small sticky patches on our bodies: one on our wrist, one on our upper spine, and one on our lower back. I suddenly remember one of our drip biology lessons. These must be the optic needle injection points. The patches are cool against the skin and no bigger than a quarter. Their tops have a single circular dot in the middle—probably so they know where to stick the needle—and a series of metallic lines that look similar to what you might find on a computer chip.

"Do not be alarmed. These are temporary BDP and NDP patches. Because you have not yet been fitted with permanent ones, these will serve the purpose for today. They are only good for one drip session and reanimation. Because of this, the pinch you feel when the optic needles are attached will be slightly more painful. This is normal. Please try to stay calm," the doctor says.

Staying calm seems like an impossibility. He's basically

telling us it's going to hurt and hurt bad. I remember how bad it looked like it hurt Garcia, and this is supposed to hurt worse. Stay calm. Ha. Here's for trying.

With a push of a button, the doctor makes all of our chairs extend and flatten into tables. The nurse makes her way around the circle once again to strap our ankles to the legs of the chairs. Now we're trapped. It's a horrifying feeling, not being able to willfully move your body. I give the wrist straps a little tug, but my arms aren't going any- where. Scary. Not being in control of your own body.

The nurse moves from chair to chair, attaching our sur- gical drips in our wrists. She pulls each drip from large spaghetti-like tubing dangling from the ceiling. Then comes the prick.

The needles pierce my skin and a horrific burning sensa- tion fills my spinal column. I convulse forward, trying to escape the pain, but that only makes it worse. I force myself to relax and lean back into the chair. Then, the pinching feeling. The needles expand slightly once they make contact with the nerves in the spine. They only expand about two millimeters, but it feels like someone is using the Jaws of Life to rip open my body. They have to expand so the optic cable can move through the needle like a snake and sink its fangs into the nerves. The feeling is close to what I imagine it must be like to get shot with a bullet, and then fried in an electric chair.

Through our screams and agony, I can see the doctor hit another button on his remote. I know that means the ice-bath. The floor opens beneath me, and the bath emerges from the floor. The touch of the water on my skin stings because it's so cold, but its frigid breath soothes the pain of the needles. For the first time, my body feels safe enough to relax.

My body shivers under the flow of cold water. The tube in my wrist starts to fill with my blood. I see it moving north and disappearing into the white tile ceiling. I'm not sure why they make these rooms white. It seems stupid to me. One little mistake and you've got a mess on your hands. Watching the blood flow makes me drowsy. The last thing I remember is the nurse placing the biometric mask over my nose and mouth and the sight of the large black zeros on the room's walls growing fainter until they seem not to exist at all.

. . .

I come to. My eyes are already open, but my vision takes a second to kick in. I quickly jump to my feet. I had been lying down. An obvious mirror of how our bodies had been presented for insertion. I look around. I'm alone in a dingy slum of a room. The walls are dirty and look weathered with time. I can barely make out the large black numeral ones painted on the walls. I made it.

There's a small table in the center of the room. On the table is a closed pelican case. I move over to the table and open the case. Inside, I immediately notice the CAR-20 rifle and sidearm. Next to those are a tactical uniform, two magazines with live ammunition, and an envelope. I put on the tactical uniform, load one of the clips, and pocket the second. I reach for the envelope and open it.

The envelope contains a piece of paper with instructions.

The instructions are simple. All it says is that there is a small Sector 6 disturbance in Block 8. I am to see to the disturbance and fix it. I'm not, however, to deviate from the objective.

I put down the instructions and make sure my gun is cocked and loaded. It's strange to me that they would send us—well, me—on a mission like this with no prior drip experience. It seems dangerous and foolish, but if I'm to find anything out, I have to leave this room. What other choice do I have? We're in a safe zone. What do I have to worry about? I wonder how much of me they can see.

The room does have a door, so I try it. The knob turns easily and the door swings open. Outside the room, there's a small hallway and staircase. I walk slowly down the staircase, gun at the ready. They gave it to me for a reason; I should be on my guard. A man quickly rounds the bend of the staircase and reaches for the guide rail. I raise my gun and he flinches.

"Don't shoot!" the man says.

He looks normal, like a living and breathing person, but this is the world of the dead. I guess I had assumed everyone would look different here, like a scene out of an old B-horror movie—gross pale skin, maybe an eyeball hanging out of the socket—but this guy doesn't. His skin is pink and both of his eyes are where they should be. Even the touch of his shoulder against mine as he passes feels very *real*. Maybe this world isn't so different from ours.

I reach the bottom of the staircase. It's clear I'm in some type of low-income housing building. Men, women, and children fill the dirty hallway. I move through them. They look at me with fear. But why? As I move down the hall, they look at me for a moment, but only long enough to keep me from noticing. They make way for me, parting from one side of the hall to the next. One or two plan on leaving their homes, but as soon as they see me coming, they quickly retreat back inside and lock their doors.

I have no idea where I'm going, so I take a look around. An exit sign hangs in the hallway with an arrow pointing farther down my current direction. I follow it and come to a door. It's opened for me as another man tries to make his way inside. He's startled by my sudden appearance and slams himself up against the wall. I can smell him. He doesn't smell bad, not like the rotting flesh of a dead corpse, but like fresh, citrusy cologne. If I didn't know better, I'd say this man could be alive.

It's bright out and it takes my eyes a few moments to adjust. This world has a sun. I can't believe it. I don't know what I was expecting, but there it is, a sun. It has the slightest gray tinge to it, but other than that it provides daylight and warmth. The warmth feels strange. It doesn't penetrate my skin. I can feel the heat on the top layer of my skin, but underneath I still feel the cold of the ice-bath. It's a clear reminder that my real body is still half dead, lying on a table in a drip room on ground zero. The thought sends a chill up my spine. The chill makes me realize I can feel here, which is great, but being able to feel, while holding a gun, makes me think of the possible pain I could also experience. Then there's the possibility that I might actually die out here if I'm not careful. And once you die here there's no going back.

Once I can see straight, I'm astonished. It feels like déjà vu. The city, streets, and people filling them seem so familiar, so identical to our city in the world of the living. If I had to guess, where I am now could be an exact replica of Mid-City. There are people everywhere. I'm not sure if that's what we call them. Are they people if they aren't alive? They seem as alive as I am or anybody for that matter. I pass by people who are smiling and laughing. There is joy and happiness here. For all intents and purposes, these people, these things, are very real and living what appears to be a life of their own in their own mirror of a world.

I still don't know where I'm headed other than I'm supposed to find Block 8. I try to stop people on the street, but when I do they are too petrified to answer me. It's like they are instinctively afraid of me. A few blocks into Mid-City and I see it. It's a monstrosity. Block 8 is a massive building, much like the design of GET, except the gray, white, and glass facade has been replaced with a hulking black mass. The top of the seemingly endless tower has a giant sign that reads: BLOCK 8.

I quickly cross the street and walk into the front entrance. It's a lot like GET level 1, but there are no employees filling the lobby. Instead, only two receptionists sit behind an information desk. My presence instantly alerts them. One of the receptionists stands abruptly. He's older and looks spooked. He rushes to greet me.

"Thank god you've arrived," he says.

"My name's—"

"Evie," he says. "GET informed us you were coming. My name's Carl Hanson. I oversee Block 8."

"I was told there's a disturbance of some kind?" I say.

"Yes. Yes, there is. A few members of Sector 6 are trying to infiltrate floor seven's vault. We don't have security personnel on-site. They always send someone like, well, you."

I suddenly have the brutal realization that I might have to actually use my weapon today. I'm not sure how I feel about it, but then again, this is a safe zone and an exam; maybe this isn't real, maybe we aren't actually shooting anyone. Maybe this is all staged, just to see how we will react. But what if it's not?

"You mind showing me how to get to level seven?" I ask.

"The elevators are right around the corner. Just walk in and punch seven. There isn't much to each floor. Floor seven is no different. There's one vault on each floor. No other doors or exits. One way in and one way out."

"What about the vault?" I ask.

"I wouldn't know. Never been in one of them," he says.

Carl motions with his hand toward the elevators. He's done talking, but I have a lot of questions. How can he be one of the only employees in the building and not have been in the vault? Not even know what's in them.

I round the corner and get in an elevator. I search for the floor seven button. There are eighty floors. That's a lot of buttons. I finally find seven and give it a push. The elevator takes off. I can feel my adrenaline starting to pump. I can't be nervous. My life may depend on it, but fear is good. Keets said so herself. She always says it, every chance she gets. I double-check my gun to make sure it's loaded. I'm ready.

The door to the elevator opens and I step out. The

hallway isn't that long compared to the HD facility hallways. It's probably fifty or sixty feet from me to the vault door. I can see five people. All of them have weapons except one who is working on the vault door with some kind of laser-torch. Blue sparks fly and scatter on the ground. The crackle of heat on steel bounces off the walls.

It's only moments before they see me. They fire first and without warning. I don't even have time to say anything. The shots ring out. Bullets fly and casings clang and clatter as they hit the ground. I take aim and squeeze my trigger. The CAR-20 screams with short, controlled bursts of mayhem. Three shots take one of them down. I can see the blood paint the face of another just a few feet away. They hunker down. One pulls out a baton-looking device and presses a button on its far end. The baton opens and a thick holographic shield opens. He lifts it up and with all his force jams it hard into the ground. The tip of the shield lodges itself into the floor. The four of them crouch down behind it.

"Keep cutting!" one of them yells to the other.

They start firing again, and my training and survival instincts take over. I lay down suppressive fire and work my way backward toward the elevator. I reach for the doors, but they've closed. I go for the button but a stray bullet disables it. I'm trapped. It's a miracle I haven't been shot yet. The sudden click of my CAR-20 makes me reach for a second magazine, but a bullet tears through my shoulder and stops my hand. I fall back against the wall. I can see the blood trickling down my arm, forming a small pool on the floor. This is it. This is the end. I suddenly find myself thinking of Aiden. All I want is to see Aiden.

My thoughts are interrupted by silence. Floor seven has gone quiet. I see three of them panicking as the fourth continues with the laser-torch. They've run out of ammunition. They aren't as heavily armed as I am. This is my only chance. I throw down my rifle. It's too heavy to hold and reload now that I'm injured. I'll have to make do with my sidearm, my lifesaver. I reach for it, but pain shoots through my body. It might be easier from my feet, so I scramble to stand.

When I reach for my gun a second time, I am attacked by one of the three. He's taller than I am, and he's going to be difficult to take down. He slaps the gun out of my hand and slams me against the wall. I force my knee up into his chest and push. He inches backward just enough for me to lay a few hard hits into his face. Blood spills from his nose. He reaches back and throws forward with his right fist. A solid punch to the gut sends me to my knees. I play possum. I'll try to make him think I'm an easy target. He pulls a knife from his belt and goes for my throat. I dodge right and answer back with a swift uppercut to his chin followed by a strong kick to his chest. The kick knocks him backward and onto his back.

I see my window of opportunity. I dive for the gun and scoop it up. I point it right at his face. He holds for a moment, a confused look coming over him. I can tell there's something about me pointing this gun at him, something about the small break in our fight, which has given him the chance to realize something. Something important. He takes a step toward me.

"Don't you fucking move," I say.

The two others pop up from behind the shield and rush

toward us. He holds out his hand behind him. "Stay where you are. I got this," he says.

"I'm the one holding the gun," I say.

"You're right. You are, Evie."

I can feel the gun start to waver in my hand. How does he know my name? What's going on? Does he know me? Do I know him and I don't even realize it?

"I've got it. It's open. Let's go!" the torch holder yells from down the hall. The two others turn and head for the vault door.

"I'm going to go," he says.

"You're not going anywhere," I say.

He begins to back away slowly. He points behind himself at the vault.

"The answers. Everything you are looking for. It's all there," he says.

"But—"

"Trust yourself, Evie. Come find us when you do."

I hear the elevator door open behind me. A single shot rings out. The man's head blows back, a spray of red explodes behind it, and his body tumbles to the ground.

I'm in shock. From everything. All of it. I don't know what to think. Aiden emerges from the elevator, holsters his gun, and brings me into his arms. He pulls me quickly into the elevator.

"It's going to be okay. You're safe now. You're safe. Everything's going to be okay. I'm here," Aiden says.

The doors close, but not before I see the three remaining men from Sector 6 slip away behind the vault door.

CHAPTER TWENTY

AIDEN

ALL OF BUNK 2 is celebrating. We have beaten the supposed better team—the red team. We high-five, dance around, and chant "blue team" like a pumped-up sports team would in a huddle. I sit back on my bunk and admire our small group of misfits. We aren't the sure bet, and I like that. I like that Hop finally gained the confidence only I knew he had. I like that Charlie learned to put aside her inner rage and work with us as a single cohesive unit. I like that Kyle held his own and supported his brother without question. I like that Sonic trusted himself and my plan. But most of all, I like that I feel like I have a purpose. For the first time in a long time, I feel like I'm where I'm supposed to be.

Our rejoicing is interrupted with a notice from the HD program. Hop answers the door to receive it. An HD employee hands him a letter that's addressed to all of Bunk 2. It states that our free time is going to be cut down by an hour and that we will be having our 3rd and final exam the following morning at 0800. When Hop finishes reading the letter, Charlie quickly snatches it from his hands. She reads it over again, like she thinks he made it up, then passes it around the room. After we've all seen it, the energy in the room changes. Our former joyous camaraderie has been replaced by scared frustration.

I feel their eyes jump to me. Somehow I know they blame me. I don't know why they make that connection, but they do. They assume our free time had been cut and our third exam being tomorrow is somehow my fault. I don't see how it can be my fault. I didn't cheat *this* time. At least I don't think I did. Maybe I had and I just don't know it. That would be unfortunate. But if we had unfairly won exam two, then why didn't the program pull me aside and chew me out. Maybe that's just not how they run things. I mean they didn't do that during the first exam either.

I realize something. I realize that my team's upset at me because they're *my* team. They no longer see me as just another member. They see me as their leader. They have always put more faith in me than any other, ever since I passed the first exam. I wonder if they would have made the same decision if they had known that Evie passed too. I'm not even sure how she managed to keep that secret when my passing was so readily available for conversation.

I guess if I'm to be the team leader, then I have to start acting like it. I decide to take the blame, but in return, they have to listen to me. I apologize and tell them this is a good thing. They can take away our free time and try to scare us by giving us the third exam so quickly, but they can never take away our ability to succeed. That power is in our hands.

My little speech manages to boost morale, and Bunk 2 feels like a team again, a solid team. I tell them the celebrating is over and if we are going to do well again tomorrow then we should all turn in early and get some much-needed sleep.

They listen.

Hop leans over his bunk and asks me if I think the third exam is going to be our first drip. I think about it for a second, but only to give the impression that I *have* to think about it. I know the answer. I tell Hop the truth. I tell him, yes, I do think it's going to be our first drip. He looks dissatisfied with an uneasiness that could very well turn infectious. I have to change the subject quickly or at the very least reassure him, everyone, that tomorrow morning is going to be just fine, but words fail to find my lips. I don't know what to say. I usually do. I can usually talk my way out of or into anything. I'm a real grade-A bullshitter. Instead, my silence leads to a feeling of dread. The dread of the unknown. Like a thick, heavy blanket, it covers us all. None of us, not a single one, knows what to expect, not even a guess.

I lie back down on my bed, shut my eyes, and try to fall asleep. I wonder why I never got a note from Evie today. I wonder if she's mad at me too for beating her in exam two.

. . .

Nater comes for us early. The exam isn't supposed to be until 0800, but he's here a good 10 minutes early. We weren't expecting an escort so we aren't exactly ready to go. I'd planned on getting a good face wash and hair comb in, but there isn't any time. He forces us out of the room and gives

Charlie an extra minute to throw on a sports bra under her top. Once she emerges, we head off down the hall. We stop by Bunk 1 to retrieve the red team. I think it's strange, but I guess I just didn't expect exam 3 to be another 2-team exam, but you should never assume anything in life. Assumptions usually end in disappointment and confusion.

On the way to the exam, I notice an HD program employee installing more cameras in the hallway. One specifically gets me thinking. It's pointed directly at the girls' locker room door. I'm beginning to think that maybe the free time punishment and the lack of Evie's letter might relate directly to this sudden and unexpected beefing up of security. Maybe the program has found out that we're talking to one another in secret. Furthermore, maybe they know we've been meeting up. I look back over my shoulder. I want to see if Evie notices what I just have. Her expression tells me to turn back around. I do, but I know she's well aware of what I've seen. I can also tell she's nervous and more on edge than I've ever seen her. I'm worried about her. I'm worried about how this might affect the third exam. I'm worried it might endanger her during the drip. I don't know enough about how it all works, and that's what concerns me.

The room they bring us to is similar to the drip we had observed weeks before, except this room has ten chairs. We each have our own chairs, assigned by name, and we all take our spots next to them. Nater has left us with Keets, who's clearly been waiting for us to arrive. She immediately picks up on all of our concerns and dives right into how everything is going to work. She introduces the doctor and nurse who will be administering our drips, then throws around words like *safe zone*. Keets tells us she and others will be watching every step of the way, and though it is very real, we have nothing to worry about. We should just trust in our training. Keets tells us she thinks we are ready, but the tone in her voice makes me think she doesn't believe the words coming out of her own mouth.

Then Keets leaves us and the doctor takes over. We all sit. They put temporary neuro-patches on our spines and wrists. They go through the entire process that we once viewed from behind the safety of a two-way mirror.

Everything building up to the actual insertion is horrific. The injection of the optic needles feels like I'm being murdered, stabbed in the back with a shank that's then wrenched around in a circular motion before being broken off inside me. It's absolutely awful. The warning of its pain can't even begin to do its actuality any justice. Fixing the IV tube to my wrist isn't that bad. It's something you're used to if you've ever had to get blood drawn or been given a vaccination. No biggie. What makes it strange is when you're lying on your back, hands and feet strapped down, and you get to watch your blood slowly leave your body. That's odd and incredibly unnatural, but it's the ice-bath that shocks me the most. The second the cold water touches my skin, I freak-out inside. I feel my arms and legs tense, fighting against the pull of the restraints. The icy prick of the water surrounding my body reminds me of the last time I saw my brother.

He was four years older than I was, but people used to say we looked a lot alike. He had sweeping brown hair and vivid blue eyes. He was tall and his large, goofy feet projected growth well into his teens. He was prone to sunspots. After only a few hours in the sun, his face and arms would freckle up. But the freckles suited him. They added a unique gentleness to his rugged skin. I remember thinking it was the greatest thing in the world looking like my older brother. Perhaps this is true for any younger sibling who looks up to their older, tougher, and generally all-around cooler brother.

He looked out for me, that I remember. He was like a third parent really. He'd often take me with him wherever he went. When our parents would argue, he'd show me how to safely climb a tree or mystify me by telling me that small rodent holes in our backyard were really entrances to the elf and fairy homes.

He was one of a kind. He never put himself before me, and he always made sure I could keep up. Even though I was much younger, our age gap was filled by his enormous amount of patience. I never knew a more patient, kind, and respectful person. No one was like my brother.

Our grandparents had retired to a small patch of land in southwestern Montana near Big Sky. It was their little piece of heaven. Twice a year we got to taste a little piece of it. My parents never quite understood the allure of that part of the country, but my brother and I worshipped it. Their home was nestled in the woods about twenty minutes south of Lone Mountain—a ski resort that brought most of the income to the little town. To the south was Cinnamon Mountain, to the east the peaceful ebb and flow of the Gallatin River—mecca for trout fisherman from around the world. To the west was, well, Idaho. It was an untouched beauty, something we envied our entire childhoods. It was an escape from the busy metropolis of our everyday lives. We looked forward to those two times a year when we could take in the peace and quiet and just have fun as brothers.

In the summer, we'd spend two weeks with our grandparents. It was hot and dry during the day, so we'd spend our waking hours out in the wilderness. My brother taught me to fish, he showed me the difference between poison oak and poison ivy, and he'd point out moose tracks and eagles' nests. When night came and the temperature would dip just low enough to warrant a fire, he'd show me how to gather tinder and look for dry pine. We'd sit by the fire drinking warm cups of hot chocolate. We'd fill the tops of our mugs with mini-marshmallows or whip cream—with each sip filling the extra space with either more whip or marshmallow, whichever we had at our disposal. He'd stare in the flames and tell me adventure stories of treasure hunters or cowboys. Sometimes, he'd spook me with scary stories about wandering spirits or deranged killers. Then he'd comfort me and tell me they weren't real, they were just for fun and I shouldn't be afraid. But it didn't always calm my nerves, so he said he'd stay up far after I went to sleep and stand guard. That way if anything did try to sneak into the room and get me, he'd be there to stop it. I never managed to stay awake long enough to see if he stood guard all night, but he was awake when I'd shut my eyes and would still be awake in the morning when I opened them.

In the winter, we'd fly out for a week after Christmas. All the presents in the world wouldn't amount to the same excitement we felt when we got on a plane to fly to Montana. Montana is freezing in the winter, but we didn't mind. Maybe it was because we were children, and children always seem to have thicker blood than adults—undeniably because there's simply less surface area for the heart to have to circulate blood to. All day and night we'd play in the snow or sit inside and battle each other in card games like war and poker. I was never that good at card games, but my brother never wanted me to think he would take pity on me. He said pity doesn't build a strong character. Still, he could have let me win once, just once.

Every visit, my brother and my grandfather would go ice-fishing. I was never allowed to participate. I begged and begged, but it was no use. I always got the same answer—I was too young. It didn't stop me from asking every year. I was determined to go. That doesn't mean that thirteen years ago, when I asked my grandfather one last time if I could attend the cold excursion, it didn't completely catch me off guard when he said yes.

They bundled me up and packed me a peanut butter and jelly sandwich. I had to carry my fair share of the gear. It was a rule. If you wanted to fish, you had to carry your own pole, tackle, and bait. It took me a while to get used to walking with all the gear and my thick layers of clothing. I wobbled side to side like a flat-footed duck.

I can remember how cold it was that day. I was woken up at the crack of dawn, when the sun had just kissed the horizon. As we walked across the frozen lake, our breath made cloudlike smokestacks from our mouths. We must have looked like three locomotives trudging across an icy tundra.

My legs were small and the gear grew increasingly heavy. They had a fishing hut about a quarter of a mile out, and they didn't like to stop until they got there—especially in this cold. I was promised the warmth of a wood-burning stove and a mug of something piping hot to keep me motivated. After a good ten minutes of slopping over the lake and through the ice and snow, my frail little body needed a rest, so I stopped.

It only took about three seconds after I stopped for me to fall through the ice. Luckily, I had just finished taking in a deep breath of air when I broke through and went under. The water was freezing. It pierced through my layers of clothes and attacked my skin with thousands of frigid pricks. At first, the sudden fracture of the ice sent me plunging deep over my head. I fought hard to make it to the surface. When the ice water turned to air, I screamed for help and grasped for the sides of the hole in which I fell, but the sides were slippery and fragile. Groping them only made the hole larger.

My brother must have heard or felt the crack in the ice. Maybe he no longer heard the crunch of my tiny and awkward footsteps behind him. Whatever it was, he had come faster than anyone could have imagined—a real feat of athleticism. After submerging for a second time, I remember looking up and seeing his shadow of a figure above me. I fought extra hard to resurface. When I did, I felt comfort in seeing his face. He looked calm. He must have been nervous beyond all belief, but he didn't show it. He was calm and resolute like he had a plan to save me, like this was no big deal. But it was a big deal. My body knew it, and he most certainly knew it.

I could hear my grandfather screaming for help as he made his way toward us. He was much older and had been leading our group, so he had the farthest to travel to get to us. The problem with ice water in the winter is that it can kill you in minutes. I reached for my brother's hands, but they were out of reach. I could feel all the layers of clothing they had put on me to keep me warm growing heavier and heavier as they absorbed more and more liquid. It was an uphill battle that seemed to be favoring Mother Nature. It seemed like the harder I fought, the quicker I began to sink. My feet had gone numb, and I was sure I was going to drown.

The third time I submerged, I sank like a rock. The fight in me had given way to exhaustion, and I made peace with my demise. My brother wouldn't give up. Without hesitation, he came in after me. He dove in headfirst and swam as hard as he could. He positioned himself under me and used his shoulders to push me to the surface. The first thing I saw was my grandfather's hand. I reached for it and he pulled me to safety. My brother's upward push combined with my grandfather's determination landed me sopping wet, near frozen to death, on the safety of the hard ice.

There was no time to rest. My brother was still in the water. I panicked and my adrenaline flowed. I cried as I reached out for my brother. He flailed around in the water. He desperately grabbed the sides of the hole. His extra body weight chipped away at the edges. As the hole grew larger and larger, he yelled out for our help. I was useless, my arms too short to be of any help. Our grandfather tried to hold onto him, but his age limited his strength. I had been just small enough for him to pull me to safety, but my brother was posing a dreadful problem. We bellowed for help but no one was around. Normally our voices would travel a great distance across the lake, but the snowpack and ice acted as a muting sound barrier. It was no use.

When hypothermia took control of my brother's limbs, he was no longer able to tread water. My grandfather brought me in close to his chest and shielded my eyes as my brother's lungs filled with water and his body drifted slowly to the bottom of the lake. His death had been peacefully tragic.

After we had gotten back to the house, the police and paramedics arrived. They kept me warm by the fire while my parents were contacted. They were on the next flight and arrived the following morning. I can't imagine what that plane ride must have been like for them. They never spoke about it, what it was like to lose a child.

The next day, a rescue team sent in a dry diver to retrieve my brother's frozen, lifeless body. They didn't wait for a funeral; they had one two days later. My parents agreed that he would have wanted to lie to rest there if he had the choice. It was an open casket. My parents didn't want me to look, but I had to say goodbye. I insisted that I go up to the casket alone. I looked in at his face and body. His drowning had preserved his body the last way I had seen him, the only way that I knew him. His face showed nothing but a calm and gentle smile. His brown hair was swept to one side. His eyes were closed, but I knew how blue they truly were. I smiled as I noticed the freckles that dazzled the bridge of his nose and crest of his cheeks.

Tucker gave his life to save mine. That's how I remember him. I never went back to Montana, and I would never forget the cold water.

This water, now, in the drip, feels so similar to that in Montana. How could I not think about my brother? *Focus. I need to focus.* Then I think about what the world of the dead will really be like. I've been there before, in the black and white room with Arthur, but now, this time will most certainly be different. I wonder if it's possible to run into my brother. He died some years ago, but I wonder if it's possible. My parents too, for that matter. It's never occurred to me to ask that question during class. Not once. If nothing else, this program has taught me that anything is possible.

The nurse starts with Josh, then Russell, then Evie, and so on around the circle. I'm just to the right, or left, depending on how you look at it, of Josh, so that makes me last in line to drip. I fight to stay awake, if that's even the right term for it, for as long as I can, but when someone's deliberately trying to kill you and you physically can't do anything about it, it's really hard to hold on. I feel my body give in, and a dark haze sweeps over me.

Then something happens. During the dark, I don't feel alone. I feel Evie as if she's right there next to me. I smell her sweet smell, I hear her vivid voice, but something is wrong. I feel stuck, as if I'm being pulled in two different directions. We were told we'd be inserted on our own in individual safe zones, but there's a part of me that wants to be where Evie is, and I don't know why.

Flashes of a large building, the words *Block 8*, and the faces of two security guards zip past my eyes in momentary glimpses of light. Then I hear it again—Evie's voice. Well, not her voice, her thoughts. I can tell it's a thought because I can see her. In my mind, she's in a hallway, a long black hallway. She's hunkered down, shooting at five others at the opposite end of the hallway. Her lips don't move, but I can see she's in trouble. I can see she's afraid. I can see that she needs me, wants me. Then the image is gone and I feel a burning tear in my spine. Everything turns to white. A flooding warm and white light.

I squint hard. I feel the warmth of the sun trying to penetrate the thick cold of my skin. The world finally comes into view. I look around. I'm standing in the middle of a crosswalk in what appears to be Mid-City. I'm wearing protective battle gear and I have a sidearm holstered on my hip. There's a CAR-20 mag in my pocket, but no rifle.

There are people around me. Lots of people. If I wasn't so sure that I'm in a drip, I'd think I was in the real world, the world of the living, but I'm not. While this place looks very much the same, it does have its differences. For one thing, all these people are staring at me. I guess I'm wearing a weapon and look a lot like I'm paramilitary, but that's not it. They look at me like they are afraid of what I'm going to do. They give me a wide berth, like a boulder cutting the flow of a mighty river. The light here, too, is different. It's warm, and there's a sun and atmosphere, but the light has a slight gray tint to it. It's the oddest thing, but this is a different world after all.

I take a few steps forward. The sudden rush of pedestrians brings my attention to a changing traffic light. Through the parting legs I can see my CAR-20 rifle sitting in the middle of the street, but how did it get there? This isn't at all how I thought a drip insertion would go. It seems so messy and unplanned, like I'm supposed to be somewhere else, but now I'm here. It's as if I jumped out of a plane without a parachute.

I rush for the rifle, but it's too late. The light turns green, and a large truck barrels over the rifle, nearly missing my own body. The tires roll past and the gun is crushed into nothing more than some bent metal and polymer fragments. I reach down and pick up the mag—the only thing that might turn out to be of some use. I look up and see something familiar. A giant black, GET-like building with a sign that reads: BLOCK 8. Evie?

I'm in full sprint now, over the crosswalk and up the street. I move as quickly as I can, shoving my way through the bustling city crowd. My fingertips land on a few arms and shoulders as I push my way to Block 8. I notice how cold these people's skin is. But Evie's in trouble and I'm here. She has to be here. I can feel it.

I burst through the front doors of the building. It's eerily like GET level 1 except there are no employees, just two security guard types behind an information kiosk. One of them stands up quickly, almost too quickly, like he thinks it's odd that I'm here. The other looks nervous and itchy.

"Can . . . can I help you with something, sir?" the man says. I spot a small name tag on the left breast of his shirt.

"Carl is it?" I say.

"Yes, that's right."

"I'm looking for someone."

"That's strange. You aren't supposed to be here."

"I'm not?"

"Oh no. You most certainly are not," he says.

I don't have time for any dumb exam rules crap. I take a few steps closer. Maybe I'm moving too aggressively because Carl flinches a little, like I'm going to hit him.

"Listen, Carl, I need to find a girl. She's about—"

"Evie," he says. I don't know how I should feel about him knowing her name like that, without me telling him anything about her, but Carl knowing that fast does mean that she's been here, or is here.

"That's right. Could you tell me where I can find her?"

"I'm not supposed to. Well, this has never happened before, so I guess, well, I don't—"

I take another aggressive step toward Carl and feel my hand instinctually reach for my sidearm. Wow. What am I doing? I keep myself from pulling it from the holster. I calmly rest my hand over it. Carl's eyes float to my hand. He understands all too well.

"I really need to know where she is. Please, just tell me where she is."

"She's on floor seven." Carl points in the direction of the elevators.

"Thanks," I say as I make a run for the elevators.

The doors open and I slide inside. There are eighty floors in this building. That's big. I find the button for floor seven and give it a push. The elevator takes off. So much rushes through my mind. I had seen this, during the drip. I had seen this building, I had seen Evie, and I had seen her in trouble. I saw five other men with guns. I saw Evie and the others in a firefight.

As I draw nearer I can hear a barrage of gunshots, then silence. I hope I'm not too late.

Floor five.

Floor six.

Floor seven.

The elevator comes to a stop. I have to be ready for anything. I have to save her. I pull out my sidearm and cock back the slide. It's loaded and ready. *I'm* ready, I think. The door opens and I see one of the men standing a few yards down the hallway. I take one step out of the elevator and notice Evie just ahead of me. She's injured and bleeding. I feel a rage come over me. My gun finds its way up until the sights align with the man's head. My finger pulls the trigger without hesitation. One round twists out the barrel and sails through the air. It cuts down the man. He falls backward and hits the floor. Blood spills out of his body, making a small red lake on the floor. Now's my chance.

I jump out and grab Evie. I pull her into the elevator and slam on the lobby button. I don't want to wait around and see what the other men might try to do. The elevator doors close and I pull Evie in close. I wrap my arms around her and gently kiss her forehead. She's hurt, but she's safe, for now. I've got her.

She's silent. She's in shock. She's scared. I tell her that everything is going to be okay. I tell her she's safe. I tell her I'm there.

CHAPTER TWENTY-ONE

THE OTHERS

THE DRIP CONTROL and monitoring room is a complex series of switchboards, screens, and equipment. It's dark; only the light spilling from the machines fills the room. Nater, Keets, and Arthur all stand and watch. There are four other HD employees sitting and operating the machines. There are individual monitors for each HD recruit. The monitors show close-up, live feeds of each recruit's face. Every slight movement and facial fluctuation can be seen and recorded. Under each monitor, there are racks of life support signals. Each recruit has a heart rate screen, neuro-impulse screen, and blood pressure screen. All of the essential drip information flows in a constant and steady readout.

"Status report," Nater says.

"All recruits are in their final stage of insertion," one employee says.

"All vitals are nominal and holding steady," another says.

"Sir," the third employee says with nervousness about his voice.

"What is it?" Nater replies.

"You might want to take a look at this."

Nater walks over to the employee and leans into one of the neuro-screens.

The employee points to fluctuating numbers. They are ever-changing, ranging from ten all the way up to 287. Nater stands up straight.

"Hm."

"What is it? Something wrong?" Keets asks.

"I'm not entirely sure," Nater replies.

"Nater," Arthur says, "talk to me."

Nater looks at the employee. "Whose neuro is this?"

"Aiden Bishop."

Nater turns to Arthur.

"Aiden's neuro is bouncing all over the place. Usually, this happens when the body doesn't take to the drip. We should reanimate before we fry him."

Nater reaches for an intercom button on the wall.

"Stop," Arthur commands.

"Are you kidding?" Keets says. "Tell the doctor to reanimate."

"Nater. Don't you do it! I want to see how this plays out," Arthur yells.

"Are you crazy? You'll kill him," Keets yells back.

"Maybe, maybe not," Arthur says.

Keets pushes her way toward the intercom button.

"This is nuts," she says firmly.

"Do it and I'll have your job," Arthur commands.

Keets whips around and looks at Arthur, his finger resting gently on the button.

A warning alarm sounds.

"What now?" Nater says.

"Evie Fox's heart rate and blood pressure are dropping. She must have experienced trauma," the employee says.

"You mean, she must have gotten herself shot," Keets says.

"What do you want to do, sir?" the employee asks.

"Timeframe?" Nater says.

"It's hard to say. Could be a few minutes, could be an hour. But she will bleed out if we don't reanimate."

"Uh, sir?"

"Speak. Jesus Christ!"

"Aiden's neuro has spiked and is holding steady around two-fifty."

"We've got to reanimate, both of them, and now," Keets says.

Arthur puts a hand on his chin. He's thinking.

"Blood pressure still dropping. Heart rate minimal," the employee calls out.

Nater walks up to Arthur. He keeps his voice low.

"Sir, you are running out of time. I'm not sure I know what choice you have. If you don't want to lose them both, we should reanimate immediately."

Arthur nods yes and Nater turns to Keets, who's ready and waiting by the intercom button. She pushes the button, "Reanimate Aiden Bishop and Evie Fox."

The doctor and nurse jump to it. They reverse the blood

flow and drain the bathwater. Aiden and Evie's heart rate and blood pressure start to increase.

"Vitals returning to normal. Reanimation in T-minus sixty seconds," the employee says.

Arthur pulls Nater aside.

"I want you to keep them separate, do you hear me? I don't want them talking. Is that understood?" he says.

"The others will wonder where they are. What will I say? How would you like me to go about keeping them separate?" Nater asks.

"I don't care. Bring her to medical. She needs to be checked out anyway. Who knows what that kind of stress did to her heart. You can send Aiden back to the bunks. That work for you?"

Nater understands and turns back to the room. He walks over to the intercom button. Evie and Aiden are just coming to.

"Reanimation process complete. Vitals look good," the employee says.

The doctor and nurse unhook the optic needles and unbuckle the restraints. Aiden and Evie look frantically around the room in an intoxicated daze. The nurse wraps a blanket around Evie's shivering body. The door to the room opens and two HD employees enter. The nurse helps Evie to her feet. She can barely stand, the intensity of the drip still wearing off.

"Take her to medical. Leave him. And go ahead and reanimate the others. The exam is over," Nater says through the intercom.

The doctor acknowledges with a nod, and the two men take Evie from the nurse.

"Aiden! No! Stop it!" Evie screams out.

Aiden tries to jump to his feet, but he can't walk. He struggles to hold his balance and hits the floor.

"Evie!" Aiden yells. "Where are you taking her?"

The doctor and nurse rush to Aiden. They grab him and pull his dead weight back into the chair. They restrain him the best they can until the two employees finish removing Evie from the room. The door shuts, but Evie's screams can be heard through the door and down the hall. The nurse reaches into her pocket and pulls out a syringe, and Aiden remembers the weird green liquid. He remembers how it knocked him out. He resists, but the needle finds his arm, and his body finally relaxes into the hard metal of the chair.

"Everyone, leave the room," Arthur says. Nater and Keets look at him, confused. "Yes. You too."

The room clears and Arthur is alone. He watches as the other recruits start to come to. He picks up a phone sitting on a desktop in front of him and dials. The phone rings three times before someone picks up.

"Mr. Parker? I was right. Aiden Bishop is a skip-tracer," Arthur says into the phone. He waits and listens. Winston Parker is giving him an earful on the other end of the line. He tells Arthur how important Aiden is, that he must be protected at all costs. He tells him Aiden must be assigned as a reaper. He tells him they need to be sure Aiden can be trusted. Then he asks if Arthur has found out if Evie will pose a problem or not. Arthur takes his time to respond. He likes Evie. She's a strong recruit and intelligent. She could be a great asset to GET, but his time is up. Winston Parker wants an answer.

"You were right. They have an undeniable connection. I know what I have to do. I'll take care of it," Arthur says.

He hangs up the phone and stands in the darkness watching as the low murmur of the remaining recruits coming back from their very first drip fills the room. Their training has come to an end. There's nothing else they can be prepared for. They will be on their own now. They will be given their assignments and they'll be inserted into the field on their first real mission. When they return they will no longer be recruits. They will all be HD operatives. Well, maybe not all of them.

CHAPTER TWENTY-TWO

EVIE

THEY'VE GOT ME running again. I'm in medical and I've been running for a solid hour, and so far there's no sign of letting up. I think they're worried about my injury while in the drip. The doctor had said something about monitoring the strength of my heart. I guess the longer I run, the more stress they put my heart under. I'm not convinced they aren't *trying* to make my heart explode, but I have a strong heart, one that the program has ensured to be even stronger, what with all its constant training. I was strong before I entered the HD program. Now, hell, I'm like Superwoman. Too bad I can't deflect bullets. They don't bounce off my skin like marbles on metal. Bullets, I found out, can still kill me. And they almost did. But seeing Aiden kill that man was far more shocking.

I saw a man get shot at a house in New York State. Our cabin hideaway had been relatively sheltered from the mayhem of the rest of the world, something that I took for granted. Even now, I remember that time as being the best in my life. Once we were back on the road, the cruel dangers of a land in constant peril crept into our lives. My father kept us on the move, and we were always as careful as we could be not to leave a trail. It becomes like second nature, covering your tracks. When your life depends on it, a primal instinct takes over. It's funny thinking about how much people try to maintain a civilized society. How we exert an enormous amount of energy on trying to evolve away from our animalistic attributes. We are, as a species, just that—animals.

We had been on the road for months and lost track of how far we had gone. We did our best to keep track as we went. My father and I took turns counting steps. He figured 2,000 steps to a mile for him and around 2,500 for me because I had smaller legs and smaller strides. You can count steps all you want, but after a while, your mind can't hold on to the large numbers anymore. We tried tallying every mile on a small notepad, but after one day took up a full page, we decided our limited paper should be reserved for more important or more dire circumstances. So we eventually lost track of how far we had gone.

My father never told me where we were going exactly, and it never occurred to me to ask. It just didn't matter. The only thing I had left was him, so as long as I had that, I could be anywhere, but we didn't end up anywhere. We had been following a stream for days. We had little, if any, contact with any other people.

I can remember the house very clearly. It was white with black shutters, and it had two stories with a widow's peak and a full wraparound porch in front. It was getting late and the sun had already started to slip beyond the horizon. The thick of the forest grew sparse and thin just sixty or so yards from the house.

When my father saw it, we froze and kneeled. Our usual protocol was to steer clear of houses altogether, but I could tell what my father was thinking. We were low on food supply, and a house in this rural of an area might lie untouched from the ravaging hands of looters. But was it worth the risk? After watching the house for movement and candlelight, my father decided he'd check it out. The coast looked clear enough. He told me to wait for him behind the tree line, and then he kissed me on the forehead and gave me a hug. He reached around to his back and came forward with our rifle. He forced it in my hands and told me if anything were to happen, I should use it if I had to. I nodded and watched as he turned and slipped out of the safety of the forest. He slinked across the lawn and gently jimmied open the back screen door. In moments he was inside.

I remember having a bad feeling in the pit of my stomach, but I never spoke up about it, nor would I ever in the future. I had only been waiting about three minutes when the shot rang out. It echoed through the open field behind the house and smacked me dead in the ear. For a moment I thought it was a crack of lightning, but the rifle clutched in my hand reminded me of the indisputable sound of a bullet.

My body sprang before my mind could decide what to do. My father would later scold me for it, but I was in a full sprint toward the house. I went the same way my father had, through the screen door. I burst in with no real plan in mind and yelled for my father, but he didn't answer . . . no one answered. I feared the worst. I searched the ground floor and then climbed the stairs to the second. I searched the small bedroom that was painted pink and a bathroom, but they were both empty. Finally, I searched the second room. That's where I found them.

It was clear there had been a struggle. A side table had been knocked over. There was broken glass on the floor, and drapes had been torn from the boarded-up windows. My father was crouched in one corner of the room. Beneath him an older man, maybe in his late sixties, with clean white hair and a thick white mustache to match. His face was weathered and worn. At first, I thought my father had been hurt because his hands were covered in blood, but when I reached them, I saw it was the man who had been injured.

Only moments after my father had opened the bedroom door, the older man pulled a revolver on him. My father grabbed the man's gun hand and forced him backward against the wall. The man fought for his life and so did my father. They wrestled around the room, both trying to break the gun free, but my father's younger, stronger arms eventually won out. When the man had tired enough, the gun tweaked in his hand, forcing his finger to press the trigger just enough for it to fire. The barrel had been jerked in his direction, and the gun shot him in the stomach.

There was a lot of blood, and my father was using his hands to try to subdue the bleeding. He told me to run to the bathroom and grab anything I could find to help. I returned with two small hand towels and an Ace bandage from under the vanity. My father used the bandage to secure the towels over the wound. The man winced and moaned with pain, but my father insisted that it had to be as tight as possible. My father asked the man if he could stand, and with my help, we hoisted him to his feet and got him to his own bed.

We stayed the night. The man had given us permission and my father had a keen sense of character, so when the man told him there would be no one else to surprise us, he believed him. The man's name turned out to be Raymond. He told us we could help ourselves to what little food he had in the kitchen. He said he had a few cans of soup left and some unleavened bread. We went to the kitchen and explored the cabinets. We found a few cans of chicken noodle soup. Raymond had a stove powered by propane, and it made cooking the soup a delight. Anything beats cooking over the open flame of a fire, no matter how good you get at it.

We brought the soup up to Raymond's room, and my father helped him eat. Raymond told my father it was a waste of good food, but my father insisted. We developed a good rapport, the three of us. It was clear Raymond saw the shooting as an accident. An accident brought on by his own fear. He told us about how he used to farm corn. He told us his wife had passed gently in her sleep a few years back. He told us about how he had lost a granddaughter when it all started. She used to sleep in the room down the hall. He had taken her in when her parents didn't make it. He told me that I reminded him of her. He asked where we were going, and my father threw out the first name of a city he could think of. He said Boston. Raymond told us we were more than welcome to stay the night since we still had a long way to go. He told us in the morning we should pack up what we could and head northeast along Route 30. That would put us on course.

The next morning when we woke up, Raymond had passed. The hole in his gut was too much for his frail body to withstand. My father took the time to bury him in the backyard under a large oak tree that overlooked the house Raymond and his beloved wife had built together. My father hoped it was something the man would have wanted. He hoped it was good enough. He hoped it brought Raymond some peace.

Like the man had said, we packed up what little food the house had left, and we were on our way. We headed northeast and had no problem finding Route 30. The road wasn't that much different than any other we had come across except this one was marked with a sign. We turned and looked at the sign as we passed. It read: READBURN, NEW YORK POP. 3,130. My father stared at the sign until I grabbed hold of his hand and pulled him away from it. No matter what Raymond could have told him, my father would forever think he was responsible for killing that nice, old, innocent man. He had made the difference between 3,130 and 3,129. With the death of Raymond, we now knew we had crossed into New York.

I had never understood the pain Raymond had gone through that night, until I felt the bullet rip through my shoulder. The doctor told me that the bullet must have penetrated close to my heart because they thought I wouldn't make it back from the drip alive. He told me I was lucky, but luck didn't have anything to do with it. The man from

Sector 6 could have easily finished me off, or at least tried, but he didn't. He knew me. Somehow, someway, he knew me. It's that very thought that's been keeping me going on the treadmill. If you can keep your mind off the physicality of the running, then you can run forever, and my mind is most certainly occupied.

I have a billion questions I'd like to ask that man from Sector 6. Aside from how he knew who I was, I'd ask him what they were doing there. Why did they want to get into the vault? Did he know what was behind the vault? Each step of my foot pounds one notion deeper and deeper into my mind—I need to know what's in the vault. Somehow, I know that the key to what GET is all about lies beyond those vault doors. If Sector 6 wanted to get in so badly, there must be a reason for it. Good or bad, I need to find out why they'd risk their lives like that.

I don't blame Aiden for shooting the man from Sector 6. He did what he thought he needed to do. I know he was only trying to protect me. I guess knowing he'd kill for me is kind of a turn-on in a morbid sort of way. I wonder how he's taking it. It's a hard thing to do, take another life. Shooting one of them myself seems a bit surreal. I don't blame him. I hope he knows that. I was scared; I did want him to help me. I was the one who thought it. Aiden just happened to deliver.

But how did he find me? Aiden being special is slowly starting to make a lot of sense. He must have somehow sensed that I was in trouble—that I had called out for him in my mind. The concept of dripping is simple in nature, but our bodies are not. When we drip we are connected in one seemingly large neurological network. It's not entirely impossible to think that Aiden somehow connected with my thoughts from my drip and inserted himself to where my mind was telling him I was. I don't know if he's aware of it or even if he controls it, but his fondness for me might have been what fueled this capability, if, in fact, that's what happened. Keets was adamant that we would be inserted separately and in different safe zones. Aiden had somehow entered mine and found me. It was only when he found me that we were reanimated. The program can't visually see what we see, but it can monitor our body's reactions to stimuli. They must have made the connection when both our vitals went berserk. If Aiden's able to enter my drip, he could potentially do the same with anyone and anywhere. He might be able to find Sector 6's own drip headquarters. Finding it could bring an end to their terrorist cell for good, which is something GET would certainly appreciate.

The door to medical opens and interrupts my thoughts. A man walks in—a man I've never seen before in all my time in the HD facility, not even in passing. He has to be in his fifties. He's got peppered black hair and a distinguished look about him. The only person he kind of reminds me of is a man by the name of Arthur, whom Aiden had told me about. The man Aiden had met with. The very man who told Aiden he was chosen.

He walks over to the treadmill and hits the off button. The treadmill slows before it comes to a halt. He picks up a paper readout of the data collected and looks through it. Once done he looks at me and motions for me to take off the oxygen mask.

"Your readings look good. You have a very strong heart," he says.

"I'm sorry, what's your name?" I ask.

"And an equally strong attitude. I can see your reputation precedes you." He puts down the chart and clasps his hands together. "My name is Arthur."

Just as I suspected.

"You had quite the close call during your drip exam. Didn't you?" Arthur says.

"If you call being shot in a safe zone close, then yeah, I had a close call."

Arthur motions for me to step off the treadmill. He hands me a towel to dab the sweat from my face. He takes a seat on a stool, like a doctor would in front of an examination table. He motions again. I can tell he wants me to sit. I don't think I really have a choice. It seems like there are going to be a lot of questions. I'm not so sure I should tell him anything. I'm good at that.

"Why are you so fiery? If I didn't know any better, I'd say you don't like us very much. I'd say you don't like this program."

"Well, you'd be wrong," I lie. "I think nothing but the best. I'm just fiery because that's who I am. I can't wait to get back in the field."

Arthur mulls over what I just said. He looks at me hard. I can tell he's trying to get a read on how truthful I'm being. I can't tell how well I'm putting it on or if he sees right through me. Regardless, he doesn't trust me. That's as clear as day. I bet he's only here to see what I know or remember about what happened.

"I really must apologize. All ten drip insertion points had been prescreened for Sector 6 activity, but sometimes things sneak by us. You were there. The guards at the gate must have thought we had sent you to handle it. Again, I apologize. It would have been a real shame had you been killed," Arthur says.

Yeah, a real shame indeed. We had learned in class that if you're killed in the world of the dead while in a drip, you don't come back. That's it, the end of the road; you're gone for good. There's no second life waiting for you. Only death in the real world grants you a second chance. It's obvious by the tone in Arthur's voice that my dying in the drip would have been a convenience, not a shame. I think he thinks the connection between Aiden and me is dangerous. Suddenly, I'm beginning to feel that he's the dangerous one.

"Yeah. It would have been. But I'm here. Stronger than ever," I say.

"Yes, you are. I'd love to know what you remember about the drip. I know for first-timers it's plausible to not remember anything at all. For others, it can be fuzzy and disjointed. Your body isn't used to the shock of the drip, and those pesky temporary neuro-patches can cause gaps in your synapses."

"What would you like to know? I can try to remember as much as I can."

I try to make nice. I want him to think I don't remember everything or at least it's hard for me to remember everything. That way I can choose what information to divulge and what to withhold. I'm not sure yet if it makes sense to tell him I asked for Aiden to help me and he came. I'm not entirely positive they know he came for me, but if they do, then lying about it might make things worse. I'm in a tricky situation.

"What happened up there? On level seven?" Arthur says.

"Well, I took the elevator up, and when the doors opened, I saw five men from Sector 6 trying to break into the vault at the end of the hall," I answer.

"Is that it?" Arthur pries.

"Hmm. Come to think of it, one of them was welding the entire time. The others opened fire at me. That's when I fired back and shot one of them."

"You shot one of them. Did you kill him?"

"I think I did."

"But you're not sure?"

"No. No, I guess I'm not sure. But I—"

"Did they get into the vault?"

"They did."

"How do you know?"

"Because I saw them enter it."

"I see. Did you happen to see into the vault yourself?"

"No."

But I wish I had. Especially now that Arthur seems concerned if I had or not.

"Do you remember anything else?"

"I remember being shot. That one hurt."

I've decided I'm not going to mention that one of the men seemed to know me. Somehow I don't think that would help my situation. I'm already getting a bad vibe. I don't want Arthur to make any false connection with Sector 6 and me. That would surely be the end of me.

"I remember being reanimated."

"Anything else?"

"Hmm."

"Do you remember Aiden?"

There it is, the real question he wants answered. He could have saved himself some time if he had just gotten right to the meat of it.

"I remember him."

"Were you thinking of him before he appeared?"

I'm not prepared for how to answer this question. I think it over. Perhaps for too long.

"Let me ask you this." Arthur leans in close to me. "When you were slowly bleeding out, was Aiden the only thing you could think of?"

I'm angry now. Arthur's distaste for me oozes from his mouth. I can only think of one thing to say.

"No."

Arthur pops up from his seat. His entire attitude changes in an instant. A sudden fake sense of joy coats his voice.

"That's it then! I think that's just about all the questions I have for you. Any questions for me?"

"Just one. When do I get out of here?"

"Oh, I'm no doctor, but I'd say soon. Very soon. It was a pleasure finally getting to meet you, Evie."

"Likewise."

Arthur turns and leaves medical. The door shuts and locks behind him. Our meeting has been strange. I'm not entirely sure why he chose to speak to me personally. He seems like one of the higher-ups and could have easily sent a minion like Nater or even one of the doctors or nurses to ask the questions. Something about him makes me think he wants me to know who he is. He wants me to know who controls my fate. He just wanted to look me in the eyes to make sure I knew.

CHAPTER TWENTY-THREE

THE OTHERS

NATER IS WAITING for Arthur outside of medical. Arthur shuts the door and locks it with his key fob. He turns and starts walking. Nater rushes to keep up with Arthur's angry strides.

"Did you get what you needed?" Nater says.

"She's lying."

"Why would she lie to you?"

"I'm not sure, but we don't have time to find out. It's time to cut our losses. Aiden is all that matters now."

"What do I do with her?" Nater asks.

"Wait another day, then send her back to her bunk. I'll handle it from there."

"But—"

"I said I'll handle it. A week from now, Evie will be nothing more than an afterthought."

Arthur rounds the corner, leaving Nater behind. He has a mission to plan and it needs to go off without a hitch. The fewer people who know about it, the less chance it has to fail. Even Nater, whom he trusts wholeheartedly, needs to be kept in the dark on this one. For now, Nater has to be nothing more than a pawn.

CHAPTER TWENTY-FOUR

AIDEN

THE BUNK IS quiet. It's been three days since my last communication with Evie. One day before the final exam and two days after the exam incident. I call it an incident because it's clear, by Evie's absence, that I wasn't supposed to be in her drip. I'm not sure where they're keeping her or even if she's okay. I try not to hold on to the very real possibility that she may have failed medical and, without notice, got kicked from the program. I know how much that would crush her. Despite her odd obsession with distrusting GET, I know that deep down she loves the excitement. She loves the rush. She can say otherwise, but Evie *wants* to be here. I'm sure of that. I wish I knew how she really felt about me. I think I've tried to make it clear how I feel about her. All my instincts tell me that Evie feels the same way, but for some reason, she's fighting it.

We haven't had class or training since the third exam. Waiting has been like torture. We aren't allowed to leave our bunk unless we have to go to the locker room to use the bathroom or take a shower. We're given 3 hours a day to eat in the mess hall. Once at 7 a.m., once at noon, and once at 7 p.m. Free time is all time now, although you can only play so many games with a single deck of cards.

The first day back in the bunk was spent talking about everyone's drip experiences. They were all run of the mill and boring. They didn't really have anything to do other than sit guard outside one of the vaults. The more each of them talks, the more I realize Evie's experience wasn't planned. Coming into contact with Sector 6 terrorists should never have happened. It was a risk that the program took with sending in recruits, but the safe zones were supposed to be a calculated risk. One that almost ensured we'd reanimate without a problem. GET wanted us to pass. They need fresh HD operatives to keep things running smoothly. They wouldn't put one of us in harm's way if they could help it. Would they?

The twins are starting to drive me, Charlie, Hop, nuts. The bunk isn't big enough for their personalities. They're close brothers, but they love to pick on one another. Something none of us paid much mind to until we were locked up with them for a few days straight with nothing to do. I think spending most of our days in class and training had distracted us enough that we never noticed how annoying they could be. Maybe I'm just irritable because I haven't heard from Evie, but when two people argue over everything, even little things like moving around too much on one of the mattresses or leaving shoes too close to the other's locker, you really start pulling your hair out. I'm convinced Charlie might actually kill one of them. She wouldn't need to take out both; one would do. Without one of them, the other would have no one to argue with. She might take down both of them if given the chance. That way she could ensure total peace and quiet.

Hop handles all the commotion by taking two and sometimes three showers a day. I know it's bad in here, but I don't know how he does it. My skin would permanently prune with that much showering. Still, at least he keeps our side of the bunk smelling nice and fresh.

No one has decided to ask me about my drip session. I think they can tell by my overall silence the past few days that I just don't want to talk about it. All of them had reanimated and noticed that Evie was the only recruit not in the drip room. They must have assumed something had happened. I had been upset, so they knew that something must have involved me. I appreciate my teammates not making a big deal about it because they certainly could have. They also could use my silence as a way to topple me from the leadership position, but they don't. Despite my lack of communication and my not-so-friendly demeanor, they still trust me the most. For some reason, they still look to me for guidance.

Hop storms into the bunk, a towel slung over his shoulder. His hair is still wet and it's clear he's taken yet another shower. His face looks purposeful. There's something he needs to say. He makes sure the door to the bunk locks behind him.

"Another shower? If I didn't know better, I'd say your parents were fish," Kyle says.

"That was stupid. Where'd you come up with that one? Your mom teach you that?" Sonic says to Kyle.

"That doesn't even make sense. Your mom *is* my mom."

"Stop talking about my mom." Sonic tackles Kyle to the ground.

Hop ignores the twins' squabble and heads directly for my bed. I'd been thinking about what I would say to Evie if I saw her. I'd been trying to sleep too. At least in my sleep, I can see her.

"I've got to tell you something. It's about Evie," Hop says.

My ears perk up. The rest of the room grows silent. Charlie breaks up the twins' fight. I sit up.

"You mind if—"

"Yeah, of course," I say.

Hop sits on the edge of my bed and takes a deep breath. He's either run all the way back here or couldn't believe what he saw or heard. Something. I just want him to speak.

"Evie. I saw her," Hop says.

"Where?" I say.

"I was taking a shower. I was trying to make it a long one, you know . . . less time here." He shoots an angry look at the twins and then turns back to me. "Had I taken a minute shorter or a minute longer, I would have missed her."

The rest of the team huddles around my bed. They know how much I've been waiting to hear about Evie. In fact, my obsession with knowing what happened to her has transformed into a team concern.

"So? Go on," Sonic says.

"I got out of the shower, put on my clothes, stepped out of the boys' locker room, and bam! Right there in front of me, Evie Fox being escorted by medical personnel."

"How'd she look? Was she okay? Where were they taking her?" I ask. I have a billion questions. None of which Hop should really be able to answer, but I have no one else to ask.

"She looked fine," Hop says.

"What do you mean fine?" I say.

"I don't know. She looked healthy. She didn't look hurt or anything."

"Was she headed back to Bunk 1?"

"I can't say for sure, but they were headed in that direction. I'd guess that's where they were bringing her."

I reach over and give Hop a hug. This is the first sign of actual gratitude I've expressed. Hop is obviously surprised and isn't sure what to do. After a moment he hugs me back.

"Thanks," I say.

"I didn't really do anything, but you're welcome."

I sit back on my bed.

"So what are you gonna do?" Charlie says.

There isn't much to do. I'm sure Evie will get in contact with me when she can. I look up at the attentive eyes of my teammates.

"Wait," I say. "Just wait."

. . .

It's been hours now. I haven't moved from my bed, not even for a moment; not for food, not for water, not to use the bathroom. I'm convinced she'll send a note. My eyes are fixed on the bottom of Bunk 2's door. I don't know how much longer I can wait. Then it occurs to me: maybe she's waiting for a letter from me. This is something that had slipped my mind entirely. She knows that Hop saw her, and she knows Hop would immediately tell me. So why wouldn't I try sending a note? No, that's too risky. What if she hadn't been taken back to her bunk? The sudden sadness and disappointment steamroll me. If she hadn't been taken back to her room, then there would be no letter coming.

I lie back in my bed. This seems more probable than not, but then comes the note. Like all the notes before, it slides under the small crack at the bottom of our door. I've come to know the sound of paper sliding on pavement all too well. I jump up and make a dash for it. I pick it up and open it. There's a key, but from the looks of it, the message isn't a long one. In the upper right corner of the key are the numbers three and two. Thirty-two, that's page twenty-three of the packet. Page twenty-three has become a popular page of ours to use for notes because the entire page is packed from top to bottom with text. It makes forming sentences easier.

"What's it say?" Hop asks.

"You got your packet?"

Hop reaches into his locker and pulls it out. He tosses it to me. I catch it with one hand and flip through the pages until I find page twenty-three. I run the key over the page. The note is simple, but important.

The note says: MUST MEET. USUAL TIME. USUAL PLACE. LAST NOTE. ASSUME THEY KNOW EVERY-THING. I'M WELL. BE CAREFUL.

She kept sentences to a minimum. She must have not had a lot of time to make it. Or she might have had to make the key under watchful eyes. She might have just kept it short so I wouldn't question anything and try to send a note back to her. I'm nervous, but excited to see her. At least she took the time to tell me she's okay. She's thinking about me, and that's all that matters, but her telling me to "be careful" is worrisome. I thought we were always careful. Maybe she means because of the new cameras? I'll have to think of something.

I'll need some help this time. I look around the room. I could ask Hop and he'd be all too eager to help, but when he gets nervous it affects his judgment. Sonic would help, but I'm not so sure Kyle would be on board with risking his neck for something like this, and I can't get Sonic without Kyle; they come as a pair. That leaves Charlie. I know how she feels about Evie, but she's my only real option. Plus she's not the type to rat on a teammate. Not to mention she's a girl, which certainly pertains to where I need to be to meet Evie. Charlie is my only option. Now I just have to convince her.

I look up from the packet and toss it back to Hop.

"Charlie, can I talk to you for a moment?"

She looks up at me. I can tell by the look in her eyes that regardless of what it is, she'll help me. I recognize the look. It's the same look I give to Evie so that she'll always know I'm there for her.

CHAPTER TWENTY-FIVE
EVIE

My window of opportunity is pretty small. I have the sneaking suspicion that they've got me on twenty-four-hour surveillance. Medical said it's for my own health and safety, but I feel fine and even Arthur said my charts looked good. They just want to keep an eye on me. It's clear they think I can't be trusted. For some reason, I feel like my time here is limited. So I rush to the girls' locker room, slip into the drain, and wait for Aiden. I'd say I have about an hour before someone from GET starts wondering where I went and comes looking for me. My only hope is that Aiden shows up when he's supposed to.

Echoed footsteps come toward me in the tunnel, splashing in the low water. For a moment I hold my breath, fearful of being caught, but as the body draws nearer, I can see Aiden's face and I'm overcome with relief. I reach out, bringing him into my arms.

"You all right?" Aiden says.

"Yeah, I'm good. They—"

"You two better keep it PG down there and hurry it up. I don't want to have to cover if someone comes in," Charlie says through the drain.

I take a few quick steps backward.

"Who the hell is that? Is that Charlie?" I ask Aiden. I can't believe he brought someone with him.

"I had to bring her. I wasn't sure if entering through the boys' room would work. It did, but if it hadn't I thought she might be of some help. You know, the new cameras."

"You think you can trust her?"

"I can. We can. Do you trust me?"

There's the question. Do I trust him? I want to, I feel like I do, but my father told me never to trust anyone—but he's not here. He doesn't know Aiden as I do. I like to think my father would like him.

"I do," I say.

"Then trust me when I say, she's the only way this was possible."

Aiden hugs me one more time. I can tell he doesn't want to let go.

"I'm just glad you're all right," he says. I gently push him off of me. "What is it? What's the matter?"

"I met Arthur."

"You did? Why?"

"He came in, to medical, and asked me all sorts of questions. Questions about you. Questions about the drip. He wanted to know everything I could remember. It didn't feel right, Aiden. He specifically wanted to know about you."

"What about me?"

"Like how you managed to enter my drip?"

"What did you tell him?"

"I told him what I remembered. How am I supposed to know how you ended up there?"

Aiden puts his hand on mine.

"I'm sorry by the way."

"For what?"

"For shooting that man."

"Aiden. It's not your fault."

"I thought you were in trouble. You were shot. I just wanted to—"

"It wasn't your fault."

I can see he's upset. I rest my hand on his and let him know that I don't judge him for what he did. After all, it's what the program trained us to do.

"That man, Aiden, he was from Sector 6."

"Yeah, I figured as much."

"They were trying to break into the vault. One of many vaults." I look Aiden directly in the eyes. I want him to really hear what I'm about to say. "He knew me, Aiden."

"What do you mean?"

"I don't know how to explain it, but he knew me. My name and everything. I could see it in his eyes. He had seen me before."

"And you have no idea who he was?"

"No idea."

"That's crazy. There's—"

"Crazy like we felt like we knew one another? Crazy like we dreamt about each other before we even met? I'm beginning to think crazy doesn't exist. I'm beginning to think everything happens for a reason."

It's true. I do think everything is happening for a reason. I don't doubt that that man from Sector 6 knew who I was. I just want to find out how and why.

"Did you tell Arthur about that man?"

"Of course not."

"Why not?"

"Are you kidding me?"

"No, I'm not kidding. What if you're in danger? What if that man knew who you were because you're important somehow? Maybe they'll come back for you the next time you drip."

"I don't think so. I really don't. Yes, they shot at me, but that's before this man realized who I was. Once that happened—"

"Once that happened, what?"

"Once that happened, he gave up. Like my life was more important than his. Why would someone who was a danger to me look at me that way?"

"I don't know."

"Exactly. And I don't think I'm the important one. I think you are."

"You don't know that. How could you?"

"It was the way Arthur talked to me. It was like he was hoping that I didn't recover from the gunshot. He was hoping that I wouldn't make it. All the while he was more concerned with you, Aiden. Don't you get it? What's important about you is you were able to enter my drip. That's huge. I don't think that kind of gift comes around every day. You yourself stood here and told me that Arthur had told you that you were chosen and had a gift. A gift they were hoping you had. A gift that you broadcasted when you came for me."

"What does it matter? So I entered your drip, but I don't know how I did it. I just heard your voice. I heard your voice and I could see where you were. I wanted to be there for you. I wanted to save you. Next thing I know I'm standing outside Block 8."

"Aiden. I'm going to tell you something and I don't want you to freak out."

"Okay, now I'm definitely going to freak out."

I take my time with this one. If Aiden loses it, I might lose him forever. The last thing I need is for him to take the side of the program.

"I need to get back to Block 8."

Aiden throws up his hands in a fuss. He stomps around and turns to me.

"That's mad. You know that? Absolutely ridiculous. How do you even think you're going to do it?"

"I need to see what's behind the vault doors. It's the only way. I need to know what Sector 6 is trying so desperately to get to. I need to know why they are so quick to put their lives on the line and why GET will try so hard to stop them. It could be the very answer we're looking for, Aiden. It could answer everything. Why we're here. Why they chose you. Why you are so important. Don't you want to know?"

Aiden doesn't know what to say. I've hit him with a lot. I'll let him think about it, but we don't have much time left. Both of us need to be getting back to our bunks.

"What do you need from me? That is why you wanted to meet, right?"

I can tell he's a little angry, like he was hoping I had wanted to meet because I missed him so badly. I do miss him and I do want to see him, but I also need his help.

"I need you to help me break into a drip lab."

Aiden laughs. It's a nervous laughter, one of disbelief.

"You're insane. You know that?"

A smile creeps over Aiden's face. He's always liked the gung-ho, nutso side of me. I think he thinks my foolishness is in some way adorable.

"I know, but I'm serious."

"Sure, what the hell, right? It's not like I've got anything better to do."

He tries to play it off like he doesn't care what I'm asking him to do, but I know he does. It's a lot to ask of anyone. Breaking into a drip room and doing an unsanctioned drip is a direct violation of HD policy. An action that, if caught, would certainly get us both booted from the program and probably worse. What I don't want to tell him is that I think it doesn't make much difference for me either way. I will figure out a way to do this with or without him.

"We've got to do it soon. Real soon," I say.

"What's the hurry?"

"The doctor told me that we receive our assignment tomorrow morning. After our assignment, we get fitted with permanent neuro-ports. But after that—"

"After that what?"

"After that, we could be sent out on a mission or assigned to another city. We'd be active operatives. There's no telling what could happen. We've got to do it tomorrow night before that can happen."

"So what's the plan?"

I tell him the plan is to use the group drip room. It's only reserved for recruit training and the least likely to be monitored on a regular basis, seeing as we have just completed our third exam. We'll have to go at 11:50 p.m. when the hall guards change shifts. It leaves us a twenty-five-minute window to get into the room undetected. That's how long they normally take from start to finish. We'll be caught on surveillance tapes, but if no one sees it happen live, they won't review the tapes unless something triggers an alert. The hard part will be getting a key fob that can open the door to the drip lab. I tell him not to worry and that I'll figure it out.

He asks again why we need to go so soon. He's noticed the plan has a lot of holes in it. The truth is, the plan does have a low chance of success, but there really isn't another option. I'm not sure I'll be coming back from our first real drip mission alive, so if this is going to happen, it has to be tomorrow night.

That's not what I tell Aiden. I can't tell him that. I just can't.

CHAPTER TWENTY-SIX

AIDEN

WE ALL SIT in the orientation room, still separated by our teams' red and blue jumpsuits. Maybe now, after today, we'll be allowed to freely intermingle. Maybe now, *team* won't be a word that applies anymore. Probably not. Why would they go through all the trouble of training us within our teams, just to cast them aside when we're assigned to positions? I think I'm stuck with these ugly mugs for the duration. That is, if I don't get kicked out for good by tomorrow morning.

The very thought brings my attention to Evie. She's sitting calmly in her chair next to Tasha. Tasha's talking to her about something, but Evie just listens. I wonder if Evie has made friends with anyone on her team. I can say honestly that the members of my team, barring Charlie because I'm not sure where she stands on her opinion of Evie, genuinely like her. I think it would be safe enough to say that the blue team considers Evie a friend. Not because they've spent an exorbitant amount of time with her, but because they've been exposed to how much time I've personally spent talking and meeting with her in secret. Secret from the program, but not so secret from the blue team. Every single one of them is involved with Evie and my relationship. Come to think of it, any one of them could have ratted us out at any given point. The amount of trust built over the weeks is really quite astounding. I'm not sure there's anything any of them wouldn't do for me—their team leader.

I always sit next to Hop. I don't think I choose to sit next to him; it's just a habit. Ever since day one when he invited me to sit next to him, it stuck. Now, sitting anywhere else would feel strange or out of place. He's never missed a moment to get a word in edgewise either. At this very second, he is still trying to talk to me, about anything and everything.

"You think you'll get reaper?" Hop asks.

"I don't know. Why don't we wait and see? Keets isn't even here yet."

"This is so exciting, isn't it?"

Hop can't sit still. He wobbles back and forth in his seat like a child who needs to use the potty.

"Stop moving around so much, would ya?" Charlie gives Hop a much-needed shove.

I'm glad she took action. Any more of his jostling around and it would have been me putting my hands on Hop.

"You're totally gonna get reaper. You wait and see. I'd bet on it. What you think I'm going to get?"

"Hop, it's not like it's your birthday, you know. These aren't gifts they're giving out, they're jobs. Dangerous jobs." I realize he's excited, extremely, and he's been looking forward to this day for some time, maybe even his entire career at GET.

I don't really know Hop's story. Now that I think of it, he's never divulged that much information. Neither have I, but no one asked me to elaborate on anything, ever. The others, though, had volunteered their stories willingly and with pride.

Sonic and Kyle's backstories, like most everything else in their lives, intertwine. They had both been working within the GET NTD, or New Technologies Division. They were both far above average in intelligence and, when it came to advancement, soared through each department. A girl named Josie Lemon—yes, like the tangy citrus fruit—had suggested applying to the HD program as nothing more than a dare. As silly and juvenile as it may seem, both Kyle and Sonic were pining for little Miss Josie Lemon's affections. She noticed all too quickly and played the brothers against one another to get things that she wanted. They were her little puppets. They took the dare all too seriously and both applied thinking the one to get in would surely win her heart forever. The only problem was, they both were admitted. Afraid that declining would seal their fate with Josie, they both accepted. I don't think they ever think about Miss Lemon anymore. They've become a part of the program, and once you've committed fully to it, everything else seems lame and trivial. It's a double-edged sword. It's a love-hate relationship. You may hate the program, but now you can never see yourself doing anything else.

Charlie on the other hand is one of those people who found out about the HD program at a very young age. She grew up living next to a legacy family, which is probably where her general disdain for them comes from. The youngest son of that family, Striker Taylor, would torment her on a day-to-day basis about how he was going to follow in his family's footsteps and join the HD program as soon as he could, and that even if Charlie tried really hard, she'd never get the chance to be in the program. Even though Charlie thought his hurtful words might in fact be the truth, the way Striker talked about the dangers and mysteries of the HD program only made Charlie want it more. She vowed she would one day be a part of it, and used the daily tormenting as a source of fuel to feed her desire. She worked hard. Harder than any recruit probably had ever worked to be in the program. Book smarts and proficiency never came easy to Charlie, and because of this, she always had to work two or three times as hard as the average person next to her. Her sheer determination gave her a tough skin and the willpower to do anything. When she applied to the program, she fought and tore her way so loudly into it that GET had no choice but to notice her. And they did. Charlie got into the program. Arrogant Striker Taylor did not. She made sure to tell us that.

Hop was and still is a mystery. He never volunteered his story. Maybe he had told all of the team something before I arrived late that first day, but I bet he just told them he applied and by chance got in. Nothing interesting and nothing exciting, just a reason. A reason that wouldn't spark any unnecessary interest in him. He might be like me. He might not like talking about the past, the long chain of horrible events in his life that led to this very moment. Much like me, he might have had a tough life growing up. He might have lost everything as I did and signed up for GET because he had no other means to survive. He might very well be a product of the system. He might not be proud of his past, and talking about it might stir up unwanted feelings.

If that's the way Hop wants to be known, then it's good enough for me. I like Hop because I don't have to ask questions to be his friend. We accept one another as we are. Everything else, all the baggage, doesn't matter.

I can tell by his face, his questions, and his inability to sit still that this moment is a long time coming. This very moment, when Hop is assigned a position within the HD program, he will feel like he can finally be proud of something in his life again. The world broke him and GET would put him back together again. I just hope he remembers who he really is. Letting this program define him would be what puts him in the grave.

"I'm sure you'll get the position you want," I say to him.

"Nah, I want to be a reaper, but that's just not me. You're built for that, we all know it, but any other assignment will do. It's just the waiting that's killing me," Hop says.

"Yeah, I hear that."

The waiting is annoying. It seems like we've been doing a lot of waiting recently. I'm not sure it's a good thing.

The door finally opens and Keets enters the orientation room. Nater is close behind. In Keets' hands is a plain old box. My bet is they're going to give us some sort of medal, certificate, or doohickey that will provide us with some sort of physical validation that we are official HD Operatives. It's a whole bunch of baloney if you ask me.

I thought this entire process would be a little more elaborate. Then again, nothing in this program has been showy. That's laughable. Even using that word is a gross overstatement. This program is secretive and GET likes to keep it that way. The most important person I've met is Arthur, and both Evie and I know he's not even at the top of the food chain. Still, I bet that he's in some room somewhere watching today's "graduation" like a proud father might. I think back to how Evie had been taken from the locker room and brought to a private dark room and tortured because she was trying to get close to me. I wonder now if Arthur had something to do with all of that. If he did, or if I find out he did, I'm not sure what I'll do the next time I see him. Only a coward would do what they did to her.

Keets nods to us all as she enters. She stands just to the right of the podium, and Nater takes his place at the podium. I can tell this is going to be short and sweet. I'm sure they both have better things to do than hand out cheesy trophies, whatever they are.

"Sonic Kim," Nater says aloud.

Sonic stands and takes a deep breath. It looks like they are going to start with the blue team, my team. Sonic weaves down through the seats and isn't sure where to go. Does he see Nater or Keets? Keets finds Sonic's gaze and draws him to her with her eyes. At least we all know what to do now. Someone had to be the guinea pig. Sonic stands in front of Keets. Keets reaches into the box and pulls out a shiny pin. The pin is small. The HD logo sits firmly placed over what looks like a map of the world. The world is half silver, half black. If I would guess, I'd say Sonic is the Navigation Operative.

"Navigation Operative. Congratulations," Keets says as she shakes Sonic's hand.

Sonic turns and heads back toward his seat. He looks back at us with wide eyes and makes a *beat that* face at Kyle. He sits and Nater continues.

"Kyle Kim."

Kyle follows in his brother's footsteps and meets Keets, who reaches into the box and pulls out another pin. This pin has the same HD logo, but instead of covering a map, it overlays the image of a drip chair.

"Engineering Operative. Congratulations."

Kyle returns to his seat.

"Charlie Dawson."

Charlie follows suit and bounds down to Keets with quick, large strides, larger than her short legs would normally manage, but she can't get assigned quick enough. She stands at attention in front of Keets. Keets reaches into the box once again and pulls out a third button. This button shows the HD symbol covering what appears to be two crossed CAR-20 rifles.

"Security Operative. Congratulations."

"Thank you, sir," Charlie says.

She's the first to say something in response. The others now wonder if they, too, should have expressed some sort of gratitude. She takes her seat and the two twins are eager to see what her pin looks like. They prod and push at one another to be the first to get a look. Charlie holds up a hand like she's going to hit them if they don't stop being so annoying. They park their butts back in their seats. Security Operative fits her like a glove.

"Matthew Hopper."

This is the first time any of us have heard Hop being called by his actual name. It's weird and doesn't fit him. The others can't help but let out a tiny chuckle as he makes his way to Keets. Hop's sure I'm going to be a reaper and I probably agree with him, which means he's going to be the Medical Operative. Now that I think about it, I couldn't trust anyone more with that job. I don't know if he realizes it, but it's probably the most important job on the team. He might have to save any one of our lives in the field. That means he has to be someone we can all trust. He should take solace in that.

Keets pulls out Hop's pin. It shows the HD logo over a stereotypical red cross. He takes the pin and heads back to his seat next to me. He looks a little defeated. I think he thinks his job isn't as cool as the others, but he couldn't be more wrong.

"Looks like you won that bet," I say.

I try to get a little bit of a smile out of him. It works. He smiles and takes his seat.

"Aiden Bishop."

I stand and make my way to Keets. I can hear the rest of my team cheering for me on my way down. They're such idiots, goofballs really. Keets reaches into the box one last time for the blue team. She pulls out a pin that has the same HD logo everyone else has. The logo covers nothing else other than the obvious: the silhouette of a grim reaper holding a scythe. I take the pin, attach it to my jumpsuit, and head back to my seat. I'm met with high-fives and more cheers. I put a smile on, but I feel stupid. I'm not sure if I should be proud, or what. I feel a little proud, but Evie's voice of reason echoes in my head. We'll have to see how the red team goes. I wonder what they'll give Evie. I could tell the other night that she didn't care what she's assigned. I'm not sure it matters to her. I don't really know what her intentions are if she finds out something negative about GET and the program. I've never asked her that. To me, it seems like she'll leave the program if she has to, but I'm not sure they just let you leave. Not after everything we've learned about GET; it's a liability. I need to start thinking about what I will do if she decides to leave. What happens if she asks me to go with her? It's something I haven't thought about before, but I probably should have.

"Russell Baker."

Nater calls the first of the red team. Keets gives Russell the Medical Operative pin. Nater moves on down the line. Gwiz is given the Navigation Operative pin, and Tasha is given the Engineering Operative pin.

There are only two seats left on the team. Security and the coveted team leader position of reaper. I think everyone is convinced that Josh is going to be given the reaper position. He's the likely candidate seeing as his very own father was a reaper, and supposedly one of the best. Evie makes sense as a Security Operative. She's the best shot in our class and has a gung-ho attitude backed by a strong intelligence and a heightened sense of survival. Even Josh seems certain of his assignment. He welcomes his teammates' whispers and assurances, but when Nater calls Josh's name next, his confident smile turns to an ugly frown filled with disgust and disbelief.

I smile. I think it's funny. Everyone else in the room is surprised. So much so that you could knock any one of them out of their seats with a subtle gust of wind. Josh stands and heads down toward Keets. He yanks the Security Officer pin from her hands. He wants everyone in the room to know he thinks this decision is bullshit. He whips around and locks eyes with Evie. He glares at her with hate and envy the entire way back to his seat. Gwiz tries to console Josh by putting a hand on his shoulder, but Josh slaps it away. He wants to wallow in self-pity.

This can only mean one thing. Evie is the red team's reaper. For some reason, I feel excited, like her being a reaper means we'll be able to hang out or something, but as she stands and takes the pin from Keets, I can see on her face that she thinks it means something terrible. I'm not sure what is so terrible, but maybe she'll tell me tonight. Or maybe she won't. I've noticed that whenever she's thinking or feeling something that really bothers or worries her, she tries to hide it from me. Maybe *hide* is too strong a word. She doesn't hide it, she just pushes it aside and won't address it. It's fine. She always manages to tell me in other ways. She's not always direct, but I don't mind having to dig through the weeds.

Before she can turn to take her seat, she does something unexpected and very uncharacteristic of her personality. Evie leans in and hugs Keets. Something that surprises Keets just as much as it does the rest of us. She gives her a nice long, firm hug, one that makes Keets blush. She's embarrassed. None of us have ever seen Keets taken off guard like this before. Keets slowly pushes Evie away, and as she does I notice why Evie had hugged Keets in the first place. She used the contact and Keets being flustered to masterfully snag Keets' security key fob from around her waist. She did it so well that Keets never noticed for a second. I don't even know how she did it, but she did. You have to admire the amount of guts it takes to do something like that in front of everyone, but I don't think anyone else noticed but me. She turns back toward her seat and manages to slide it into her right pants pocket undetected. One thing I have to say is that she is a girl of her word. When I had asked how we would get into the drip room, she simply told me she'd *handle it*. Well, handle it she has. It looks like tonight is a go.

Evie takes her seat. Tasha is the only one on the red team who seems happy for Evie. She smiles and congratulates her. Evie thanks her and then sits. I'm trying to get Evie to look at me, but she won't. It's like that feeling where you don't look at someone when you are upset because you know looking at them will make you cry. I can tell she's upset, and that's enough to upset me.

Nater straightens up and clears his throat.

"Today marks the end of your HD recruit training. From this day forward, you are no longer recruits. When you wear that badge you are considered working operatives of the HD program."

Everyone in the room claps. It's what Nater wants. Sometimes you can just feel the anticipated reaction within someone's speech. Even Josh claps. He may not like the assignment, but at least he's made it.

"We have high expectations of you all. We have put a lot

of time and effort into your individual assignments. Take a good look around. The people next to you are going to be in the field with you. If you don't already know, you must learn to trust each and every person in this room. You will still be working within your current teams; however, we no longer look at you as a cohesive unit. You are coworkers and as such you will treat one another with the utmost respect. Thank you for all of your hard work. We look forward to the fine jobs we know you will do in the future."

Nater steps down from the podium. On his way out of the room, he gives way to Keets. Keets takes the podium. She looks a little emotional. She's proud.

"First off. Congratulations to all of you." We all cheer again out of gratitude. Keets, love her or hate her, has been there through all of this with us. "I'd like to thank all of you for bringing 100 percent of you all the time to this training period. I can personally say that you are one of my best classes in years. And I'm not just saying that. I firmly believe that you will all do great things for this program. Now, down to business. Sector 6 terrorist activities have increased rapidly over the past month. The program wants to get you guys into action as quickly as possible. And when I say quickly I mean two days quickly. First thing tomorrow you will all be sent to medical to get retrofitted with your permanent neuro-ports. The day after that you'll all have your first HD mission in the field. We'll have a briefing at 0800 hours; then you'll be inserted. I wish you the best of luck out there in the field. Thank you all again for being a class I can be proud of."

Keets steps down from the podium, but none of us

move. We haven't heard those three words we have come to rely on so heavily. Keets turns back to us.

"Okay, you are dismissed," she says.

And with that, we all stand and push our way out of the orientation room. I watch Evie as she leaves, one hand firmly against her right pocket. She doesn't want that key fob to fall out by mistake.

CHAPTER TWENTY-SEVEN

EVIE

T HE REST OF Bunk 1 call it an early night. Josh is still upset about his assignment. I don't really blame him. After all, even I was pretty sure he'd be assigned to the reaper role. He cared so much about getting it and I cared so little. I do feel a little bad for him. Tasha's another story. She couldn't have been more excited about my recent appointment to leader of the red team. I think she thinks it will help her gain some favor within the group—if she's friends with the team leader, then everyone else will have to accept her. The exact opposite of that is more likely. Nonetheless, she's become incredibly difficult to throw from my shoulder. She wants to talk all night about what our first real HD mission will be like and if I have some kind of plan.

What I don't want to tell her is that the reaper assignment means nothing good for me. In light of how my time has been spent here in the program, assigning me to reaper feels like a death sentence, almost like a warning of what's to come. I can't explain why I feel that way. I just do. I can sense it. Just as I can sense how Arthur secretly hates me for surviving my first drip. It just doesn't feel right. Not now.

I finally convince Tasha to go to sleep. I use my new power as team leader to basically force her. I simply tell her that I need my very important engineering operative to be well-rested for insertion. She buys it and goes to bed immediately.

It's quiet now and dark. The lights have been off since 10 p.m., and I've been lying on my back waiting, just waiting for 11:49 p.m. It takes exactly 7 minutes to get from Bunk 1 to the drip lab. I timed it on the way back from our assignment ceremony. I counted my steps like I used to do with my father: 423 steps. That's just about 7 minutes, give or take a minute or two. Best-case scenario it takes 5 or 6 minutes. Worst case it takes 8 or 9, but that's cutting it real close. Setting up the drip will take at least another 5 to 6 minutes, and we need 3 to 4 minutes to reanimate. That leaves us with 1, maybe 2 minutes of actual real-world time in the drip. Lucky for us that's 1 to 2 hours of time in the world of the dead, but still, it's not much time. That's a really small margin of error. A margin that assumes the guards will take the usual 25-minute changeover. Not to mention the narrow 5-minute window we may or may not have to run back to our rooms. It's not ideal.

I'm scared, naturally, but I'll have Aiden with me, and that will calm my nerves. I wonder what the world of the dead will be like when it's nighttime here. Is the sun always up there? Or will it be dark too? I hadn't thought about that.

Aiden had asked me what the plan was. My plan is pretty simple. Get into the drip lab, which to me is the hardest part, and then make the drip to Block 8. With any luck, the gun load-outs will be there again, and we can make our way to the GET Block 8 building armed and ready for the worst. Once inside we'll tell the guards we need to go to floor seven. If they refuse or want to call and check, I'll simply say it's in direct correlation to the breach from Sector 6 that had happened a few days before. I had seen firsthand the destruction the Sector 6 team had performed on the vault door. Hopefully, the door will still be under repair. That's about the extent of my plan. Once we are inside the vault, we'll have to see where it takes us. If any speed bumps pop up along the way, we'll just have to wing it. The entire thing is going to require a lot of luck.

I take a quick glance at the clock. It's 11:49 p.m. Here we go.

I climb softly out of bed, my heart racing. I can't believe I'm doing this. I take two steps toward the door.

"Where are you going?" Tasha says.

I freeze. Freezing probably makes me look more guilty. I should say something, and quick. I turn around. I can just make out the edges of her face in the darkness.

"Shh. You don't want to wake the others. I'm just nervous. You know, about the mission. I'm going to run to the bathroom real quick."

"Oh. Okay. You need company?"

"No. No. You go right back to sleep. I should only be a few minutes."

Tasha turns back over and closes her eyes. That was a close one. She could have ruined everything. I look at the clock. It's 11:50 p.m. I'm already behind schedule. Not good. I head for the door.

Now that I'm out, there's no turning back. I'm already on camera, and if the program wants to come after me, they will. I walk briskly, but not any faster than I normally would. I don't want to draw any unnecessary attention to myself. I've gone 137 steps and I still need to pass both the girls' and boys' locker rooms. That's another 82 steps. After that, it's a right turn and then straight ahead for the last 201 steps.

So far, so good. I haven't heard anything or seen anyone. I can only imagine what I must look like on the surveillance monitors. If there were someone watching, I'd be detained already. The boost of confidence quickens my steps. I round the corner; the locker rooms are in sight, but I can also see something that scares me. Two guards are walking down the hall toward me. They're at least forty or fifty steps beyond the bathrooms and deep in conversation. They don't seem to be paying much attention to what they could easily see if they just stopped talking for one second and did their jobs. I'm only about fifteen steps from the boys' locker room. I'll have to go for it and let them pass.

My steps are even faster now, but I move on the front outer edge of my feet—a technique that allows you to move with speed and silence. My father called it fox walking. I'm almost there, but the guards are closing in; they'll surely notice me. I can see one of the guard's heads beginning to look up. For some reason, I close my eyes. It seems stupid, but I do it. Suddenly, someone grabs me by the arm.

I open my eyes and see that I'm in the boys' locker room, but I'm not alone. The entire blue team is here: Sonic, Kyle, Hop, Charlie, and Aiden, who's looking out a small crack in the door.

"What the hell are—"

In unison, they tell me to *shush*. I'm angry, but they're right. My tirade will have to wait a minute until the guards pass. I cross my arms and Aiden steps away from the door.

"Coast's clear," he says.

There's an audible sigh of relief in the room. I uncross my arms long enough to smack Aiden in the chest. The rest of the team winces like I just hit them.

"So, you mind telling me why your entire damn team is here?" I ask.

"They wanted to come," Aiden says.

"What do you mean they wanted to come? You told them? I told you not to tell anyone."

"Don't blame him. He had to. You need us," Charlie chimes in.

I pivot around on one foot. I don't want to hear it, especially not from her.

"Excuse me? Was I talking to you?"

I can feel Aiden's hand on my shoulder. He doesn't want things to get messy.

"Charlie's right. We need a team. After thinking about the plan, I knew I'd have to drip with you."

"But—"

"What if something goes wrong or you need an extra set of hands? I'm not going to let you go in there alone. That meant we needed someone to control the drip and to reanimate us. Charlie already knew about it, so—"

"Wait, she already knew?" I say.

"Guilllllty. You know that secret meeting place of yours

is real private, but it doesn't hide your voices too well," Charlie says.

"Once Charlie knew, well—"

"Then I found out," Sonic says.

"Then I found out," Kyle says.

"Yeah, then I found out," Hop says with a disappointed look on his face. "You know I'm still pretty bummed I was the last one to know."

"We know," Sonic says.

"So there you have it. I didn't mean to tell them, but once they already sort of knew, I couldn't very well lie to them. And once they knew the crazy plan, they wanted to be a part of it."

"Where our reaper goes, we go," Charlie says.

Aiden looks at me with his deadly blue eyes. I can tell I'm not going to win this one.

"It's really for the best. This way I can be with you, we'll spend less time in the drip, and we'll have a safer reanimation with a full team behind us," Aiden says softly.

"And a set of eyes to keep you out of trouble up here," Hop adds.

I can't take my eyes off of Aiden. I hate to admit it, but he does have a point. They all do. Having more people involved will only help us, not hurt us. The fastest and safest way to make this mission a success is to involve them.

"We don't have much time left. We better get moving," I say.

The blue team looks just about as excited as I am. They're waiting for my approval, which tells me Aiden had told them this entire operation is a no go if I say they can't come along. I can't be mad at him for that. I know he's just looking out for me and I need him. If I have to play ball to have him along, then I'll play. Besides, I like the blue team, even Charlie, but we really are running out of time to get to the drip lab. I move to the front of the group and lead the charge. I've got the key fob and will need to have the door unlocked, open, and ready to let us all in.

. . .

We're in, and just about one minute to spare. Our little spat in the locker room must have eaten up a good two or three minutes. On top of that, we realized the rest of the blue team would need access to the control room so they could keep a close eye on our vitals. The control room door was only fifteen steps before the drip lab. Luckily, the key fob worked on both. We parted ways. Sonic, Hop, and Charlie went inside the control room. We figured navigation, medical, and security could keep tabs on vitals, how long we were in the drip, and if anyone from the program was coming to stop us. Aiden, Kyle, and I went straight into the drip lab.

We move quickly, not wanting to waste any more time. Aiden and I remove our shirts and jump into two chairs next to one another. Kyle moves around to each of us and straps our hands down. He reaches for the remote, and then we pause. He looks scared and confused.

"What about the neuro-patches? We don't go to medical until tomorrow," he says.

Aiden and I look at one another. This mission might be doomed before it even starts. Neither of us had thought about the logistics of the drip.

"Was nobody paying attention during our first drip," Sonic says through the intercom. We're surprised to hear his voice, but we could really do without his arrogance right now. "The temporary patches. I saw the nurse get them from the first drawer closest to the door; then she handed them to the doctor."

Kyle rushes to the drawers by the door. He opens the top drawer and pulls out six patches. He holds them up, then rushes back to our chairs.

"You're welcome, Kyle," Sonic says through the intercom.

Kyle places the patches on our spines and wrists. Their cool gel melds to our warm skin. I'm not looking forward to the impending pain. Kyle reaches for the remote and hits the first and second button back-to-back. The chair begins to flatten out and the optic needles pierce our skin. It's excruciating. I let out a squeal like a stuck pig. I could be wrong, but it feels more painful than the last time. Maybe doing things out of order makes it more agonizing.

We're flat now and Kyle moves to strap down our legs. It doesn't help the pain, being able to move our legs. Now I see why they strap you down. He reaches for our BDP tubes and connects them to our wrists. Then it hits me. How are we going to drip to Block 8? I don't think any of us know the drip coordinates. Even Sonic, the navigation operative, won't have the coordinates. He knows how to input them into the system, but the insertion points would normally be given to us in a briefing before the drip. Kyle reaches for the remote.

"Stop!" I cry out. Kyle stops and looks at me.

"What is it? Is everything okay?" Aiden says.

"The insertion point for Block 8. We don't know the coordinates."

"I was actually just about to bring that up," Sonic says through the intercom.

"So what do we do?" Aiden asks.

The answer is so obvious. I'm surprised I didn't think of it sooner. I knew there was a reason I needed Aiden here with me. But can he do it? Can he exercise his gift, the gift GET wants him so badly for?

"Sonic. Just make sure Aiden and I are linked to the same drip. Can you do that?" I say.

"Sure thing. Already done," Sonic replies.

"Where are you going with this?" Aiden asks nervously. It's clear he can tell what I'm getting at.

"You can do this, Aiden. You just have to trust me," I say.

"I don't know if this is such a good idea. I don't even know how I did it," he says.

"You remember what Block 8 looks like, right?"

"Yeah, but—"

"So just concentrate on that."

"I don't want to get us killed."

"Do you trust me?" I can tell by the way Aiden is looking at me that he does. "Then just close your eyes and picture Block 8. Tell me what you see."

Aiden closes his eyes and concentrates hard. His eyes squirm under his eyelids. He's searching for as many details as he can remember.

"I see the crosswalk where I appeared the first time," Aiden begins.

I look up at Kyle and tell him to proceed. I tell him to time it. We only get one minute in the drip and not a second more. It's hard to say how long our locker room debacle and patch situation took away from us, so it's better to be safe than sorry. Timing is everything. Kyle nods, reaches for the remote, and then hits the last two buttons in the sequence. Our blood starts to leave our bodies and soar to its container in the ceiling. The icy baths emerge from the floor and start to fill; the cold nip grapples our skin.

"I can see my rifle in the street. There's traffic; the city is full of people. I go for the gun, but a car destroys it, and that's what makes me notice the building. It's enormous. Its black and steel structure towers over me. I can see its giant sign, BLOCK 8," Aiden says.

It's night here—finally something working in our favor. Aiden performed on cue and that deserves a hug. I grab him hard with my arms and he hugs me back. I don't want to let go, but the clock is ticking and the end of our mission is out of our control. We have one hour.

The blaring honk of a car horn ends the hug. We're standing right in the middle of the street where Aiden had inserted himself the last time. We both turn and see the CAR-20 on the pavement. Aiden makes a run for it. He dives and tumbles, snagging it up from the street, narrowly missing a sure death blow from an oncoming car. I follow swiftly, weaving through the traffic, and find him on the other side. We stop for a moment and look up at the giant Block 8 building. It really is massive. Then we're on the move again.

We pass through the front doors. It's dark inside. Only

a little bit of warm amber light from desk lamps behind the information kiosk spills into the lobby. There's only one guard on duty and he's more than surprised to see us—to see anyone. He jumps to his feet and takes a step back. He sees our gun and is afraid. He hadn't been notified of any HD insertion, so he's uneasy. He reaches for a sidearm on his hip.

"I wouldn't do that if I were you," I say as I motion for Aiden to lower his gun. We don't need this guard getting any jumpier than he is.

"Who are you?" the guard says.

"That's not important. What's important is that we were sent here to inspect the level seven vault."

"Really? That can't be."

I need to lay on the heat. This guy is dumber than I could have expected. I wanted the guard to be dumb, but not so dumb he can't be manipulated.

"You're going to tell two HD reapers they aren't allowed to carry out their direct orders from ground zero?" I ask.

"That might be a bad idea for you," Aiden says.

"Two reapers? I didn't know. I'm sorry, it's just I didn't expect GET to send anyone just yet," the guard says.

"Why's that?" I ask.

"The level seven vault hasn't been fixed yet. We've closed access to the floor."

Perfect. If the vault hasn't been fixed yet, then getting in won't be a problem, just convincing this goober to bring us up there.

"You really think we'd come all the way down here if we weren't ordered to?" I call our own bluff.

Aiden looks at me with uneasy eyes. He can't believe I would volunteer the truth like that. The guard eases up a bit and removes his hand from his sidearm. He reaches forward and grabs a key fob from his desk.

"No. I guess not. I'll let you up." The guard moves out from the safety of the kiosk and leads us over to the elevators. He swipes his fob and reaches inside the elevator and hits the button for floor seven. "There you go. Just make sure you check in with me at the front desk before you leave."

Aiden and I step into the elevator.

"Sure. No problem," Aiden says.

The doors shut, the elevator starts to move, and we look at one another. We can't help but smile.

"I can't believe that worked," I say.

"You don't have to tell me. You were fantastic," Aiden says.

"You weren't so bad yourself."

I could kiss him. Right then and there. The adrenaline has me woozy, and he's never looked so good. Maybe that's just the excitement talking. Regardless, I want to. I look at him, but the elevator coming to a stop and the doors opening interrupt the moment. Aiden asserts his bravado. He remembers the last time he was here and it wasn't pretty. He raises his gun and moves out of the elevator. I follow slowly. We don't have much time, but we don't exactly know what to expect.

The long black hallway is still riddled with bullet holes. We move past where I had been shot in the shoulder. Traces of blood still adorn the wall and ground. The shootout seems like it was only moments ago. I can still see where each one of the Sector 6 team had been. We walk down the hall and right through where the body of the man who knew me would have been. It's not long before we're standing right where the man who was drilling stood, the phosphorus blue from his ion drill sparkling as it hammered away at the reinforced door, but before us, there is no door. The door to the vault has been removed, its empty hinges vacant and with no purpose.

In place of the door, a large double-paned sheet of semi-transparent, medical grade tarp has been fastened with gelatin tape—a sticky substance that once adhered can only be removed with a chemically stimulated resin, one we most certainly don't have on us. The only other option is to cut through it, but I don't have a knife. I was never given one with my battle gear the last time I dripped, so if Aiden hadn't seen one, he wouldn't have given me one this time.

"You don't by any chance have a—"

"Blade?"

Aiden reaches into one of the breast pockets of his battle vest and pulls out a small knife. Well, not exactly a knife. It's more of a utility blade.

"That's it?" I ask.

"What? I didn't know we'd need one. This is all I got."

Aiden hands it over and I flip out the knife. I stab at the tarp door with all my might. The knife punctures the tarp, but cutting a slit for us to pass through is another story. This stuff is tough. It has to be. Its purpose is to seal off entire areas tight enough that no germs or bacteria can get in or out. It's used to build portable hospitals in the field. It's meant to take a beating.

I can't make the cut alone, so Aiden helps me. He slings the CAR-20 around his back and wraps his hands around mine. Together we pull down on the handle of the knife. Slowly but surely, the material gives way and we manage to cut a slit large enough for both of us to climb through. I lead the way. I tuck one foot after the other and snake my body through the slit. My feet meet a metal grated walkway. It's dark, so I turn to help Aiden through. Once inside, he flips on the flashlight fastened to the bottom of the CAR-20.

My heart almost drops out of my chest. The metal walkway leads out into a vast open room. All along the walkway are bodies. The bodies are suspended by a series of metal stirrups like a slimmed-down version of our drip chairs. BDP tubes stick out of both arms on each of the bodies, circle back, and connect to large blood containers fastened to steel braces behind the chairs. What looks like one large optic needle is inserted just below where the spinal column connects to each of their skulls. A thick electrical cable runs up from each lifeless body and connects to a power grid that leads to a massive circular center column one hundred feet or so in front of us. I trace the column with my eyes and see that this is not the only floor like this. Above us, each sequential floor has the same layout. There must be thousands, if not tens of thousands of bodies in here.

As we move down the walkway, I look at each body. I notice on their necks, just below their right ears are small barcodes tattooed on their flesh. Below each barcode is a number and below that two haunting words: SECTOR 6.

"Do you see that?" I say to Aiden.

"Yeah, this is weird. What is this place?"

"No, the barcodes. On the necks," I say.

Aiden looks closely.

"Sector 6. You really think all these bodies in here are citizens of Sector 6?"

"I'd be willing to bet on it," I say.

We walk closer and closer to the cylindrical center mass. A small beacon of green and blue light draws our attention. The light comes from a small computer screen fixed to the side of the column. Looking up, I can make out one on each floor—at least one on the two floors above us. I can't see much beyond that because it's otherwise so dark. The screen shows a readout diagram of the floor seven vault. It corresponds to a number for each body, and each number has a digital percentage under it. Some show 100 percent; others are as low as 12 or 15 percent. To the far right is one large blue bar that kind of looks like the battery life symbol on a phone. The blue bar hovers right around the top of its capacity. I look at Aiden.

"They're draining them for energy," Aiden says before I can mutter those exact words.

GET found their energy source all right. They found it in the world of the dead. But why Sector 6? My only guess is they found a way to kill two birds with one stone. They get rid of the rebellious citizens and in turn reap the benefits of their energy. But the electromagnetic energy can only be harvested in the world of the dead, which can only mean one thing.

"They're killing them," I say to Aiden. "Everything makes so much sense now. I don't know how, but GET must go into Sector 6 and take however many they need. They must have to kill them to bring them here, Aiden. GET is murdering people to give the rest of the world power."

I can feel the tears starting down my face. Aiden brings me into his arms and wipes them away.

"I can't stay here anymore. I can't be a part of all of this. I have to find a way out. I have to. Will you help me? Please tell me you'll help me."

"Of course, Evie. It's going to be okay," he whispers into my ear. "It will be okay."

But I know it's not. Nothing will ever be okay again. I can't be a part of this program. I look up at Aiden and stare into his eyes. The tears have stopped and left nothing but anger. Aiden can see it in my expression; I can feel that he does when his body gets tense.

"We need a plan," I say.

"I might have an idea," Aiden says.

. . .

My eyes open. Alarms are blaring, which means something must have gone wrong. Kyle's frantically unhooking my leg and arm straps. I turn my head and see Aiden coming to. We've reanimated into chaos.

"We've got to get out of here," Kyle says.

I go to move my legs, but the heaviness from the drip sends me to the ground. Kyle tries to lift me up.

"A little help in here!" he screams.

Charlie, Sonic, and Hop burst into the drip lab. Charlie and Hop scoop up Aiden, and Sonic helps Kyle get me to my feet.

"What happened?" Aiden says.

"Someone in your drip must have called it in because this place is going nuts," Hop says.

It must have been the guard in the lobby of Block 8. He probably called it in just to make sure he saved his own butt. Maybe he wasn't so dumb after all. We all limp to the door. Aiden and I still can't walk on our own; there's no way we can make it back to our bunks without being caught. We'll be too slow. We look down the halls. We can all hear the sounds of hurried footsteps and the shouts from armed HD guards. This could be it, for all of us.

"Yo, Hop, you think you can handle him on your own?" Charlie says. Hop nods his head.

"No, I know what you're thinking, and it's a bad idea," Aiden manages to push out.

"Guys, we don't have time for this. We've got to get going. If we're not in our bunks when they come to check on us, we're dead meat," Sonic says.

"Aiden, he's right," I say.

"Looks like you're the odd man out on this one. I can handle it," Charlie says.

"I'm the team leader and I'm telling you no. We stick together," Aiden says.

"You may be team leader, but that doesn't mean I gotta follow everything you say. It's the only way."

Charlie turns and runs down the hall away from us. She begins to scream at the top of her lungs, things like, *come and get me, you bastards,* and *wrong way idiots!* As she disappears around the corner we know her little diversion won't last more than a few minutes, ten at most, so we better get a move on.

The blue team drags us back toward the bunks. Bunk 1 is before 2, so they drop me off. I can stand just enough on my own now that I feel confident I'll have no problem making it to my bed. Before entering, I turn to Aiden.

"Are you in?" I say.

He nods his head yes.

"Come on, we gotta go. We're running out of time," Hop tells Aiden. I open the door to my bunk and slide in. I watch for a moment as Aiden and the rest of the blue team make it back to their bunk. I can't believe how many lives GET has destroyed. I can't believe how everything they have shown us is inevitably a lie. The videos and news of Sector 6 terrorism are nothing more than an elaborate cover-up. Sector 6 is only fighting for survival. For the citizens of Sector 6, the only thing that has changed after The Great Event is that their lives have gotten worse, more fearful, and even more dangerous. GET is everything my father thought and knew it would be. I have to leave. My purpose here is done. I've seen what I needed to see.

I close the door to Bunk 1. I hope Charlie is okay.

CHAPTER TWENTY-EIGHT

AIDEN

WE'RE ALL IN Med-Bay 1. After a long night of waiting, the morning finally comes, and it is time to get fitted for our permanent neuro-ports. I don't think any one of us got any sleep last night. The sirens wailed for a good hour after we got back to Bunk 2. After that we laid in our beds and waited for Nater, Arthur, someone to come in and haul us away for what we had done, but no one did. No one ever came for us. So then we waited for Charlie to return, but she never did. It probably wasn't smart staying up all night; we all look like hell with our giant bags, deep black circles, puffy cheeks and eyelids, and greasy hair, but how could we have slept knowing Charlie had sacrificed herself for the team. I'm not sure any of us know what has happened to her, but if the silence in the room is any indication, then we all assume the worst.

Med-Bay 1 is large. It's designed for pre-op teams before or after insertions. There must be fifteen individual medical beds, enough to fit three full drip teams. They have us lined up like ducks in a row. I can't help but think we're just waiting for the slaughter. It seems odd to me that they didn't pull us out of our rooms last night and get right to punishment. Something isn't right, unless they're waiting for the right time to enact swift justice.

We all try to play it cool. None of us look at one another. We thought it best to act as if nothing was out of the ordinary. Of course, Charlie not being part of the row definitely makes some of the red team turn heads. For now, we'll stand here, waiting at attention, for Keets or Nater, or whoever will be briefing us on the neuro-ports.

The door opens and Keets enters. Nater follows, leading Charlie in with one hand on her shoulder. She has a pretty severe black eye, and both her arms are covered in bruises. It's clear she was interrogated, or at the very least, punished brutally. If she was interrogated, that means they never saw us on camera, and from the looks of the bruises, it doesn't seem like she ratted on a single one of us. But why did they not check the tapes?

Nater gives Charlie a good push into the end of our formed line.

"Watch it," Charlie says.

We all smile, even Evie. I'm not sure if Charlie gave Nater attitude because that's just who she is, or because she wants all of us to know that she's okay and still her same old sassy, no-bullshit-taking self.

Keets paces in front of us. It seems like she's looking for the right words to say. She looks angry, well, frustrated, but not livid. Not like the seething hate that drips from Nater's malicious stare. Keets stops pacing and looks right at me. Not in my general vicinity or between a few others, but directly at me. She wants to make sure I hear what she's about to say. She's tailored it for my ears. I take a deep gulp of air.

"Last night, you may have heard our emergency alert system go off," Keets says. "I'm sorry if we woke you, but it seems we had a bit of an emergency. A little after midnight an unsanctioned drip session was performed."

The few members of the red team who hadn't been included in our field trip gasp and shift uncomfortably. They can't believe some of us would have tried such a thing.

"We did catch operative Charlie here running through the halls last night. When asked if she was involved with the drip, she never denied it. When asked who else was involved, she refused to name anyone else. She was dealt with accordingly. Normally, we'd just check the surveillance tapes, but somehow, they mysteriously didn't record a damn thing. Consider yourselves lucky; somehow they were turned off."

It's hard to keep from grinning ear to ear, but we've got to keep our composure. I think it's safe to say they know the blue team was involved in the session. If you'd asked Keets or Nater to pick the names of everyone involved, they'd most certainly pick the five of us. But with no actual proof, and Charlie's mouth staying zipped, it's looking like we're in the clear.

"We do know that there were more of you involved in last night's little breach of conduct. But unless any of you want to step forward and give yourselves up, which I highly doubt is going to happen, we have no choice but to move on and move forward. We have your first active HD mission tomorrow, and you need to be ready. These neuro-ports aren't going to fit themselves. But know this, dripping on your own was dangerous and could have killed you. You might want to think twice before pulling a stunt like that again. Oh, and you might want to thank Charlie."

Keets is eager to let the events of last night go, but Nater still seems a little bit annoyed. He takes a few steps forward as if he's going to say something, but Keets is quick to jump in.

"That should be all. Thank you, Nater, for helping us this morning."

Nater looks disgusted and angry that Keets clearly doesn't want him to speak. He turns and leaves the med-bay in a huff. He'll probably head straight to the shooting range and unload a hundred rounds or so. He should too, might cool his head. Keets holds up an NDP. It's small, black, and metal with a tiny hole in the center. She rotates it between her fingers; one side is flat and smooth, the other bumpy and rough with a series of seated teeth circling the outer rim.

"This here is a permanent NDP. You will each have two installed along your spine. This is a permanent BDP." Keets lowers the NDP and holds up a small metal rectangle very similar to the texture and characteristics of the NDP, but instead of a hole there's a valve. "It will be installed into your left wrist. You've already seen how these ports work together; now it's time to officially become part of the HD team."

As Keets finishes, the door to the med-bay opens again,

and ten doctors file into the room. There's one doctor for each operative. They stand across from us.

"These doctors will be installing your ports. It's not a painful process, but it is unpleasant. It only takes twenty or thirty minutes to complete. Not as easy as ripping off a Band-Aid, but not as difficult as open-heart surgery either." Keets laughs at her own joke. "Let's get started. Good luck." Keets leaves us alone with the doctors.

They lead us backward and tell us all to remove our shirts and lie down, face first, on our beds. Holographic medical walls pop up on all sides of each bay. Here we go.

The beds have neat little holes in the headrests so you can breathe during the process. That's what the doctor keeps telling me anyway—*just remember to breathe*. As if I might forget. He probably means breathe in a manner to keep myself calm. Everything we do here demands the ability to keep calm. Keeping calm makes things hurt less. GET and the program seem to like to inflict pain. Something not all of us are built for. I can only imagine what's going through Evie's head right now. Being branded with neuro-ports is, at this point, her worst nightmare. She doesn't want anything to do with the program anymore, and these ports will be a constant reminder.

I have agreed to help her escape. With one little head nod, I have agreed to go with her. I'm not sure what I was thinking. I just couldn't tell her no. She was looking at me with those eyes of hers, those soul-searching eyes. How can you say no to them? She assured me we'd get to the bottom of everything. We had found more than we bargained for. She had told me we should still go through with medical today, that we didn't know when or if we might need to get back into the world of the dead. If we did, we'd need the ports.

We had formulated an escape plan during our drip. It wasn't much as far as genius plans go. Our only choice was to stick to what we already knew. We couldn't very well get in the elevator and walk out the front door. The HD facility would definitely be on lockdown now that we had already tripped the alarms. The only thing we could think of would be to follow the tunnel of our secret meeting place. We had never explored where it went and knew very little about how long it actually is, but it seems like our only option. We know that one direction leads to access to the boys' locker room. By our best guess, the boys' locker room is farther away from the elevator, which means it has to be farther away from the main lobby of the GET building and subsequently farther from the street. So, once in the tunnel, we would head in the opposite direction. The tunnel only goes in those two directions, so we'll have a fifty-fifty chance of getting it right.

We won't bring anything with us. A gun or two would be nice, but we have no easy way of accessing them. We'll just bring ourselves. Staying light means we can move fast, and moving fast is paramount. With any luck, they won't notice for a good hour that we are missing. Hopefully, that's enough time to make it to the street. Once we get to the surface, we aren't sure where or what we should do next. I think just getting topside is all we have to focus on for the moment. After that, we'll roll with the punches.

Evie is set on leaving tonight. I'm not sure why she wants

to leave so quickly. I told her I thought we should wait until after our first HD mission. That way, the program would be more unsuspecting. If it looked like we were playing ball, then they might think we weren't going to try anything fishy. But Evie wouldn't let up on the timetable, so we will leave tonight. The hard part will be saying goodbye to the rest of the blue team. I can't ask them to come with me. I'm sure if I tell them about what we have seen, they might even volunteer for an early departure, but telling them would mean I'm putting them in danger. If they came with us and got caught, it would most certainly be a death sentence. I don't think I could live with their blood on my hands.

The doctor pulls out a large metal syringe. It's different looking than most syringes. The needle is long and thin, and the tube is solid and rectangular.

"This will sting a little, but it will make the installation of the neuro-ports tolerable," the doctor says.

The doctor pushes my left ear forward and slowly inserts the needle. I can feel the cold prick pushing farther and farther into my head. My teeth clench together involuntarily, something the doctor tells me is normal, but nothing about this feels normal. The single, steady pressure of his thumb on the back of the syringe sends something into the back of my skull. The farther his thumb comes down on the syringe, the more my head begins to pulsate. It feels like my head is being filled with concrete. The pressure is immense, so much so that my ears pop twice to relieve some of the buildup.

The doctor removes the needle and places it on a small surgical table next to the bed. Then he takes a small tube of some kind of aqua-sonic, sticky, cold gel. He flips a switch on the side of the bed, and a bright light turns on overhead. In his hand, he holds what looks like a wall stud finder or a price check gun. He places it at the top of my spine, just beneath where my neck and head meet, and pulls the trigger. I hear the gun beep and it makes me jump a bit. The doctor puts a hand on my shoulder and tells me to relax. He traces my spine with the gun. It beeps every time he passes over one of my vertebrae. He stops, removes the gun, and squeezes out a small glob of the gel on where he had just had the gun. The gel is cool, so cold in fact that I can feel my skin go numb. I can also smell something terrible, like what happens when you singe some arm hair over an open flame.

He moves on. He starts tracing my spine again. This time he starts just below where he had placed the gel. It's clear now that the gun is for finding where the ports are supposed to be installed. He stops a second time and applies more gel. He puts the gun and the gel on the surgical table and stands. I hear him walk a few steps away, then return, sliding his chair away from the table. He stands next to me.

"Aiden, I'm going to install your first neuro-port now. I'll be using a port drill. You are going to feel some discomfort, but it shouldn't take more than a few moments," the doctor says.

The drill touches my skin, and the NDP is screwed into my back. There's pain, but not tons. Keets had been right about that at least, but the feeling itself is unpleasant, to say the least. It feels like someone is inside my body, tugging at my skin, muscle, and tendons. It feels gross. The smell of burning flesh fills my nostrils, and the hum of the drill subsides. At least mine does, but I can still hear the faint sound of other drills in other bays still hard at work.

"That's one. Now I'm going to move on to the second."

The drill starts up again and with it the same grotesque tug at my skin. The second port is more disturbing than the first. I'm not sure if it's just my mind getting to me or because it's physically farther down my spine. Either way, I can't wait for this to be over. The drill stops and the doctor plops it down on the surgical table.

"Okay. Go ahead and turn over on your back for me. You might feel a little soreness as you lie back down. That's normal. You should feel some soreness until your skin has a chance to grow back around the teeth of the ports."

There's that word again, *normal.* I turn over and lie on my back. The ports feel strange against the top of the bed. It's almost like I'm lying on two small rocks. The doctor moves around to the other side of the bed and tells me to hold out my left arm. He pulls his stool around and takes a seat. Here comes the BDP. I can't imagine this one will be any worse than the two in my back, but I'm wrong.

The BDP is installed with a prehistoric-looking device. It's a frighteningly large pistol-shaped hunk of metal. The tip is a 1-inch-by-1-inch square opening. The edges of the opening have some sort of thin light strip built into it. The doctor loads the BDP into the bottom of the gun like a bullet magazine from our CAR-20 rifles. He lines the tip of the gun up with my left wrist and pulls the trigger.

The BDP tears through my skin and lodges itself deep into my wrist. If it wasn't for the valve on the top, I'm pretty sure it would have shot clean through. Only milliseconds after, the thin strip on the gun barrel lights up a blazing red. It's no light strip at all. It's a laser strip. The heat from the laser cauterizes my skin around the BDP insertion point, sealing and sanitizing any loose skin or escaping blood.

"All done," the doctor says.

He puts down the BDP gun and stands up from his seat.

"You can go ahead and put your shirt back on."

I lean forward and swing my legs over the side of the bed. I look down at my wrist, then over at the sheet covering the medical bed. On it, there are two little circles of blood and pus. The doctor can see my face wince at the sight of my own bodily fluids.

"Don't worry, that's normal." There it is *again*. "They might leak a little until—"

"The skin grows back," I say.

"Very good." The doctor reaches into a drawer, pulls out a small tube of antiseptic, and hands it to me. "Now I want you to put this on the ports twice today and twice tomorrow. You shouldn't need more than that."

I take the tube and stand up.

"I'm all done?" I ask.

"All done."

The doctor flips a switch and the holographic partitions disappear. I can see a few of the others are just finishing up too—Charlie and Sonic, Josh and Tasha. I can't decide if I should wait for Evie and the rest of my team to finish before heading back to the bunks, but maybe it's better if I don't. At least now I'll have an excuse to leave the room later and head to the locker room. I can say I need to check on my ports and put some of this goo on them. It won't be what I'd wish my last words to my teammates to be, but it's all I can let myself say. The less they know the better. The more unsuspecting they are the better. If they're inter-rogated again after Evie and I leave, I genuinely want them to know nothing. It will be better that way.

I leave Med-Bay 1 and head back to Bunk 2 for the last time.

CHAPTER TWENTY-NINE

EVIE

THE CLOCK IS once again ticking. Getting out of Bunk 1 was easy. I told Tasha my neuro-ports were itchy. The rest of the team was giving me the cold shoulder. I could tell that even Tasha was upset with me. I didn't like the idea of leaving without saying goodbye to her, but I had to.

Now that I'm in the girls' locker room, I don't have much time. It's funny to think just how important the water tunnels have been for me. They started out as a juvenile means of seeing and flirting with Aiden, but they have evolved into a headquarters for plotting and now escaping.

I didn't lie to Tasha. My neuro-ports *are* itchy. I walk over to a mirror and lift up my shirt. I have to turn my head pretty hard to see them. They're gross-looking, unnatural. The very sight of them makes me sick with guilt. If I could I'd rip them out right now, but who knows if I'll end up needing them. I pull down my shirt and head for the storm drain. By now Aiden should be on his way to the boys' locker room, doing the exact same thing I am. He'll remove the drain cover and slide down into the tunnel to meet me. He'll probably have a hard time saying goodbye to the blue team. I know how close they have all become.

I reach for the drain and give it my usual pull, but for some reason, it won't budge. I give it another try—still nothing. I feel a nervous sweat forming on my face and under my arms. This can't be happening. I wonder if Aiden is having the same trouble.

"I thought you were checking your ports."

I freeze. The sudden and unexpected voice brings a shiver to my already aching spine. I have been caught red-handed. How could I have been so stupid? But the voice is calm, familiar, and friendly. I turn around. It's Tasha.

"I was . . . I mean I did . . . I was just—"

Tasha takes a few steps toward me. "Don't worry about it. I get it. I'm not a complete idiot, you know."

I can't read the situation. It's unclear whether she knows what's going on or she just thinks she does. I think it's best not to ask.

"I'm sorry," I say.

"For what?"

"I don't know, for everything."

"Well, it was pretty stupid of you to go into a drip with the blue team. I know you're into Aiden, but, girl, please, you should have at least brought me along with you."

Tasha smiles. She normally doesn't talk with all that sass, but she thinks it might lighten the mood. I appreciate it. I can't help but laugh.

"Can I at least get a hug?" I ask.

Tasha wraps her arms around me. We hug, a good, long

hug. The truth is, I will miss her. It's been a really long time, probably not since Susan, that I've had an actual friend.

"Thank you," Tasha says. "Thank you for being there. Thank you for giving me a chance."

I can hear the beginning sniffles of a good cry. As much as I love her, I don't have the time for this. Besides, if she starts crying, I won't be far behind.

"You're welcome," I say.

She picks up on it and laughs as she releases from our hug. She looks down at the drain.

"Did you need help with that?" It's a rhetorical question. She saw me struggling with it. "Well, let's get to it."

We kneel beside one another, our hands firmly on the drain, fingers laced through the small slits. It's an all too familiar feeling. I really have to stop running. Maybe someday, somehow, but today won't be that day. We give one last strong pull, and the drain cover pops off from the wall.

"Well, you better get going," Tasha says.

"Tasha, I—"

"Don't worry. I won't say anything. You were never here."

I can tell from the sincerity in Tasha's voice that she won't. She'll never tell anyone what she saw, even if she is tortured. She's stronger than I had thought, which makes leaving all the harder. I wish I could take her with me, but I can't.

"Thanks," I say. I can't think of anything better.

I slide my feet into the drain and start my descent to freedom. Tasha and I make eye contact one more time before I disappear for good.

"Catch ya later," I say.

"Say hello to Aiden for me," Tasha says.

Then, like the many times before, I drop down into the tunnel. When my feet hit the ground, I'm quickly reminded of the dangerous road ahead. The uncertainty of the journey is palpable. I look up at the drain. I can hear Tasha replacing the cover. Smart girl. I should have thought of that. Might end up buying us a few more minutes.

"Can you trust her?" Aiden says as he emerges from the surrounding darkness of the tunnel.

"I think so."

"Because if you don't think you can, it's not too late to turn back. This is the last chance we'll get. One step in that direction and we have to commit to this. There will be no turning back, not down there."

"I can trust her. I'm sure of it," I say again.

"Okay. Good. We should get a move on then. Who knows what lies ahead."

"And who knows how long before they come after us."

"You think they'll come after us?"

"You're their prize pony; of course they'll come."

It's true. Once GET figures out we're trying to escape, they'll come after us with all they've got. Letting me go might not matter all that much, but letting Aiden go too would be unacceptable. They'll do anything to get him back, or at least not fall into the wrong hands. Thinking about it now, they might kill both of us if it came to that. We'd be better off dead than out in the free world. They have no idea what we may have seen during our drip, and that's scary. Scary enough to kill to protect.

. . .

We stand at a crossroads. Our brilliant water tunnel escape plan has turned into a bit of a nightmare. The once single tunnel has now split off into three different directions. The first tunnel we took led us a good twenty minutes to a dead end. By the time we got back to the split, we had wasted almost forty minutes. Between that and the time spent already getting to this point, we're well over the hour I had allotted for our escape to the surface. By now GET has been alerted to our disappearance and is probably on their way to come and retrieve us.

There are two other tunnel options, neither of which we can be sure lead to anything. For all we know, we should have gone the other direction completely. One wrong decision and we'll be caught.

"Which one?" I ask.

"I don't know. I picked the last one. I'm not sure I want to pick again."

"You think it matters? At this point, a coin flip might be as good as anything."

"Why? You happen to have a coin we could flip?"

We both laugh. If we're going to get caught, we might as well enjoy the last few moments we have together, but our laughter is interrupted.

"No one is going to be flipping a coin," a voice says from behind us.

Our first instinct is to make a run for it. Just pick a direction, any direction, and make the move, but we know the voice. It's Keets. I make a break for it, but Aiden grabs me by the arm. I fight to wriggle free. What is he doing? Why isn't he trying to run too? Then I see it. Keets is holding a CAR-20. My arms go limp and Aiden takes my hand in his. We both think these might be our last seconds together.

Instead, Keets tosses the rifle through the air, and Aiden catches it.

"Here. You might need this," she says.

Aiden and I look at one another, confused. Why is Keets helping us? Is this a trick? Who is she working for?

"But—"

"What? You think I didn't realize when you took the key fob from me? The program's had its suspicions, but when you did that, I knew," Keets says.

"So you were the one who got rid of the tapes?" Aiden says.

"I didn't get rid of them. I just made sure they were turned off during the shift change."

"But what if you were caught?" I say.

"What if *you* were caught?" Keets replies. "I couldn't have you, either of you, getting caught. Especially since I've seen firsthand that Aiden's a skip-tracer."

"That's what they call it?" Aiden says.

"So you know? Well, that saves me some explanation at least."

"But why are you helping us?" I ask.

"Aiden is too powerful a tool. Him being here would surely bring about the end of Sector 6."

"So you're part of Sector 6?"

"I am," Keets says.

"But you've been in the program since the beginning," Aiden says.

"I have. We thought there would be no better way to put an end to GET than to have one of us on the inside. But I've never managed to get into one of the vaults, I've never been able to provide any real proof of what GET is doing, but you two have, haven't you?"

Aiden and I look at one another.

"I thought so. We have to get you out of here. It's the only hope. But you don't have long. They know you're using the drainage tunnels, but they aren't sending anyone down here after you. I convinced them to run a purge."

"What the hell is a purge?" Aiden says.

"Well, it doesn't sound good, that's for sure," I say.

"They're going to flood the tunnels, try and flush you out."

"Yeah, or drown us," Aiden says.

"It's the best I could do without blowing my cover. It buys you a little more time, but move as fast as you can. Once that wave of water comes, you don't want to be there for it."

"Thanks for the advice," Aiden says.

"One little problem. We don't know how to get out of here," I say.

"Take the middle tunnel. It's a straight shot. When the tunnel dead-ends, there'll be a ladder. Climb it. It's a long climb, but don't stop. Once you get to the surface, climb out the grate and run. Run as fast as you can. The best thing you can do is head for Sector 6. You'll be safe there. That is if they haven't already shut down the access roads. If they have, you'll have to think of something else, but you better get going."

"What about you?" Aiden asks.

"I'll be fine. Go. Just go!" Keets shoves us off with her words. I'm not sure she will be okay, but she's willing to take the risk. She knows what will happen if Aiden is caught.

Aiden slings the rifle around his shoulders, grabs hold of my hand, and we make a run for it down the middle tunnel.

. . .

It seems like we've been in this tunnel forever. Our quick pace has slowed to a painstaking trudge because the water in the center channel has risen. At first, it slowly seeped over the edges and sloshed at our feet. But now, the water is making its way up above our knees. Each step requires us to lift our legs high above the water line or wade through, which sucks up a lot of our energy. At this rate, we'll never make it to the ladder in time. I wonder if this is the purge. Somehow, I feel like this is the calm before the storm. So we trudge on.

"How much farther do you think this ladder is?" I ask. Maybe some conversation will help the time pass. Anything to take my mind off the burning exhaustion starting in my legs.

"Shh."

"What?"

"Shhhh," Aiden says again.

"What's the matter?"

Aiden stops walking and holds up a hand. I take it as a signal to stop too. His pause is for a purpose. He looks like he's listening for something. "Did you hear that?"

"Hear what?" I listen really hard for a good couple of seconds, but I don't hear anything.

"You don't hear that?"

"No. What is it?"

"Maybe I'm just letting my head get to me," Aiden says as he takes a few steps forward.

I wait for a moment and let him get a few paces ahead of me. Now I think I do hear something. A sloshing? Yes, it's like a slight slosh followed by a low rumble. The kind of rumble you might hear while walking through the woods and you hear a nearby river.

"You coming?" Aiden asks, but as soon as he does, the once low rumble almost instantly becomes a thunderous boom. We both turn to look behind us, and we see a thick wall of water racing toward us. I turn back around to face Aiden.

It's the purge.

"RUN!" I yell.

We both hop to it. We never knew we could move that fast in such high water. We make our own little whitecaps as our knees clap to our chests and we high-step as fast as we can. In the panic, my feet slip out from under me and I fall face-first into the waist-deep water.

"AIDEN!" I scream, but he's already come back for me. He scoops me up and helps me move. A shooting pain runs through my left ankle. Like an idiot, I must have twisted it. I wince in pain.

"You all right?" Aiden asks.

"I'm fine, just keep moving!"

"I think I can see the ladder!" Aiden cries out. "Come on!"

Our adrenaline pumps into overdrive, and we move as fast as we can. We reach the ladder and Aiden insists I go first. I get one hand on the first rung of the ladder when the purge hits us. Aiden is instantly swept away. The water hits me like a block of concrete. I can feel my legs tear away from the ground. I hold on for dear life with my hand. I manage to get the other hand on the ladder, but the water rises fast, and it's only moments before I'm fully submerged. I hold my breath and try not to let go of the ladder.

Once the water fills the entire tunnel, the force of the purge settles enough that I can make my way up the ladder. One foot, then the other, I climb up to a break in the water. I spit water from my mouth and take giant gulps of air, then look back down below me.

"AIDEN!"

Somewhere, below, he's trapped underwater. I scream his name again as if that will miraculously bring him back, but before I know it, my body instinctually sends me plunging back into the frigid water. I have to save him.

Once underwater, I open my eyes. I've never been that good at this; it always made my eyes sting. This time is no different, but I have to suck it up. Aidan's life depends on me. I swim as hard as I can in the direction the purge took him, the pain of my twisted ankle wrenching with every kick, but it's not long before I see Aiden. Keets had been right. The tunnel did dead-end. It stopped only twenty or so feet past the ladder. Aiden had been swept away with the purge and slammed against the grated wall of the tunnel, a grate that lets water flow through, but nothing solid that's any bigger than a penny.

Aiden's unconscious, knocked out by the force of the hit. I wrap my left arm under his arms and across his chest.

I swim as hard as I can back toward the ladder, but the subtle current is made hard by the extra weight and my ruined ankle. I manage to get to the ladder. I just hope I'm not too late. I grab hold and hoist Aiden up. It's easy under the water, but as we start to breach, his earthly weight makes it hard to hold on to him and the ladder at the same time. I put his back to the metal rungs and use my legs to hold us both upright. I shake him with my hands.

"Aiden. Aiden!"

I give him one, then two slaps across the cheek. He's not waking up until, suddenly, he heaves his head forward and coughs up a good slop of water right in my face. I wipe it from my eyes only to find him staring right back at me.

"Hey, beautiful," Aiden says with a smile. He's trying to make light of his near-death experience. I don't like it. What would I have done without him? I don't think it's very funny. Not at all. I let go and let him slip from the ladder and bob back into the water. I start to climb. His hands find the rungs and he starts up after me.

"Hey," Aiden says.

"Come on. We've got a long way to go to get to the top," I say. And we do.

We have fifty flights of stairs to climb, but in our case, fifty flights of stairs in the shape of a ladder. It's going to be tough, but we have to keep going. Up is the only direction we can go now. Up and out.

CHAPTER THIRTY

AIDEN

WE REACH THE top. We stopped numerous times during our climb to rest. It must have taken us twenty minutes until we finally reached the small grate in the street. What lies before us on the other side of it is unsure. We could be under anywhere in the city at this point, and who's to know if GET is already waiting for us. Maybe they got to Keets and made her blab. Maybe Keets was never on our side in the first place and she had set us up. With any luck, they'd think we died in the tunnel during the purge.

I'm still not entirely sure where we will go once we're out. This is as far as we had planned, if you can call it a plan—almost everything has been different than we anticipated. Keets had said we should try to find our way to Sector 6 because we'd be safe there, but she also said if the access road was blocked, we'd have to figure something else out. Once you get to the city limits, there's only one road that takes you to The Grand Wall. The wall itself is about ten miles from the edge of the city. Those ten miles are a heavily forested stretch of road riddled with armed GET guards and at least two security checkpoints. No ordinary citizen is allowed to make the trek, but those are the rumors. For all we know, it could have ten security checkpoints, one for every mile.

The ten-mile walk to The Grand Wall will take three to four hours on its own, and that's if we do it with no stopping or interruption, but GET will more likely than not be looking for us. Once they find out we didn't die in the purge, they'll scour the streets. So we'll have to spend time hiding and throwing them off our scent. The journey will be slow going, to say the least. It'll be double, maybe even triple the normal travel time, which means we might have to spend a night out there before we reach the actual wall.

We can't just walk up to The Grand Wall either. There's a constant patrol over the wall. We'll have to wait and watch, study the best times to make a move. That's saying we find a good place to try to make it through. If we make it through, what's next? That part is very unclear. We've worked so hard to escape, but for what really? What's even on the other side of the wall? What is Sector 6 like? No citizens other than those sent to Sector 6 have ever seen it. Stories of what it might be like came from those who knew the area before The Great Event, but the event itself changed things. It changed the world. Any leftover memories are only a small variation of what actually exists now. The crazier thing to think about is what's beyond Sector 6—The Great Lands.

The Great Lands are considered to be territory lost to the wilds of Mother Nature. Land with no bounds, society, or civilization. No one has gone into The Great Lands and lived to tell about it. Well, at least they've never come back to tell about it.

These are the things I plan on talking to Evie about when the time is right, but that time is not now. For now, we just need to survive.

I place both hands on the grate and push as hard as I can. This is one of those things that is probably far easier to do if you're pulling instead of pushing—not to mention pushing while standing on a narrow ladder. With some persistence, I manage to lift the grate just enough to squeeze up, out, and onto the street. I leave Evie below for a moment, just to check if the coast is clear. It is. The streets seem safe, but it's almost too clear, enough to make me think twice before pulling the grate open for Evie. It's late at night now and I'd expect the city to be a little quiet, but as I look around I notice we're on Fifth Street—the Fifth Street diner is a dead giveaway—it's only a few blocks southwest of the GET building. The plus side is we're already set up in the right direction for The Grand Wall. The bad news is, this area should be active all hours of the night. Something doesn't seem right, but then again we've also been away from this world for some time now.

I have to help Evie out. Her ankle is still bothering her. I think it twisted during the purge. I'm still impressed that she managed to swim her way through it and pull me to safety. I owe her now. I don't mind. I'd gladly sacrifice my life for hers, but now I feel like I owe her. I feel like I have a responsibility to make sure nothing happens to her, more so than ever. Once on the street, I can tell by the panicked look on her face that she's thinking the same thing as me—where is everyone?

"Something's off," Evie says.

"Tell me about it. It's a ghost town. I'd almost prefer walking into GET guards. At least then, we wouldn't be setting ourselves up to be ambushed."

"Well, we can't stay here. We have to keep moving. If we follow Fifth Street it will dump us out a block south of the road to the wall," Evie says.

She wants to be the leader of this operation, and I can't say I disagree with her. She seems to know more about this whole thing than I do; after all, it was her idea in the first place.

"How's your ankle? You think you can—"

"It's fine. Let's just keep moving. Every second counts," Evie says.

I know she's tough, but there's only so much abuse a body can take. I don't want anything happening to her. Like I said, I feel responsible now.

We move as fast as we can. I keep the rifle raised. We have to be ready for anything. I don't want to have to shoot anyone, but I'll do what I have to. Evie's limp gets more noticeable with each step. I'm worried she might really damage it. At this rate, she'll never make the ten miles. I might have to carry her. We can't risk stopping.

Even though there aren't any people, the ghostly shell of a fully populated city still brings life to the streets. Dozens of parked cars line Fifth. We use their hulking metal and fiberglass bodies to conceal our movement. We stay low, as low as we can, and look over our shoulders every ten steps or so. Evie leads the rush. I'll let her ankle set the pace; that way she won't stress about falling behind. I don't mind. It's already been a tough escape. I can use some extra time to regain some energy.

We've passed GET to the north and we're only a block from the road to The Grand Wall when we see them. GET guards line the entrance to the road. They form a solid front, stretching across the entire street. Behind them, a barricade of steel pilings and concrete roadblocks form an impenetrable barrier between Sector 6 and us. Whether or not they know if we are still alive is unknown, but it's clear they figure we'll try to head for Sector 6. There's only two of us, and there's fifty or so of them. That's fifty guns to our one. We won't stand a chance going head-to-head. We'll have to figure out a new plan. For now, Sector 6 will have to wait.

"We should take a closer look. Maybe there's a way around," Evie says.

She's trying to be optimistic, but there's no way we're getting through. Before I can say anything, she's already on her hands, crawling as close as she can. She slides under a large truck and props herself between two sedans only about thirty yards from the GET line of defense. She's crazy, but that's part of what I love so much about her: she's fearless. That's more than I can say for myself. I'm definitely scared right now, but she hasn't left me much choice. I slink my way up next to her. If we keep our heads down, we should stay out of sight.

"Look," Evie whispers. "It's Nater."

"They really brought in the big dogs."

"He wouldn't want to miss this. He hates me."

"You? I thought he hated all of us."

We watch closely as Nater barks orders. It looks like he's been waiting for this day—a day in which he can command his own militia. He tells the guards to keep their eyes open. To listen closely. He warns them that we are armed and dangerous. I can't help but smirk.

"I don't see Keets, do you?" Evie says.

I scour the crowd, but she's nowhere to be seen. I know Evie's thinking the worst, but Keets is an intelligent woman. She's probably fine.

"No. Don't see her," I say.

"Drop the gun and put your hands on the back of your heads," a cold, deep voice says from behind us. I can hear the gun cock, loading a round into the chamber. He means it.

"Just do what he wants," Evie says.

But we can't be captured. Who knows what they'll do to us. I think it's safe to say we can't ever go quietly. Our escape has to go all the way, or we have to be willing to die trying. That, and I owe Evie a life-saving gesture.

"Of course," I say as I slowly begin to lower my gun to the ground.

I can hear the GET guard reach for his radio and call out that he has found and secured us. Perfect. I use his own distraction against him. I swing into action. I spin around on a knee, bringing the rifle back up to my shoulder. The guard reacts, raising his. Evie picks up on the action and uses the underside of her forearm to hack away at the guard's aim. Her hit forces him to pull the trigger, and a single shot rings out, the bullet slamming into the door of the car next to us. I squeeze my trigger gently. The bullet finds its way through the guard's shoulder with violent destruction. He drops his gun as his body bounces backward and onto the pavement. Chaos erupts over his open walkie.

"Come on!" I say.

I reach out for Evie's hand. She takes it and we start to run. I look back only for a moment and see that they've spotted us and are in chase. The crack of gunpowder and the sound of bullets whizzing over our heads keep us moving. We have to abandon Fifth Street. They split their party into two groups. One wraps around to cut us off to the south, the other presses us forward. Our only option is to move north, but the only thing north of us is GET. Perhaps that's what they're trying to do, corral us like sheep back into a pen. For now, we have no option.

We move around cars, around building corners, up and down stairs—a real urban assault. It's hard to think while we run for our lives, but we need a plan and a good one. If we're headed back toward GET then we need to figure something out, and fast.

The sound of the chase is deafened by a grinding, metal-on-metal noise from above. I look up. The GET Railway! It connects all GET facilities around the country—the only safe way to travel between them. There are two trains a day: one at midnight and one at high noon. The railway is directly powered by GET's main power grid and as such never stops running. It's commanded by an autopilot system that is programmed to stop at each facility for five minutes and then move on to the next facility. I've never taken one, but I do know that the noon train goes east, then down the seaboard. The midnight train goes west to Seattle, then down the coast, stopping in San Francisco and Los Angeles before heading back again. It's not much of a plan, but it's the only means we have to get out of this city, or at least out of our current situation.

The train stops at the GET station on the south side of the building. We'll be coming up on it shortly. It's our best bet on making it out of here alive. Maybe our only bet.

"Evie! The train!" I yell as we run.

I don't think she has it in her to argue. We stick close to the track and follow it to the outskirts of the GET building. There's a small underpass we have to get through that separates the station and us. It passes right underneath the train track. It's just one flight of stairs down, fifteen yards of flat, and one last flight of stairs up to the station. We make a break for it.

We're two steps down the first flight of stairs and Evie's ankle gives out. It crumples under pressure, and she falls face-first down the steps. She screams in pain and I rush to her.

"Are you okay?" I ask stupidly. I saw the fall. It was hard and down a flight of stairs. Forget the ankle, we'll be lucky if she didn't break anything.

"I'm okay. Just help me to my feet."

I can tell she's not okay, but we don't have much time. I can hear the guards closing in on us. I throw my right arm around her waist and bring her to her feet. She uses my shoulder for support, and we hobble toward the station.

We're just about to the second flight of stairs when

the guards come piling into the underpass. They take aim and start firing. We swivel around and approach the stairs backward. As we climb I shoot one-handed. I'm not very accurate this way, but it's the best we can do to stay our execution. In the midst of the mayhem, I feel a sharp burn on my upper left thigh. I know I've been shot, but since I didn't fall when the bullet hit me, my best guess is it's just a graze. I should be fine if I can clean it up. We keep inching backward until the underpass disappears at our feet. I stop firing and we turn back toward the station in a hurry. It's hard to tell how much time has passed; the train might have already left. Five minutes is a short window.

The station is in sight and the train is still in the bay, but the thirty-second warning lights that tell you when the doors are closing for departure start flashing. A burst of adrenaline rushes through me. If we're going to make it, we have to move faster. In one swooping motion, I throw the rifle around to my back and drop my left hand down just below the back of Evie's knees. I pick her up, holding her in my arms like a hurt child, and make a break for the train.

The GET guards have gained again and are close in chase, discharging their weapons. We're feet from the train and the doors start to close. One last burst of energy. I can make it if I jump. I leap forward, narrowly skimming through the closing doors. I turn my body in midair so I'll land on my back, keeping Evie safe from the hard landing. We hit the floor of the train, the wind is knocked out of me, and our momentum sends us sliding up against the far wall of the train with a thud.

I hold Evie firmly in my arms as the doors to the train

close. Nater is first to the train, an evil, snarling, spit-infused face and mouth staring right at us. He paws at the door like a bear trying to pry its way into a car for food, but the train is already starting to move, and like I said, they can't stop it, not for anything. The only way to stop it before it hits the GET facility in Seattle would be to kill the main power grid, which is something they'd never do. Killing the grid would shut down the train, but also the power to every GET-controlled city in the country. That's impossible. That would be foolish. There's no telling what would happen if they did that. I don't think it's a risk they'd be willing to take over two escaped HD operatives, no matter how important they think I might be. The irony in the situation is they had designed the train to run this way as a failsafe. It's meant to prevent unwanted passengers from getting aboard, something designed with Sector 6 in mind, but now the joke's on them. We're aboard and there's nothing they can do to stop it.

The train picks up speed and the passing station leaves Nater, the guards, GET, the HD program, the red team, the blue team, and the city all behind us. Our lives, once again, are about to change. In fact, they already have. Now, all we have is one another. We may not have a plan, but we have that.

Evie is hurt and exhausted. She's tired and hungry, and her ankle is all but ruined. I rip off a piece of my jumpsuit and use it to bandage her ankle. I wrap it tightly. If she can keep it from moving too much, it will heal faster. I leave her on one of the bench seats and tell her I'm going to take a quick look around. The train isn't long, only six cars, I think. It was built for speed, not for maximum capacity. She doesn't want me to leave her, but I assure her she's safe for now. I leave her with the gun and head off down the train.

I pass through each car. I'm looking for two things: if we're alone and if there's any food or water. The train itself is like any other train I'd imagine. Each side of it is lined with clean flip-down seats. Every tenth seat there's a bench, long enough to lie on if you wanted. There's one set of doors in each car, and windows reveal the world above each seat. In a small strip of wall above each seat are pictures of all the different GET facilities. I look at them as I pass. I begin to feel sick as I remember our predicament. We'll need to find some way off this train before it stops in Seattle. GET will be waiting for us there. We can't be on this train when it arrives.

We had entered the first car and are the only ones in it. The next four cars are identical to ours—just seats, windows, and pictures. I haven't found anyone in any of the cars, and the sixth doesn't prove any different. We are in fact alone, which is good; we don't need anyone barging in on us. Being alone means we're safe, for now, but the sixth car is different from the other cars. The sixth car looks like a dining car. It has tables, a counter with snack food like chips, fruit, nuts, and drinks. Excited, I jump the counter and pile up as many goodies as I can. I stuff my pockets with all that I can carry and make sure we have at least four bottles of water. We should hydrate as much as we can now. There's no telling what our situation will be like in the morning.

Once my pockets can't possibly hold any more and my

hands and crossed arms are piled high with water bottles, I start making my way back to Evie. It's been about fifteen minutes and she must be getting worried. A jostle in the track, the slightest murmur in the wheels, sets my balance off enough that I lean against one of the tables. Regaining my balance, I look up. Just above the doorway to car five is a railway map. The map is rudimentary, but it outlines the course of the train. At first, I don't think anything of it—I know we're heading to Seattle—but then, just a twitch in the far reaches of my brain sends my eyes back to the map. I smile. I must look like a grinning fool, but at least now I'm a grinning fool with a plan.

CHAPTER THIRTY-ONE

THE OTHERS

ARTHUR ENTERS WINSTON Parker's office on level 51. He shuts the door behind him and waits. For the first time ever, Arthur fears what might happen when he tells Winston about how Evie and Aiden have escaped. Winston stares out the same large window. He looks down at the street and watches as the GET train sails along its track into the distance. It's as if he knows what happened even before Arthur will tell him, but he waits. He waits until he thinks Arthur can't stand the waiting any longer. He wants Arthur to sweat. He wants Arthur to think the worst. Winston Parker wants Arthur to know he's the lesser man.

"They're gone, aren't they?" Winston asks.

"They are."

"How did you let this happen?"

Arthur takes a few steps into the office, closing the gap between them. "They escaped through the tunnels beneath the locker rooms. We ran a purge, but they made it topside. We think they had some inside help."

"You think!" Winston turns and slams his fist down onto his desk.

"We thought they might try to head for Sector 6, but they jumped on the GET westbound train. We'll be alerting the Seattle facility that—"

"Are you really stupid enough to believe that they'd stay on that train until Seattle? You think they'd try so hard to escape only to be easily picked up once they arrived in Seattle?"

"No, sir. I don't."

"You have my permission to kill the main power grid."

Arthur takes a concerned step forward.

"But sir, that's insane. We can't just kill the power grid. The entire city, The Grand Wall would lose power. We'd be weakening our defenses. Sector 6 could use the downed grid to their advantage. We could be overrun. It's too dangerous."

"Aiden Bishop is EVERYTHING! Don't you understand that? Everything. What's insane is you not being able to put a lid on this entire situation."

"We still have the ocular camera. We installed it when he went to medical for his permanent neuro-ports."

Winston sighs and smiles, just a little. He's relieved, somewhat.

"How long until it's online?" he asks.

"It should be up and running in the next twenty-four hours. We should be able to see everything he sees. With any luck we'll be able to pinpoint his location," Arthur says.

"Will he notice? When it turns on?"

"He might get a slight headache, but nothing too out of the ordinary."

Winston pulls out his desk chair and takes a seat. He folds his hands together.

"Good. I'll give you thirty-six hours to find him and bring him in. A minute over that and it'll be *your* head. I mean that. Now get out of here."

Winston spins around in his chair to look back out over the city he created. He'll do anything to hold onto it. Arthur backs toward the door before turning to open it.

"Oh, and Arthur?" Winston says.

"Yes."

"Do me a favor and kill the girl. Show me you're a man of your word."

And with that, Arthur leaves the office, shutting the door tight behind him.

CHAPTER THIRTY-TWO

EVIE

AIDEN IS FAST asleep. It wasn't long after he told me all about his plan that he asked if I felt safe enough for him to catch a little bit of rest. I still think it's adorable the way he fears for me. He's so protective, like a loving husband over a beloved wife. Only after a few seconds of his eyes shutting, he slipped into a deep sleep. He must need it. With the amount he worries, I can't imagine he's slept more than six hours in the past few days. I'll let him rest as long as he needs. We should be more than safe for now.

I'm still amazed that Aiden managed to get us on the train. I thought for sure my bad ankle would be the end of us. I'm mad at myself for twisting it. I know it wasn't my fault, but I feel stupid and weak. I hate feeling weak, especially around Aiden. I don't want him to think he has to pull any more weight than he already does. I don't know whether it's just the crisis situation or something more, but as I watch him sleep all curled up in a seat, his back using the wall for support, I can't help the feeling I get in my chest. I feel a warmth, and not just a warm feeling because we did what we'd said we'd do or because he makes me feel safe, but because I need him. I've said I need him before and it's always been out of necessity, but as I look at him now, it's more than that. I need him because I can no longer picture my life without him. I need him because he makes me feel whole, like the last piece of a puzzle. I think, no, I *know* that I'm falling in love with him. I've never felt this feeling before, so I'm not sure exactly what it's like or should be like, but when people say *you know when you know*, I understand that now. This must be love, and if it isn't then I don't think I'll ever experience it. This is as real as it gets, and we haven't even kissed. I want to tell him how I feel, but it's not the right time. I'm not sure when that time will be, but it's not now. I want to let him sleep. He needs it. He deserves it.

Aiden's plan is simple in theory but hard to execute and even harder to survive. He told me he found a map of the train track when he was in the sixth car grabbing some food and water. He told me the importance of the track was that it passed through Montana, precisely a place he called Big Sky Country. He said we couldn't be on this train when it pulled into the GET station in Seattle and he's right. So his plan is to jump from the train when it crosses through Big Sky, Montana. He said he knows of a place there, a place we can stay while my ankle heals and we figure out our next move.

At first, I told him I thought the plan didn't make any sense. We have to get to Sector 6, and we are already going in the wrong direction, but I didn't have a better plan, so I had to agree. I'm in no condition for another firefight, so a little quiet time might be nice. Aiden told me about the place he knows. It's a cabin in the woods, close to a lake, that used to belong to his grandparents. He told me he used to visit there for a few weeks in the summer and winter. He said, based on where the track crosses, if we jump in the right place, he'd be able to get us there. I don't doubt he can find it, but I'm worried someone else might have taken it over, or that it might be burnt to its foundation, just like my father had done to our little cabin in the woods.

It doesn't scare me so much that we'll be jumping from a train moving at ninety miles per hour. It doesn't even scare me that we'll be on our own in the unknown of The Great Lands. Nor does it scare me that if we don't find the cabin, we'll be stuck in the middle of the woods with no more plan. What does scare me is that any of these things, like jumping from the train, The Great Lands, or surviving in the wild, might take Aiden from me. That's what's scary. I don't want to lose him. Ever.

. . .

The sun is just starting to break over the horizon. Its warmth peeks through the glass of the train windows, cozying up to my skin. It's nice. For a moment it makes me forget everything that has happened, and everything that will happen. Right now, the sun is liberating. It's beautiful too. Rays of light pierce through thick, frothy clouds spilling down onto the lush nature of The Great Lands—something my father used to call *God light* because only God could make something so divine. We're far from any city now. Vast plains freckled with looming pines find their way toward mountainous peaks towering high above, cutting through the thick air with jagged rock. A few of the peaks wear little white caps of snow, like hats keeping their ears warm. It's only spring and I'm sure the world here has finally sprung to life. Everything is so beautiful. I can't imagine a prettier place—not even in my dreams.

A small stream of golden light streaks across Aiden's face. He stirs, but it doesn't wake him. It's the following gentle jostle in the train track that makes his eyes open. He squints at first, using his hand to block the morning rays. He jolts up quickly, and then he relaxes his body when he sees that I'm still here, and safe. Aiden stretches, raising his arms high above his head, and then arching his back like a stirring cat. He looks rested. He looks refreshed. He looks good.

"Where are we?" Aiden asks.

"No good morning?" I mess with him.

"Sorry. Good morning." Aiden smiles. "So where are we?"

"The sun's just come up. We've been going for about ten hours now."

"How long was I out?" Aiden says.

"About seven."

"You could have woken me if you—"

"No, it's okay, I thought you needed it."

"Thanks," he says, but I can tell he's a little disappointed in himself that he didn't stay awake and keep a close watch.

"We should be coming up on our jump point soon. I figure we have about a twenty or thirty-minute window before we get out of walking range of the cabin."

"How will you know when we get there?"

"Well, time will put us within shot, and I'll keep an eye out for Cinnamon Mountain. The train should pass close enough to see it. I think I can remember what it looks like."

"You *think*?" I say.

"I will. You trust me, remember?"

Now he's being a little bit of a smart-ass, but he's still cute about it. I don't know if I want to punch him or hug him.

"So, genius, how are we going to make the jump?" I ask jokingly, but it's no joke. I really do want to know. I've already got a bum ankle and I'd sure love to avoid any further injuries.

"Follow me," Aiden says.

We work our way into the control room of the first train car. It's big enough for one person to work as a conductor, but since the train is automated, it's unmanned. The door is welded shut, but a small overhead electrical panel is easily removed. Aiden breaks the panel free with his hands, and I climb in and slip through. I quickly search for an emergency stop switch. I hear Aiden shouting directions to me from outside the door. There's no switch, but we don't need one. All we need to do is cut the main power line from the control room to the battery packs. Cutting the line won't stop the train, but it will slow the train, hopefully enough to make the jump safe.

I rip the control console away to expose the ignition housing where the battery power line should have a lead. I cut the line by ripping it free with a good yank, and the train almost instantly brakes backward. I climb back through the electrical hatch and into the first car. The train continues to slow.

"You're a genius," Aiden says.

"I know," I say as I pass by him and head for a set of double doors toward the back of the car.

We have to pry them open to make the jump. We both grab hold of the CAR-20 and use it for leverage against the door. It opens just enough for us to squeeze our hands through, get a good hold, and push it open the rest of the way. We gather a few more water bottles and some prepackaged food and prepare for our departure.

It doesn't take long for Aiden to spot his mountain. It has a dark brown hue that stands out from the surrounding scenery, which is probably how it got its name.

"Together," Aiden says.

I take Aiden's hand. The ground still looks like it's whipping by us. My heart is pounding out of my chest. It's exciting and horrifying at the same time.

"Just remember, when we hit the ground, tuck in your legs."

For some reason, I hold my breath, and then we jump.

We both hit the ground hard, maybe harder than we had anticipated, but our tuck-and-roll technique works flawlessly. Lucky for us, the ground here is soft and plush with overgrown grass. We stand up, cheer and hug, and congratulate ourselves on surviving it. We watch the train as it barrels away from us on its course to Seattle. We don't move until we no longer see or hear it. Then, without delay, we move on.

This is the hard part. The walk to the cabin is longer

than Aiden thought, or remembered. What he said would only take three hours ends up taking six. Try walking six hours on a bad ankle. It's tough and incredibly painful.

I'm impressed with how well he still knows the way. He had told me how young he was the last time he had been there, too young for any normal person to remember something this well, but Aiden's not normal. The country is an untamed wilderness. Thick forestation, overgrowth, and vegetation hide little, if any, signs of human life. We move as quickly and quietly as we can, unsure if anyone, any wild ones, might be lurking or looking. I don't think either of us would quite know what to expect if we ran into someone out here. I can't imagine it's any better than during The Great Event. People must still live in fear and rely on instinct to survive. My guess is we don't want to come in contact with anyone else if we can avoid it.

And we don't. Not a single person. We do, however, cross paths with a few dozen deer, a handful of rabbits, hundreds of birds, squirrels, and chipmunks. We even cross paths with a moose. Something I thought had gone extinct years ago. It's clear that Mother Nature waited for no one to evolve over the years. To her, GET, the HD program, us, all of it means nothing.

. . .

Through hard, gravelly plains, up into the green foothills and the thick pine forest, we finally see Aiden's cabin. Time hasn't been kind to the place, but nevertheless, it's still standing. Thick vines have crept their way around the cabin's wood frame. Dust and debris cover a once vibrant screened-in porch. It's not small by any means, not like my cabin had been. You could fit five of my cabins inside of this one. I resent Aiden a little, now that I've seen his family cabin. Even in its decrepit state, it's nicer than anything I could have ever hoped to have in my life as a child. I haven't even been inside yet, and I can tell he and his family were well-off, wealthy even, but Aiden never acts like other wealthy people I know. Had I not seen this cabin, I would have never known. So I guess I can't hold it against him.

"I can't believe it's still here!" Aiden shouts. He's excited. I don't blame him. I'd be the same way if I got to see my little cabin again, but that's impossible. "Come on!" Aiden climbs up the steps and into the front porch.

The front door is locked, but a firm push with his shoulder opens it. Time weakens all things, even locks. I step inside and let Aiden have a minute to take it all in. He rushes between rooms, looking for any trace of people. It looks like he's anticipating running into one of his grandparents, but they'd be long dead by now. If they hadn't died before The Great Event, the event itself would have taken them.

I move through the cabin. It's more like a house than a cabin. His grandparents must have lived here full time because it's packed with things. Every counter, bookshelf, and wall is covered with photos of Aiden and his family. I look at them as I pass. He's so young in the photos; a bright innocence shines through his eyes and smiles. Many of the photos show an older boy with him, a boy who looks so similar. It must be his brother, but Aiden's never mentioned him to me. Seems odd to leave something like that out, but I guess there are still things I haven't told Aiden about myself.

There's a full kitchen, packed with high-end appliances. The cabinets still have plenty of canned goods, which is great news for us and our grumbling stomachs. There are four bedrooms: one that was obviously the grandparents' room, two others that are smaller and look like kids' rooms, and a final bedroom, which is where I find Aiden. He sits on the edge of the bed looking out of a clouded window. He's crying, silently, letting a few tears roll down his face. I stand in the doorway. I'm not sure if I'm supposed to disturb him or not. I want to run to him and hold him in my arms. I don't want to see him cry, but I also don't want to make him feel insecure. So I wait.

I shift my weight and he hears my presence. He rushes his hands to his eyes and wipes the tears from his face.

"I didn't know you were there," Aiden says.

I walk into the room and take a seat next to him on the bed. The mattress hasn't been used for years; it's still plush and soft. I haven't felt anything so comfortable in quite some time. I could sink into it and just sleep forever, but not now.

"You okay?" I ask.

"Yeah. Just happy really. It's been so long since I've been here." He points out the window. In the distance, I can see the faint shimmer of light bouncing off gentle ripples of water. A thin, sandy beach lines the outer rim of a lake. "That's the lake I told you about. There's plenty of fish in there. I'd bet the poles and boat are still in the shed. We can check tomorrow morning."

"Of course," I say reassuringly.

"I thought you could sleep here tonight. It's getting dark soon, and we might as well get a good night's sleep. I'll take one of the other rooms, or on the couch. Might be a better place to keep watch."

Aiden stands and heads to the doorway.

"I don't think there's running water, but I'll look into it tomorrow. Do you need anything else? I was going to grab some firewood from outside before we lose the light."

"No, I'm good. Thanks," I say. Then Aiden slips out of the room and leaves the cabin to go find wood. I hear the creak of the porch door open and slam shut as he leaves.

Aiden finds wood, lots of it, and just before the blanket of night covers the sky. The world is so quiet here. The sounds of nature and the intermittent crackle/snap of the fireplace fill the cabin. We eat our fine dinners of canned SpaghettiOs, two bags of potato chips, and two bottles of water. Tomorrow we will fish, Aiden had told me. And maybe we will. Fresh meat would taste great about now, and our bodies need the nourishment.

We sit apart by the fire, sipping on mugs filled with powdered hot chocolate. Aiden tells me stories about his time here. He tells me about his brother and how he died. He tells me he hasn't been here since it happened. He tells me how good it feels to be back; how this was his favorite place in the world and how happy he is to share it with me. Then we finish our hot chocolates in silence.

It's still cold, the spring air is crisp at night, and the fireplace only heats the living room. We say our goodnights and I head to my room, but it feels lonely. I wonder if it's appropriate to ask Aiden to keep me company. I wonder if he would. I wonder if I should. But I can't stop my body; it's already made its decision. It forces me to the doorway; it forces me to ask.

"Aiden," I say.

He's sitting on a ledge by the front porch, looking out into the night, the CAR-20 rifle resting on his lap. He's keeping watch. He doesn't want to be caught sleeping while I'm awake, not again. He looks up at me.

"What's wrong?" Aiden says.

"I was just wondering if you wouldn't mind holding me for a bit? I'm having trouble falling asleep and—"

"Of course."

Aiden stands from his perch and walks toward me. I lead him into the room. Neither of us says another word. He places the rifle on the night table next to the bed. I climb onto the mattress, lying on top of the covers. He slides in next to me, his warmth touching up against me from head to toe. His right arm slides under my neck and his left curls over my waist. He brings me in close, his firm grip is comforting and reassuring.

"Is this okay?" he asks.

"Yes," I tell him. And it is. It's perfect. Just perfect.

CHAPTER THIRTY-THREE
AIDEN

THE SUN IS starting to rise, and Evie is still fast asleep. We haven't moved from the time we fell asleep until my body sensed first light. I gently slide my arm free from underneath her head and fold a thick comforter around her body. She squirms some and lets out an innocent little moan as she settles into the touch of the soft fabric. I wait and watch her for a moment. Everything at this moment is perfect. If I could live one way with one person for the rest of my life, this would be it and she would be that person. Nothing has ever felt so right.

I didn't have my nightmare last night. In fact, I didn't dream about anything at all. For the first time in a long time, I slept soundly, with no interruption, no night sweats, and no sudden jerk awake.

Even though I didn't have the dream, my head hurts. The entire back of my head feels like it's going to explode, but at least I slept, best in months. I grab the rifle from the nightstand and leave Evie to sleep. I close the door slightly, only leaving it open a crack, and go in search of some aspirin, Advil, Tylenol, anything to help kill the throbbing in my head. I search the bathroom cabinets, but there's nothing. I search the kitchen cabinets and under the sink, but nothing. Finally, I search my grandparents' room.

I find some Advil in the top drawer of one of their nightstands. Thank God. The expiration on the bottle says it expired two years ago, but I figure the expiration dates have got to be a little lax with things like over-the-counter drugs. Either way, I have to try something, so I head back into the kitchen and grab a water bottle from the fridge. I notice we only have three bottles left, including this one, so we'll have to figure out how to get our hands on some clean water today. If I remember correctly, there should be a water purifier in the shed. If we have to, we can purify lake water. It'll be a slow process, but at least we'll have water. I unscrew the cap, throw two pills in my mouth, and swallow. I open one of our small bags of chips and shove some into my mouth. It's not much, but I want to leave the rest for Evie.

I have a lot to do today, so instead of whining about my head, I decide to leave Evie a note, in case she wakes up while I'm outside. I search the drawers in the kitchen for paper, pen, or a pad of some sort, but don't find anything except a single piece of chalk. I place the tip of the chalk on a small blackboard hanging next to the door and write: EVIE, WENT OUTSIDE. I'LL BE BACK SOON. HOLLER IF YOU NEED ME.

I step back and look at my message. I actually used the word *holler*. It sounds weird and I'd never say it aloud, but it's true, it really is the best way for her to get my attention. It's spring and the snow has receded back to the highest points in the mountains; now the lake has no sound obstructions. Normal talking can be heard across it. I'd have no problem hearing her if she yelled for me. Satisfied, I sling the rifle around my back and head out the front door.

. . .

Everything is new to me now. I've never been here in the spring. It's really quite beautiful. The air is crisp and cool. It bites at the skin, but the piercing warmth from the sun muzzles the nip, sending quick, close shivers and goose bumps. The ground is soft and damp. A thin layer of crystal-clear dew covers every blade of grass and every petal of the flowers. The trees are ripe with green pine cones, not yet browned and ready to fall—their sweet smell fragrant and constant. I take in a deep breath. Nature reigns supreme here. I had almost forgotten how much I love it here. As I exhale, the pain in my head dissipates. Maybe all I needed was some fresh air, some old and new memories to calm my mind.

I head around the back of the cabin. This is where the shed is. My grandparents were smart enough to lock it up, but the padlock has grown a thick layer of rust over the years. A hard hit with the butt of the rifle tears it free, and it plops to the ground. The door to the shed opens with a creak. I open it as far as I can and reach for a hinged door bolt attached to the bottom of the second door. I pull it up and swing open the second door. A pigeon flaps its way out of the opening, leaving a thin cloud of dust in the air. I cough and swat at the dust until I can see inside the shed.

It's not a big shed, but just large enough to fit three shelves—filled with old trinkets, tools, buckets, lawn equipment, a few fishing poles, a tackle box, and the water purifier—and the rowboat. Finding the purifier is one of two of my objectives. The second is the rowboat. I'm glad it's still here. I wasn't sure if it would be. It was old when I was a kid, and now it looks ancient—remnants of another time. I reach in and grab hold of the anchor ring on the bow of the little boat. I wrap two fingers through it and pull hard. It's made of wood, so it's got a decent weight to it. After a few moments of struggle, the boat gives way and slides toward me. With a few forceful tries, I manage to pull it out of the shed.

Like the lock and the cabin, time hasn't been kind to the little boat. The wood on the hull has suffered from dry rot. The wood sucks up water from the lake like a sponge and then disintegrates like bread thrown for ducks. If that isn't bad enough, there's a hole the size of a basketball near the stern, which would ensure that it sinks properly. They should have tossed this boat when they had the chance. It looks like any fishing would have to be done from the shore, which isn't a bad thing; it just might take longer, and we'd most likely only catch pumpkinseeds or perch. I pull the fishing poles, purifier, and tackle box from the shed and put them on the porch.

Now on to power and water. I don't expect either of them to work, but who knows. I told Evie last night that I'd try in the morning, so I will. The valve is under the cabin. My grandfather used to send my brother under to turn it on or off. I kneel down so I can crawl on all fours and shimmy myself under the cabin, hoping I won't come face-to-face with any large spiders or an angry raccoon. Finding the water shutoff valve is easier than I thought. The valve is marked with a yellow handle and stands out from the dingy darkness. I give it a turn, but I don't hear anything. I sit and wait; maybe it takes a few seconds, but still nothing. Just as I thought, the water doesn't work.

I climb out from under the cabin and look for the electric meter. I find it on the opposite side of the cabin. The meter is dead and when I pull down on the main breaker lever, I don't hear anything. The electricity is dead too. It looks like we'll have to live without running water or power for a while. I'm not sure how long a while is though. Evie and I haven't had the chance to talk any further about what our plan should be. We had made it out of the program, away from GET, off the train, and to the cabin, but what next? I'm sure Evie won't fight me on staying until her ankle heals, but knowing her, she's going to want to figure out a way to go back and get into Sector 6. From here, we could walk our way into Sector 6. There's no wall on this side. It would take us a few weeks, maybe even a month, to make the trip on foot, and that's if we survive the elements of The Great Lands. We have no idea what's really out there. Nevertheless, Evie would want to attempt the journey. I won't be able to talk her out of it. That's for sure.

Out of the corner of my eye, I notice something—a rectangular object about the size of an old storage chest covered by a tarp. I pull off the tarp. Beneath it is what looks like a solar generator. I can feel a smile come over my face. I squat down and look the thing over. It seems fairly simple.

There's an on switch, a choke, a battery indicator light, and a pull rope. The battery indicator shows two out of ten bars of power. I decide to give it a try. I grab hold of the rope and give it a yank. Nothing yet. I adjust the choke some and give the rope another hard pull. The generator kicks in with a sputter and a hum. It runs smoothly.

"Yes!" I say to myself.

After a series of fist pumps and an intricate little victory dance, I look up to see Evie staring and laughing at me through her bedroom window. Embarrassed that she caught me, I place my right arm on my stomach and bend over, giving an end to my performance with a subtle bow. Evie smiles. I smile back, and then she disappears from the window. I may have embarrassed myself, but at least we'll have some power.

I walk around to the front of the cabin, Evie is there, waiting for me. She's on the steps of the porch, a blanket wrapped around her shoulders, her hair loose and wavy, dangling lightly across her face and down over her shoulders. She holds a mug of something hot. The smoke billows from the outer rim as she takes cautious sips. She's beautiful.

"Good morning," I say.

"Good morning. I see you got the power on."

"I did."

She holds up the mug. "Microwave works."

"Good. At least it'll be easier than making food over the fire."

"You find the boat?"

"Yeah, but it's useless. Any fishing we'll have to do from the shore."

"That'll work?"

"Sure. It should, but I figured I might go on a hunt today. Look for some of those deer we passed on the hike in."

"You're going to go on a hunt?" she asks with surprise.

"Yeah, what's wrong with that?"

"You can't shoot."

"I can shoot."

I'm a little offended. Sure, I'm not as good as Evie, but I can hold my own. After all, I saved her butt with my shooting.

"Yeah, at like sixty yards. With hunting you'll need to be accurate at one-fifty, maybe even two-fifty."

"And you're saying I can't do that?"

"I'm not saying you can't, I mean . . ."

I can tell she's just messing with me, but I go with it.

"Okay, hotshot, why don't you come along then, show me how it's done?"

Evie puts her mug down on the steps and tosses the blanket just inside the screen door. She climbs down the steps and snatches the rifle.

"Give me that," Evie says.

"You sure you're up to it? I mean, your ankle—"

"Just come on." Evie hobbles off in front of me.

I smile and follow her. I knew taking a little jab at her would get her motivated, get her to forget about her ankle and come with me, and all I really wanted was for her to keep me company anyway.

. . .

We wrap around the lake with our eyes peeled. We keep a lookout for anything that moves. On the far side of the lake,

Evie picks up on some hoof prints on the beach. We follow them from the lake and into the woods. She's concentrating hard on tracking. I'm not so interested. I'm more concerned with watching her. I follow her every move. I watch the way she scans the woods. How she kneels every so often to touch the ground with her fingers. She's done this before, survived, and better than I ever could have. She seems at home here. It feels like home here. I wish we'd never have to leave.

The thick woods come to an end. The tree line faces a vast rolling field full of wildflowers of all kinds—daffodils, baby's breath, and dandelions. It's stunning. Spring here really is beautiful. For a moment we forget ourselves. We forget our mission. At this moment, the beauty overtakes us. Evie looks back at me with a playful, *you can't catch me* expression, and as quickly as she has looked at me, she is gone, darting into the field of flowers. I chase after her. I can tell she wants the chase, so I let her lead. I could easily overtake her and her bad ankle, but I want her to enjoy it. She looks so happy. The happiest I've ever seen her. Her face is beaming with radiance, her body twirling with an airy gaiety.

Her arms outstretch, her fingers tickling the tips of the flowers, and then she stops. She closes her eyes, takes in a deep breath, and smiles. I stand and watch her. She's celestial, like an angel sent to this Earth just for me. Then she lets go and allows herself to fall backward. The dense, soft vegetation breaks her fall. Her eyes open and she reaches a hand up for me. I take it thinking she wants me to help her back to her feet, but instead, she pulls hard, catching me off guard, and I fall to the ground next to her. We're surrounded now, looking up at the sky, flowers towering around us like skyscrapers. She looks at me and I look at her. This is the right moment, the moment to kiss her for the first time. I lean in and close my eyes. Our lips meet gently, her lips soft as pillows, warm to the touch. We kiss. A few seconds turn into the rest of my life. We are meant for one another. There's no denying it.

The kiss is perfect, but something in the back of my head creeps forward—the dream. Everything feels so familiar now. We've walked right into the dream, only it's no longer a dream; it's very real and happening. We've played out the entire dream right up until the point where it becomes a nightmare. But before I can say anything, Evie breaks the kiss and sits up. She's looking at something, intently. I reach for her. I'm panicked.

"Evie, we should—"

"Shh," she says with a finger to her lips. Then she points. I sit up and crouch next to her.

"There," she whispers.

I look, and off in the distance, across the field, a few hundred yards away, is a family of deer, five or six maybe. Evie raises the rifle and looks down the sight. Maybe the dream doesn't mean anything. Maybe it was just a way to bring us together. Evie's finger rests gently on the trigger, and then the shot rings out. A single shot. A single bullet, but no deer falls. They scatter in all directions. I look over at Evie. Her face is cold. A blankness fills her features.

"Evie?"

I can tell something is wrong. Then she collapses, her

body limp and fragile. I fall with her, shoving my arms under her head to try to protect her. Her body shakes. A thick pool of blood forms over the right side of her chest and soaks the grass beneath her. Evie's been shot. I put a hand over the exit wound and press down hard. I try my best to stop the bleeding, but she's slipping away fast. She coughs and heaves for air, but she can't seem to find any.

"Evie!" I scream. "EVIE!"

My face fills with tears. I can see them making little clear pools in her blood-soaked shirt. She reaches a hand out and touches my face. She tries to smile, but I can see the fear. She tries to speak to me.

"Aiden," Evie mutters.

"Shh," I tell her. "Save your strength. You're going to be okay."

She shakes her head. I can tell she knows better than me.

"I think I love you. You know that?" Evie says ever so softly.

I nod my head in a fury of anger. A single tear runs down her cheek, and it smudges black as it passes through the coughed-up blood on her face. Her eyes widen and her pupils spread into saucers. As she takes her last few breaths of air, I swear I can hear her say, "Save me."

Her head falls limp over my arm, and I feel the firm grip of hands on my shoulders.

"NO!" I scream.

I lash out and bring her lifeless body in closer to mine. I don't want to let go of her, but the hands pull at me, tearing me away from her. They grab me by my legs and begin to pull. I kick and I scream, but it's no use. There is no fighting it. GET has come for me. Evie was holding the gun, she was a threat, she was a liability, she was expendable, and so they killed her. They took her from me. With one shot, she is gone.

They drag me across the field, and I watch as Evie's body gets lost amongst the towering beauty of spring in Montana. A plume of dandelion spores float up from the disturbed surroundings, and as I'm being pulled back toward GET and away from Evie, all I can think is that I never should have brought her here. I should have known this would happen. It's all my fault.

END OF BOOK ONE